ME AND MY TAPEWORM

ISOBEL

Dr. E

ISBN 978-1-950818-74-7 (paperback)

Rushmore Press LLC
1 888 733 9607
www.rushmorepress.com

Printed in the United States of America

CONTENTS

INTRODUCTION

We are accustomed to everyday habits and necessities, always facing the criticism of family, neighbors and friends, always trying to look and act the best we can, always trying to make a better image and a better score, while secretly yearning to live other people's lives.

We actually live caught between the hard and unnegotiable truths of our own life and the image we would like to show about us. This photo-shopped program consumes most of our daily effort and leaves less energy for essential life fact adjustment, and when a crisis comes up, we are helplessly falling to stupid details.

We want to be happier; we need to see life in brighter colors, we want to laugh and wish the best for our children; instead, we leave them a gloomy and messy stage on which the best actor that mimics life is praised, and the dying one is glorified, even when there is no one left for applause.

How come we came to lie and still think this is normal, because this is no lie, we simply "present just the convenient part of a truth" ? How come we get to unwillingly deploy / express our true personality, so far from whatever we have wished, yearned for or dreamed about, in a sometimes schizophrenic division between our wish and our realistic potential ?

We are getting farther from ourselves at a rate we cannot even perceive, and that may be the main error- inducing factor when it comes to self- judgement, as we see in a speculative "rear mirror" our unmoved statue, while cruising ahead at 4 Warp, lacking the time to receive feed-back. The second one is society induced – the political correctness that forces us sometimes to accept and comply to rules that sometimes become not only obsolete, but silly and unrealistic, like on Facebook, Instagram or other means of sterile communication between "zombies". We get "punished" to freely express ourselves in terms of language and feelings, and there are people narrow-minded enough to try and make us ashamed of what we really are, of how we look like or what we really think, not to mention speaking our mind!

I dedicate this book to all those having the simple and natural truth in mind, honesty in their soul and the power to publicly show them both! I trust that there will be a time when political correctness will become political directness. And I promise we can do it while having a good laugh!

Oh yes! Many of the things I speak about in this book have actually happened to me, but not all of them, and- as probably expected - I also used stories I heard of, or read about. Unnecessary annoying things have been removed, and some fictional facts and characters have been added in order to serve to a superior meaning of my imaginative world. Any allegedly harmful resemblance or reference to publicly known people or entities is purely unintentional and does not represent a specific or politically assumed point of view, nor does it aim to harm anyone or anything. It was all honestly done in the name of fun and a better life, together!

The author

ARE WE REALLY RELATED TO APES?

Readers having some knowledge of anthropology must forgive me. They surely know that according to evolutionist theory, we and apes must have had a common ancestor, one we failed to locate in the framework of the past, say… 25 million years.

My above mentioned question, somehow rhetorical, is about the determinism of this afiliation, as many of the present day anthropologists and archaeologists consider this "missing link" as being a creature resembling to us and apes, in the same time.

What if we could have been able to choose our preferred animal, like in a zoo or in a zodiac, and thus modify our ascendance? Would this have been enough for us to alter our character, and also our social and economic status, our political views and ultimately, our way of life? We simply hate to be sorry over missed targets or spilt milk.

Let us take an imaginary trip around the world, and see what various nations might have chosen. Some of them already did, and they use those animals for publicity.

The Americans for instance, are fascinated with the bald eagle, only this time the eagle brought the backbone "blonde" feathers to his forehead and used a Russian stylist, they say.

The English have – ever since King Richard - a traditional choice for the lion. However, their lion has recently reconsidered sharing game with the rest of the European pack, and wants to go hunting (read starving) alone, declaring a hunger Br-exitus.

The Indians are majestically displaying the elephant, one intelligent, gentle, sociable, strong and dominating animal, packing qualities which the average Indian – between us, girls! - will never have. Not to mention that some people in India are quite secretly worshiping rats. However, rats are also intelligent mammals and in "dire straits", can also be eaten, which is an advantage the elephants lack.

Australians are undecided between the cute Koala bear (very successful when scoring on women tourists!) and the well- known kangaroo, renowned for stupidly jumping up and down, like the front wheel spring of a Russian Molotov truck, dropped on the concrete floor of a frozen garage in the Balti County of the formerly Russian Moldavia.

Chinese are fascinated by the dragon – species that went extinct right after the 'Flintstones" series was completed. Interestingly enough, because they are so many and hard to settle down (the Chinese people, not the dragons), the Communist Party observed this animal yearn nursing inside Chinese citizens, so they allowed official Animal Astrology to officially satisfy any popular particularity. Now they are having the Dog sign, I believe, never to be changed until next year.

The Arab and Muslim people in general, have chosen camel, which can eventually be eaten, as well. The animal is extremely rational, calm and enduring, which makes the choice nonetheless surprising for a warrior population frequently driven by opposite feelings.

The Dutch oscillate between the wind mill (!?) – eternal enemy of Don Quijote, and the cow, which stands in beauty standards very close to their women, if not ahead of them.

Canadian have chosen a vegan sign (the maple leaf) and hope to be excused of other diabetic implications, the Serbian are still judging between wolves and the spicy stew called "pleskavitsa" and the Swiss simply adore cheese (!?), yet without the hard to avoid mice assigned to it.

Possibly in an apparently paradoxical urge, the Romanian have chosen the Tasmanian Devil. The Tasmanian devil is a small dark-brown furred animal, size of a slipper-happy dog in our parts, but here is where all the tenderness ends.

The little critter has the teeth and the appetite of an adult hyena, the urge of a great white shark and the foul mood of a C.E.O., disturbed by the press exactly while doing Sunday overtime with his young and blonde secretary of Swedish origin, who is carelessly handling the pen with her rather cold hands.

The Tasmanian devil is a true howler; it is unconsciously howling when hungry; howling when thirsty, howling when upset, howling when it goes to sleep, howling when having sex or howling if you offend a hungry one by showing it a lettuce.

For the Tasmanian devil howling is very important, (no matter where and when, or why,) only to show its presence, otherwise, it might happen to go unnoticed and that's a situation that could make you howl! The Tasmanian devil's howling is an identity statement, with subtle connotations in our con-citizen behavior.

What other significance can a barbed wire bonded eagle tattoo can have in a dark tan fellow, (the drawing that is) looking like a chicken tied to a stick at the poultry market on Sunday morning, except for a cry- out of civilian rebellion, socially fed- up status and a little "put'em up" yearn?

How about when your neighbor, living in a 10/10 foot single room apartment goes to the corner grocery shop to buy a 10 cents bread driving - for the whole 50 yards - his Porsche Cayenne in a "Fast & Furious" style? The message is: "Hey, all of ya' MF that sees me! Keep ya' eyes open and ya' brainz too! I've got my value, drop dead all of ya' and my enemies F. -Off!" Sorry, local slang cannot be translated, but it is so much "spicier"!

What significance can a dog - leash size chain possibly have, when made out of solid gold, and worn in public around the neck at the market place or on vacation by a tanned gentleman, if not a mute and still subtle "satisfying" income declaration, which the IRS, sometimes suffering from the spinster syndrome, pretends not to see?

How is it possible not to be sentimentally touched by a group of "backstreet boys", who are trying to approach a young lady by whistling, using onomatopoeia and straight meaning gestures, when you realize that they actually yearn for sweet returning love and elevated conversation? They simply avoid looking at Oprah, because they are ashamed to cry in front of the other street chicks and punks.

These apparently upset people have a problem, they just want to be <u>bloody heard and understood</u> by someone, WTF? We're clear about that, or ye' gonna find it out the hard way, capisci?

Unfortunately, they get lucky only once in a while with the D.A. or a shrink, cause the local minister won't stop to listen to them, as last year they mugged him while being busy with Christmas Carols and collecting donations.

There's another category of citizens, having this itch of communicating, although they actually have nothing useful to communicate, still they want to be seen and heard – guess Facebook and other derivatives were invented while having them in mind! Some of these characters make it as high as the Senate or the House of Representatives, and that is because of the number of likes! The question is, who has the ability or the talent to turn a like into a vote!

Social behavior has clear correspondence in animal life, and so does sex life! With the social touch added, our sexual attraction to others may become guessable, slightly or – au contraire - very visible, and sometimes even annoying. Some of those people have this preoccupation carved so deep on their face that they need no introduction, others, however in lower numbers, commit the gesture of publicly displaying their ardor when in parks or remote streets, from under an old trench-coat, in front of the first housewife or maid that happens to pass by them holding her grocery bags! The victim is currently unaware of the positive effect she has triggered and the satisfaction she has procured to the guy. The man is not exactly a consumer of extreme (read fulfilled!) sensations, (nor can he be suspected of offering any "hard" sensation either!), but he occasionally scares off some maid in the outskirts!. It so happens that more often, he gets chased through the bushes in the park, with his "pride" hanging loose, dodging and zig-zagging like a mongoose the half a pound of sweet potatoes thrown at him. On the other hand, did you notice sometimes how possessively some executives look at their secretaries or some physicians at their nurses?

But let us get on with our quest for finding the logical connection between animal and human behavior. For instance the pig, a useful and gentle animal, so tasty (all of it!) could easily become our preferred being, when not affected by African plague virus. No wonder we have been using some of its body parts as grafts (like heart valves, for instance)! Seriously challenged when it comes to weight by "hungry" humans, the pig also displays a series of less hygienic habits, together with champing food and gulping mouthfuls while breathing in its food, not to mention mud bath and splashing, especially when mud contains its droppings, as well.

You may be surprised to find out how many "educated" people seem to surprisingly mimic such piggy manners, at least on occasions but mostly when they are alone. For example, you get up in a bus and – almost always – will closely encounter a person that has all clothes dipped into the menu list of the last few months, together with the unmistakable hint of the "exotic" places where they have been visiting, like for instance a sewage channel – possibly crawling through it!

The smelly plethora that already brings tears to your eyes will penetrate without discrimination everything around it, while being rehydrated by the sweat of the last 2000 miles spent in the same bus, at the rush hour, day by day. Pay attention and do not try to put any distance between you and the pig-man. This will be regarded as discrimination and in retaliation, he will initiate a common, otherwise boring conversation, yet enabling him to exhale- by his bad breath - some sort of toilet sewage mist that humiliates diction, spelling, and ammonia while reminding you of the subtle hunting habits of the Komodo dragon.

Having your eyes in tears from the preceding experience, you try to go down the bus corridor, delicately pushed around by a crow-man, hopping around with his claws in everybody's pockets.

But the pig-man – because he was our true character – can be found everywhere.

He might be the executive of an institution, routing in all corners for something fresh to champ. Fresh in a manner of speaking! He will turn his piggy little eyes with blonde eyelashes after all the Miss- Piggies in the institution. He grunts hysterically or beyond rational 'understanding during meetings, drinks like a pig, lays on one side instead of working, falls asleep while driving and feels good only when he comes tired at his shelter and throws himself into his own shit, sharing it with all those that get splashed on the happy occasion.

When elected as mayor or Congressman, the pig-man wins by giving the frozen -shrimps in his poll territory one sausage and then boils them properly after the elections. When invited in restaurants, he will chow ham from other pigs, when in hotels, he will chase all occasional sows and the street is not wide enough for his SUV.

One less elevated species of pig-man, the "Neanderthal" of pig-men, is the boar-man. Popular and populist, he accounts for all the qualities and bad parts of the regular pig-man, but he has something extra that makes all the charm: he is - or so he means to look like – pissed all the time, angry, grumpy, etc.

This helps him to elegantly get away from boring obligations like greeting people around him, responding to elevator conversation, shopping jokes or to conversations over a cup of wine. No Sir! He is pissed! He is upset and everybody should better understand it quickly, or they'll live to regret it if they don't!

It may be enough to cross his path and that does it: you didn't pay the right bribe, you don't have the right hat color, there's always something that stirs him up and he starts squalling. He is mounting up and curses you as he gets nervous and he may even hit you, if he sees you're scared enough.

He was the preferred character for high political jobs during communism, but comes in helpful even today, yet only in more refined versions, well shaved and perfumed and with a powerful ring-hook attached to his nose by a political party or some discrete agency.

The rat-man is frequently encountered, as is the animal he worships. Just like the species, he is very discrete and has an awesome dissembling capacity. For instance, if he ever gets to be a union leader, he will take his whistle and curse the government he hates, but which managed to double his salary.

He will conveniently take a vacation in the mountains or in Maldives when his friends come in power and his preferred government slices salaries in half.

Getting under his foul influence, other rat-men will hysterically bite and spit those who are doing them well, only to issue stupid and para-logical explanations about the odd things their preferred politicians are doing, and they will remain faithful to them even when, in the most "rat-ish" style – so to speak – those are having fun by hunting them.

The rat-man can silently and motionlessly watch how a woman or a child are molested, or an old man gets mugged in broad daylight. He will later explain his lack of action as a sample of civilized discretion, some sort of "we do not mingle in other people's lives", all meant to cover for his cowardice or carelessness that prevented him from "pissing against the wind". Kind of neighbor that grabs his beer and popcorn to his porch when your house across the street catches fire!

These days, the rat-man gets to be manager in hospitals, state agencies, ministries, schools or may become apartment block administrator. He will fawn with his tail sticking up in front of his superiors, swallowing tons of curses and shit without a blink, but will radically transform himself when confronted with his subordinates. He then suddenly becomes a merciless beast that humiliates and torments them just for fun, or to demonstrate to them how powerful he is and how much they depend on him.

The rat-man is reluctant to good-deed doing; he will become gregarious, interested and efficient when it comes to bust or frame/ compromise someone, or when it comes to plotting, staining someone's career or wrong doing, in general.

He will find the time for any argument or explanation, no matter how irrelevant, to justify his lack of implication or, on the contrary, complicity to something had gotten wrong; it was all in the name of duty regulations and so the explanation can last forever.

As manager of a health facility, the rat-man will register and approve (in front of the media, if possible) any necessity request for medication or medical gear that the patients cannot survive without. This happens while he knows perfectly that the hospital pharmacy does not have those drugs, or they are not on the approval list or the unit simply doesn't have the necessary budget to buy them.

If you ever want to do something, no matter how much you are committed to complete your project, the rat-man will find ways to stop you. He will "randomly" initiate stupid orders and regulations that actually prevent you from completing a project which is beneficial to the entire community.

He will hide behind excessive care for legality, inventing the necessity of stupid additional approvals, or behind "superior orders". Everything will be wrapped in phrases like: "it is not the way we like it: we simply have to do it this way!", "We cannot argue on this one: orders will be executed, not discussed!" or the old "We do the omelet, we need to break some eggs!", etc.

No mentioning about the people that may die or cripple because of his indolence, incompetence or his incapacity to step aside. No intention to let someone competent take over. No Sir! The rat-man grabs hold of his chair because his ass changed to the shape of it and would rather have his tail cut off than leave his position.

The ostrich —man has an apparently elevated, philosophic and detached view on things: he actually doesn't understand or care about anything. Whenever you need him, he will be in the nearest sand-pile, treating his latest migraine/headache.

The cockroach-man is not a high profile character. He is "there" anyway, covered by the crowd, fidgeting for crumbs since generations.

He sees the world in one single dimension – his own – and he is unable to conceive it could be different. After all, why bother with philosophy when we have so many scattered crumbs to gather! He will accidentally bump into another cockroach-man from time to time, ignoring each-other, sometimes fidgeting with other cockroaches towards more appetizing garbage piles in other neighborhoods; once in a while some of them die squashed by the feet of a larger animal, but cockroach-men are so plentiful! You won't get rid of them and you cannot change them. They know they are so many, defying evolutionism and insecticide, fidgeting everywhere, and they know that in case of "earthquake or nuclear disaster" they will survive and even thrive, because for them the difference between living a life and simply existing is not relevant. Haunted by such martial thoughts, they move a little their antennas, and fidget on through our lives and their own, crawling all corners in search for new crumbs.

The hyena –man is commonly a public clerk; he is boringly observing how the state and the government put you down on your knees and execute you with over 920 taxes (top statistics here this year), then jumps and rips you apart for the last few dimes left in your pockets.

Believe it or not, the green shit-fly has its own followers. The green fat fly buzzes everywhere all the time, settling upon everything in view and especially on the matter that gave its name. The fly eats hard, bathes in it, then goes around the neighborhood and regurgitates everything, spreading all around samples of its preferred menu.

The human-fly is similarly processing lies, gossip and outrageous intrigues, which smell so foul and are so easy to disseminate. The shit –fly has just two fears in its miserable life: shit crisis and the post-electoral fly-splash! When it comes to the first, we seem to be registered permanently although stained all around; the post-election punishment is forever delayed by manipulation and by under- the -counter understandings!

The shark-man can be active in usurious lending business, a bandit, a pirate but can also become president. He is naturally aggressive and launches deadly attacks without discrimination towards anything within its range! And I mean anything! If all he has around him is smaller and younger little sharks, he will not hesitate to gulp some careless ones, just because of boredom, no matter how faithful they were until the cannibal "accident".

The bottom of his sea is full of the remains of his former friends, who came in too close, like butterflies near the fire. The shark-man does not think/reason: he will swallow everything from the blue whale to the bait fish in the fisherman's basket. He is not really listening to you when you talk to him; he is thinking all this time, about what he should say or do to you. Like any dictator, he is painfully aging and deteriorating, in a small pond that he regards as being his ocean, and inside which he thinks of himself as being the macho tiger- shark.

His preferred motto is: "I am better, not because I am smarter, but because I can eat you and you cannot eat me!". Sometimes the shark-man sends his females to torment the smaller fish and lure them towards his greedy mouth.

The chameleon-man is a more exotic species, living in more exquisite environment. He is commonly a trans-party politician, always in search for the best doctrine and of course, if so we happen to mention it, the best position for him, but he can also get to be the principal of a school or a clerk. The chameleon – principal is the "man –of-the-school", commonly a boring and frustrated teacher with no didactic or management skills, totally "devoted and dedicated" to the institution's higher interest – usually dictated by the party in power, upon one condition only – that he stays forever as principal of the institution and it is him and only him that rules everything. Otherwise, it is a catastrophe!

So that the "man-of-the-school" proceeds to hungrily and industriously lick the ass of the various education inspectors taking turns, them being politically replaced so quickly, that he barely manages to wipe his mouth in between.

He will never get tired in claiming his personal sacrifice and the accomplishments of the institution as being his own, whenever he finds a bunch of suckers to listen to him. He will negotiate his position to bloodshed, implying the possibility of changing the color of his skin from yellow (liberal) to orange (democrat-liberal), red (socialist) or green (ecologist or nationalist) or any other trendy color. The chameleon is popular and well known for his long and sticky tongue, his diversity in camouflage and omnidirectional view, but he will outlive with an eternal handicap, derived from the Latin saying "Aquila non capit muscas" – he will always remain a lousy insect eater!

The snake-man is by far, the most fearsome. He sits coiled in a favoring environment, tolerated or, sometimes, even loved by someone. He is discrete, stealth, but his attack is cruel and decisive, without any warning. He will sometimes accept the touch of a warm hand, but is capable to inflict a vicious bite in it, the very next moment, without any reason at all, displaying a hatred and a ferocity which is difficult to comprehend for normal people.

He is actually capable of calmly hating everything beyond his liking or his possession. Going into the open is no longer a solution, so that he takes time in carefully preparing ambush attacks. He frequently associates in "hunting parties" organized by hyena-man, shark-man or boar – man, yet preserving his solitude and style of action, and savoring triumph by himself, a psychological triumph which does not exclude lots of money.

His way of acting is ageless: when getting old, he will spy and bite his old neighbors, savoring their agony. When used to Court paperwork, he will take pleasure in delivering unpleasant subpoenas on Easter day or Christmas Eve or on the poor victim's birthday, as only this will render him full satisfaction. The hideous remains of his shed skins are still hanging loose in the darker corners of the post-communist states. Always adaptable, the snake-man promotes actively the rattling and the spitting species. Black mamba is a good example too, for the aggressive temper.

We could endlessly talk about this parallel between our humans and various animal species, but we happen to observe that, in their eagerness to achieve power and supremacy, very few realize their species are literally starving to death.

The comparison between primates and humans is not lacking argument: we have similar height, 2 upper limbs and 2 lower limbs, all having 5 digits, one of which opposable (in apes even the lower one), similar habits and comparable moods. The ardor by which sometimes a political or social character is hunted by media, IRS, Police, political parties and social organizations, remind me of the hordes of chimps hunting for "colobus" monkeys, their preferred victims, which they sometimes simply kill for fun, without eating. The fact that monkeys have 2 more chromosomes than we do (48 instead of 46), or have opposable toes in all 4 limbs is no longer a surprise to anyone, although it might be subject to invoked superiority as in "Planet of the Apes" series.

I mean" Dude, you may have even 78 chromosomes, but my mother's son will kick your sorry ass" kind of philosophy, as easy as we peel a banana, which is something we never did the right way, if you ask monkeys.

Human society offers controversial examples: some seem to have nothing in common with primates, others seem to have had emerged from the group only recently (possibly after prom).

The resemblance is striking sometimes and so deceiving, that I'll bet in some crowded and boring Monday afternoon, the clerks from the Population Register Agency would readily issue ID cards for 3 baboons and 2 orangutans along with other people, without anybody noticing it.

There might be some problems with the signature, but we aren't going to waste time over trivial details, right? I can further bet that the baboons and the orangutans that made it to citizenship may even succeed to vote twice or three times before the whole thing gets out in the open. And then even getting a driver's license may be no sweat. There is no punishment for them, as the socialist arranged amnesty for such offenders. I've seen recently two brightly sharp clothed darker skin characters, wearing large sombrero hats, and eager to have their deceased uncle released from the hospital, as they had "urjent business in Jermany". Everything went fine until the signature episode, where they failed. That is bizarre, I said to myself, seeing that one of them was driving an X5 (BMW) and the other a SLK500 (Mercedes). I wondered where they learned to drive and where did they pass the written driving exam form?

We must have inherited passion and ardor from primates, who rarely become thoughtful, if anytime. I once saw a gorilla "silverback" male at the Barcelona zoo; it was standing with the back towards us and seemingly in a state of deep thinking. Maybe it wasn't thinking at all, maybe it was just listening to the radio news in the park, where Hugo Chavez (alive at the time!) was giving part of his favorite anti-capitalist speech.

Perhaps the gorilla was thinking of the possibility of a revolution of all caged animals in the zoo, one that would open the path for him towards a better position in the zoo – Il Comandante, Il Capo, Il Macho, Il Padrino, etc.

Meanwhile, on the other side of the vivarium, young male and female gorillas, were dedicated to happier seductive activities that came in terrible contrast with both his gloomy mood and his position as alpha male.

It is very likely that the majority of people do not aspire to existence as another shape or identity, but when it comes to "zoon politikon" - the Greek description for the political animal - we suddenly become very precious and exclusive like the white buffalo or the stripe-less tiger.

The notion of "political" defines for them another biotope, one that is complex, rich, fulfilling and exclusive, one that we, the MF-ing horned herbivores, will never dare even sniff or put hooves on.

Natural balance means that every creature of God must find a place under the sun, to live and safely multiply according to the laws of nature. Once you ruin the balance, you can get into trouble, like the Australians who brought frogs to get rid of the warms eating their crops, and now they cannot get rid of the frogs, who menace to replace them up north. I don't like frogs, they are ugly, some poisonous even and full of warts, but some can be eaten and taste quite good when not looking like Jabba-the-Hut, but I don't think they ought to be blamed in this story. Well if they start attacking kangaroos, that's a different story and we're free to go fix'em.

The question remains:

Are we really related to apes? It may seem so, but hey, we could have done worse, isn't it?

ABOUT POLITICALL CORRECTNESS AND PERSONAL ISSUES

We all know that one of the most important assets of modern civilization is social life – and we should not include here the internet social applications like Facebook or similar, supposedly having an apparently paradoxical opposite effect.

Desmond Morris, ethologist of the UK, explains in his "Bald monkey" book a lot of animal behavioral conducts – especially in apes - and how we should translate them in our modern interactive society. Basically, we are – sort of – having the same referentials and fears, the same criteria and the same approach to things and persons and their actions as apes do - or did, only we are not very much aware of it and act on a different scale or within another meaning.

For instance, is it not true that you find a person that comes to speak to you from a very close range, as being somehow annoying, to say the least? When I say close range, I mean the kind of gentleman and / or lady that comes facing you like 10 inches away, looking deep into your eyes like the aquarium fish. The kind that pathetically develops the type of subject for the listening of which you need a gasoline can and a box of premium matches, and he / she won't set you free until you light the matches.

The fact that he or she just ate, and spits you with droplets of pure, high quality garlic sauce, horse- radish marinade or fermented French cheese has nothing to do with your discomfort! By the way, there's a orange-yellow French cheese type that smells- in my imagination - like the festering peri-anal abscess of a diseased skunk; I could NEVER touch it, (and I do not remember if it is Morbier or Marouilles, very distinguished brands).

You will keep on smiling and pretend that you cry only because of emotion – if the subject of your dialogue is sad. If it was a joke, simply pretend you are crying with laughter. If the subject was something irrelevant and idiot – like a weather comment – you may be in trouble, because there is nothing to account for the tears, unless you have a sudden attack of glaucoma, which is more discreet, by all means, and would need further boring explanation.

The relevant fact is that our ancestors – and I am not talking here Abe Lincoln, Richard- the- Lionhearted, King Tut or even Cher – I mean way before them all - our truly old ancestors, used to carry weapons like knives or swords. It would commonly take some space – generally about 30-40 inches – to swing them into action against a close range attacker/ victim.

Even when going to peace with an enemy – and the habit of shaking right hand is a remainder of the ritual of showing you do not carry a concealed weapon in your right hand – you had to be careful and not come too close to your enemy. It was equally important not to allow him to come as close as rendering you unable to oppose a treacherous attack, like in the finale of the "Gladiator" drama.

That security area of 35-50 inches around us was always strictly necessary in order to feel safe. Or at least breathe safe. So next time someone comes closer than 70 cm or 30 inches to speak to you, please notice how you instinctively take a small step back, maybe concealed in a lateral one to begin with, while pretending you observe something elsewhere or do a similar trick, enabling you to get back to the "safe" distance rate.

I once had a very embarrassing adventure about this issue; while being at a New year's Eve party, there was an annoying little man who thought he knew me and insisted to come and talk to me at very close range. I strongly suspect now it was a more complex manifestation, as he sometimes grabbed my necktie and my coat and was trying to shake me into understanding his point, like maniacs do. I vaguely remember he even tried to invite me to dance a polka with him and I was finally excused because – due to the crowd – I couldn't get away from the table – and I had a bad knee!!. God knows what would have happened if I were in a more comfortable position. Love can strike with a devastating power. The fact that I was with my wife did not seem to impress him at all! However, besides being given the opportunity to have a precise and detailed account of his few resting teeth and inhale repeatedly his mesmerizing ammonia sewage - pool breath, I congratulated myself for not reacting too vigorously, as I later observed he was also wearing a hearing device. Which does not explain why he was the one talking all the time, but anyway! Maybe he was secret service or something. You never know whom you get to dance to these days!

Our privacy can be invaded in many ways; getting too close to someone is not always regarded as offensive. Young people often get together and stay so close to each other that they seem welded or conveniently "united". They are so cute and they look at each-other like the rest of the world does not exist for them, and I am pretty sure – in those moments - it doesn't! And shouldn't! It always makes me emotional and I always think that the "get a room!" cliché cannot solve their problems. By the way, their problems are commonly far greater and the answers to them, more generous than we could understand and / or admit, are partly in our hands. I remember what our late King Michael the First said before he passed away: "I do not consider this country as a heritage we got from our ancestors; I consider it is something we borrowed from our grandchildren and followers and should safely return before leaving this world". This is something he failed to do because of the fowl communist disaster and the Russian influence.

Now, getting back to our idea, I can say that sometimes, being too close to someone may trigger surprises unaccounted for. I once took my reserved seat in a train compartment near a very aggressively drunk person. Actually, he was not very selfish, as he was trying to persuade everyone around to honor his bottle of cheap wine and take a sip – or "kiss" it - as he said. I am not an ascetic type, actually, I am rather Epicurean in eating and drinking habits, but there was no way he would convince me to drink his stuff in the middle of July heat, on a train lacking AC and without sterilizing the bottle "kisser" first. I was a medical student at the time and I used to be creative, so I grabbed the bottle in a more or less clumsy way, pretending I have trouble in holding it upright. The next thing I did was raise it in a gesture like trying to drink out of it, but it slipped away from my hand and out the opened window it went. OMG, you should have seen the disappointment on his face. The "Desolation of Smaug" was nothing compared to his! He was almost ready to pull the emergency handle in trying to recuperate it, but I coldly suggested it might have already broken against the rails and the heavenly fluid spilled among rubble. The only way I calmed him down was to mention that such event might have a divine determination; maybe our dead ancestors were thirsty and they are now satisfied with the booze they got from us or, err.. …especially him, consequently, they welcome the sacrifice and cherish him. And it worked. He ultimately had some respect for ancestors. Another time I was placed between two very "consistent" ladies. Consistent was a euphemism; each of them might have sold shade in summer and milk in winter and make a good business out of it. I was so stuck I could not hear anything as my both ears were obliterated by their …generous …presence. I finally decided it was a risky place to stay if any of them – Good Heavens - fell asleep, and I struggled to get out. I did it and when I succeeded, it sounded like opening up a bottle of champagne. When I looked back, the space where I stayed was gone already, being re/claimed by their … vigorous personalities. I assumed my move was not misinterpreted as they were both still smiling while I showed myself out of the compartment. Or so I thought, because of the lipstick. Or maybe they didn't even notice my escape and they were smiling like this ever since their last plastic surgery, I could never tell. It was like in that joke: "I told my girlfriend she has painted her eyebrows way too high; and she seemed very intrigued".

I currently am very careful not to disturb someone while that particular someone is doing something, whatever that may be. They say that Japanese people are more successful because they take much care not to disturb others.

I wonder if this assessment was a genuinely psychological one, as for me it was quite puzzling.

I mean I do not want and I avoid at all cost to disturb someone. What if that someone is a burglar or a mugger? He smiles at you and winks – as a sure promise of what will happen to you if you speak up. Suppose you do upset him by disturbing him while he is doing his …"thing". You don't get excused - not in 50 years, as he will be looking for you even after 10 years when he gets "out".

There are other issues perhaps even more disturbing than this one. I travel frequently in European countries in order to participate at various professional meetings and conventions. Can't remember now all, but there were Paris, London, Berlin, Copenhagen, Amsterdam, Madrid, Rome, Athens, etc. All of these EU countries have vigorous allegations concerning their care for citizens and how they would never allow any discrimination to interfere. Ok! I said to myself every time. Now let us check it. How? It is very simple: if you are in the airport, go to the toilet. I am sure you will see at least 2 colored persons out of 3 mopping around.

Go to luggage claim or take a look under your airplane; the workers disembarking or manipulating luggage are colored, commonly black. Then go to the subway station; lower clerks and janitors are all black. Go to your hotel – the "Field-Marshall" at the entrance in shinny uniform smiling at you like a Cheshire cat is most probably black. People scrubbing floors and carrying luggage are black. Maids are black. Elevator operator is black. We're talking about countries with dominant / traditional white population, having one single common feature in the past – they all had colonies in Africa or around.

I once tried to eat something at the McDonald's on Champs D'Elysee in Paris. Most of the personnel were black, including one nice curled happy- face about 20 years old. I didn't eat my burger, but not because she was black (she was really cute!) but because she picked her nose right in front of me, just before handing me the sandwich (with the same hand and the alleged finger underneath).

Sure, the picking finger, with its sticky content most likely still lurking underneath her fingernail, was outside my package, but what if she touched food while packaging? I mean you do not die because of it, but I would be reluctant to eat the food contaminated this way even if I did it myself.

So much for non-discrimination. I didn't get any chance to visit the US so far, but if I'll see luggage carriers, janitors, cleaners or machinery operators who are exclusively black, I'll know the Americans are all the same with EU: All hat and no cattle, like they say in Texas.

One of these days, while watching the end of the winter Olympics in South Korea, a friend of mine, real joker, was staring straight through his glass of beer and said:

- You know something? I'll bet nothing in this wide world is just happening by accident; there must be a superior meaning in it!
- Wow! I said. What a philosophy! When did you realize that? What do you mean? Like God given?
- Sort of, but not exactly! What I want to say is that sometimes things match in bizarre ways that we are not ready to comprehend, or are not for us to see.
- Well tell me how it goes, now! Don't let me down! Illuminate me, bro!
- For instance, I've been watching lots of sporting events lately and I found some very disturbing combinations and coincidences!
- ?!,,,,,
- Take a look at these championships and Olympics; there are nations and individual types who are prone for a distinctive sport and result.

I got into the game:

- Yap! Like Bulgarians are always good with weight lifting! But they also have good yogurt and pickles! And Ethiopians always run the Marathon first! But which is the disturbing part?
- Well, I was wondering how come that all black people become champions in running, while the white people get so good at target rifle shooting?

In the now a days politics in my country, it scares me when I see odd circumstances putting together people that otherwise hate each-other. It would be like making a brotherly alliance between Democrats and the GOP, all in the name of public welfare and satisfaction! That's the kind of information you need to swallow with antiemetic, even when given by Reader's Digest! Like how it would be seeing President Trump inviting Hillary Clinton to a polka on a Saturday National reunion political barbeque. With a barn dance. I can imagine her keeping her lips tight in her traditional smile (which, incidentally, gives me the shivers!) and Trump laughing all the way, trying to pinch her by the cheek. Oh, come on now! I only said cheek, so please consider just the straight, classic/ official meaning of the word!

However, it doesn't always come in so cheerfully. I have seen live political debates where one of the invited politicians poured the water from his glass on the head of his opponent; in one such event, a Socialist jumped over his opposition candidate and started punching him like in a boxing game. The reporter – a nice young lady -who was actually to blame for the incident, because she knew nothing about nobody and got to their nerves – started screaming and the atmosphere was something like in Scream 5. It took a while to get the victim out of his "socialist" range.

Obviously, real hatred mounted beyond political reason, as for many people, living in a world allegedly free of communism means "payback time".

You can't just go there, meet someone you hate or dislike, to the least, and say: "Oh, Hello! You're ugly. I'm busy, so have a nice day!". That works well on a failed internet date, when you see the disastrous gap between the handsome and manly character you've been chatting with on the Net and the slimy, yellow teethed, good for nothing, bald and humped "rag-in-the-butt" person staying in front of you.

That is if he cares about having a talk, before he ties you up in the trunk of his car in order to carve your tattoos later, with his survival knife, to improve his collection.

I went one day to a meeting of my party; cannot hide from politics, still stirs me up! It is like a collective frenzy in which everybody is throwing shit upwards.

Naturally, some of it hits the fan, as Americans use to say it. Then you need an umbrella! The worst scenario is when the smell does not bother you anymore! The political party can be a good umbrella, if compromise with your own convictions does not reach dangerous levels, and it never happened to me so far (mine is a right-side party!). However, the meeting was about ganging up with the Socialist (our traditional antagonist) in some sort of National Union formation in view of the next elections.

Meanwhile, the Socialist candidates we were supposed to promote, actually the Mayor and the President of the County Council, were busy screwing us on all fronts.

Somehow they grabbed hold of the Emergency Hospital administration (decentralization!?) and their first measure was to put out of office all managers and coordinating medical stuff that was not registered as Socialist with their party. As Chief Surgeon of the T&O clinic, I discovered after a 3 day participation to a Congress that I was no longer in charge. I was to blame too, with my big mouth. However, now I was becoming in the awkward situation to politically sustain them. After they took the bread from the mouth of my children! I went to the local party leader and I said: "Friend, this is BS! These guys are traced by prosecutors for illegal business with public funds and even already prosecuted for other illegal businesses! (at this time they are history). They kicked me out of a career I have been building up for 25 years without a wink and did the same to hundreds of people, and now you want me to promote them? I'll better cut my hand off before even writing a letter for them. These soon-to-be-inmates represent the true liberal ideology – based on freedom, initiative and honesty?" (our definition of right side "Liberal" is totally different from the one in US!!). He finally admitted it was ok if I did not participate, and I never did until 2 years later, when the political cart split and broke again.

In our reality, cunningly stupid morons, based on the countless votes of even bigger morons, confiscated leadership. I am being sour, but the reality is ordinary people here lack social, political or economic education and they take everything they see on TV as grunted. And they want the state to always "give them" something, whether it is discount for medicine or fire-wood, gas or electricity, it "don't" matter, provided it is for free and "no work" demanded for it.

Which is exactly what their political socialist representatives do for them, using public funds to "bribe" this brainless mob into voting them. Did you know that after the recent congress, the social-democratic party here has 32 top national leaders, all of them short of college education? Some others do, they got even PhD degrees in Universities that functioned for as long as they have registered their degree and closed soon after.

We used to have an old saying, which could be translated like this:

"With the uneducated simple moron
You have a fight, and then you're cool
But a colossal war is going on
If the alleged moron went to school"

All my family works or worked in education: my wife and her sister as well as my brother in law are teachers.

I am faculty and my mother in law was a primary grammar school teacher. I enjoy harassing them with stories about how crippled the education system became. There's no more respect for the teachers and the teachers seem blind when it comes to understand that respect is gained, not imposed or sentenced. That comes with wit, talent and experience. In a remote neighborhood of the city, the school was full of brats. One of them gets up in the middle of the Math class and tries to harass the young and nice looking lady who was their teacher:

- Miss, how am I supposed to write a difficult test like this, after partying last night and having this mad, super-crazy, unstoppable and devastating sex experience?

All other kids started laughing and cheering and were eagerly waiting to hear what the teacher would say to this. The brat gave high fives to all his friends around him.

She looked at him with sort of sad eyes, without smiling, and answered:

- It hurts me to see how much you must have suffered, but you can try using your other hand! And she continued explaining the lesson.

But of course, there are other interesting issues we can bring up to your attention.

One of my friends went to US and – as it was summer time – they decided to go to the beach in North or South Carolina, can't remember which.

He was very upset because he went there loaded with cash, which was a very suspicious looking fact to the authorities and he almost got booked few times for forwarding hundred dollar bills. But this was not the end. Once they got to the beach, they had another problem.

His wife, considerably younger than him and with somewhat Rubensian curvy shapes, exposed herself on the beach with a minimal bathing suit, according to stylish European standards. This caused havoc amid the local busty housewives, all dressed like for Siberian traditional frozen water bathing. They even covered kid's eyes so they would not see her! "OMG here, OMG there, yada yada! Oh dear, we are so ashamed of what we saw today at the beach! It was repulsive!

(wow!) "Imagine this cheeky (she really is cheeky if we mean the bottom and I am saying that in an appreciative way) woman offering a view to her body to my innocent kids!

My friend was a bit upset about this bigot attitude and advised his wife to get a whole one-piece suit from local shop. And he said: when these 300 lbs. house wives behave like this, it looks like they never see the almost naked persons of uncertain gender, riding the subway train while wearing exactly what my wife – who surely is a woman, I can testify to that – was wearing at the beach that day. Or maybe we shouldn't talk about the adventure they had a few years back with the cable boy or the plumber, when their husband thought he got crabs because he peed in a bush of poisoned vine. Or when they caught their husband banging the baby sitter or the next-door neighbor's wife?

They do not let them kids to watch TV, they forbid sexual education at schools, and when their girls come weeping home because they got pregnant at sweet sixteen, they throw them out because they dishonored their home.

I said nothing; we have this breed as well.

But I remembered something else I wanted to point out; the "benefit" of esthetic surgery. The results are sometimes stunning, people cannot recognize themselves. I think the best job is being done on the wanted criminals and fugitives. Women come next, in order to maintain that "28 years old" look for their next 40 or even more. You cannot blame them – pregnancy and kids create deformities in most of them, and as a brilliant internal medicine professor of ours (Hatieganu) used to say: "The only glands involved in obesity are the salivary".

I once met a high- class family in my city; they were "white collar", intellectuals, well positioned and paid, with a nice house downtown and a lot of friends and admirers. Him, was a tall man, slender and a bit skinny and bony for my taste, with a bony face, big large nose but a honest smile on his face, but her was a real beauty: oval shaped face, cat's green eyes, tiny nose over curvy and juicy pink lips, dark complexion and perfectly shaped hips, thighs and legs. Not to mention the jumpy boobs! All in all the dream girl of your teenage!

The good impression lasted until I saw the kid! The boy was 7 or 8 but you couldn't say for sure. He was the ugliest kid I ever saw in my life! Brahi-cephalic skull, half closed left eye, merged eyebrows like Lombroso's criminal type, twisted teeth and a little humpy, I think. WTF is with this kid? Who does he belong to? I tried again and again in vane to find any trace of resemblance to his parents, as I knew the boy was their natural offspring! It was only after that I learned his mother underwent extensive plastic surgery in repeated sessions and I figured out how this must have affected the father.

Sometimes a husband can hardly recognize his wife in the morning without the make-up, but with such profound changes, that must be a totally different experience. It also depends on how much he drank the night before. He must take a deep breath and hold steady until he is sure he knows the person before jumping off the balcony. Some hasty brothers did it before realizing they were actually at home.

One of them was a guy I used to know; he came to me with both forearms broken and I put him in a plaster casting – for both upper limbs! He was very happy because he was no longer supposed to do anything around the house and they would have to feed him and all; he was LOL about the situation and he felt like a king. I told him: "Don't make a fuss out of it! Let's see how you wipe your ass tomorrow morning!"

Imagine you get accustomed with your spouse's body after so many years and you kind of "know" her "dimensions". Guess what happens after she puts on bigger boobs! Guess what happens if one of them blows up some day! Or worse, at night, so you have to stop whatever you do and dress up to go to the nearest hospital that can treat silicon poisoning.

Women may often get "assessed" by such parameters and it is only normal for them to try and better their image to the top! Unfortunately, the kid you give birth to remains a cruel reminder of what/ how you really are, and I think this genetic kind of print is also valid for the education you give them.

One would consider us men more fortunate than women when it comes to all these features and image necessities. Maybe we are, and we can make together a list of the reasons, like I saw one in a revue last month cherishing womanhood:

"If you are a man:

- You are in a good mood throughout the month
- Car shop mechanics do not mock you
- You don't have to carry with you a bag full of crazy stuff
- You don't give a rat's ass if someone does not observe your new haircut
- It doesn't basically matter how your body looks when you apply for a job
- None of your colleagues has the ability to make you cry, unless he ate onion;
- Intimate lingerie is waaayyyy cheaper
- You basically need only 3 pairs of shoes: wedding, sports and everyday job;
- You keep family name all your life
- When taking a bath you can be ready in 10 minutes, hair drying included;
- You can always wear white T shirts in rain or wet places
- Whatever is on your face stays the same color, unless you enter a brawl;
- You – normally - don't have to shave lower than your throat
- You can leave hotel bed a mess without second thoughts
- Grey hair and wrinkles do well on you
- You can attend a peeing, farting or burping contest without being ashamed
- You can get to be a referee, priest or president
- You can spread your legs when seated
- You don't need to be accompanied to the toilet
- You don't need to stop at the next gas-station, because the previous had a dirty toilette seat;
- You can admire Brad Pitt without starving while trying to look like him;
- You know at least 2 dozen ways to open a beer

- You can bring any idea to common reason with a simple WTF
- Any call to your friends will last at most 60 seconds
- If you fail to call a friend whenever you get laid, he will not comment with others "a subtle change" in your behavior;
- If you are still single at 35, your friends either do not care, or may even congratulate you;
- Your friends do not care if you grow fat or slim;
- You don't give a f--k on people talking at your back;
- You can scratch your balls anytime you want, more or less discretely; (this could be discussed – you don't have them, you ain't got any itch! But then we have'em, don't we?)
- You can unbutton your shirt anytime when you feel hot;
- With 400 million projectiles in every "ammo" shot, you could double the Earth population – theoretically at least! – in a couple of days;
- You can become a father every day, without having to wait for 9 months;
- You are not upset if your best friend has other friends
- You can have a banana on the street without having comments from other men, that is if you are not on the wrong side of the street;

A friend of mine told me he found out the result of an interesting fact about men. He said it was important, because it explains our night time behavior.

He agreed to share the details with me and said that, according to this statistics, men wake up at night because of these 3 reasons:

- to drink water – 5%
- to go to the bathroom – 12%
- to go home – 83%

Political correctness may kill valuable messages, we may thus fail to transmit. I am not implying being rude and offensive is better, however, a message can be delivered in a persuasive but delicate way.

For instance, Oscar Wile was saying: "Bigamy means having a wife too many; monogamy is pretty much the same".

A female friend was once invited to a coffee by my wife; they were having a discussion over manly manners and I tried to interfere and defend my gender. She got mean and said to me that I'd better mind what Robin Williams said – "Problem is that God gave man a brain and a penis, but not enough blood to use them both in the same time". I told her that right now I am concentrating on my brain because I needed to answer to an intelligent woman like her, but I can do better than that later. Also invited her to come over and check the rest. She said nothing, but smiled. My wife also said nothing, but she didn't smile, so I left.

Perhaps she remembered about Billy Crystal when he said: "Women need a reason to have sex; men only need the place to do it!"

I'll never understand how Woody Allen has got so much success with women, considering his "athletic" look. And he has the guts to deny it: "Last time I was inside a woman was when I visited the statue of Liberty". He also used to say: "Sex is like the game of bridge. If you haven't got a good partner, you'd better have a good hand!". He admitted that he is such a good lover because "he is practicing a lot alone!".

Brendan Francis said something notable – "The difference between paid sex and free sex is that paid sex ultimately gets to be a lot cheaper".

The degree of involvement is gradually decreasing in a relationship, and I saw numerous couples in which "sweetie pie", "prince charming", "tiger", "cowboy", "darling", etc. dramatically turns into "filthy pig", "brontosaurus", "moron", "witch", "stuffed cow", etc.

Romance has gone and left room to harsh words, burps, farts and lack of consideration. I heard about the daughter of a distinguished person in our city who – after one year into marriage – had to hear from her husband: "You are a miserable diseased wreck; I only took you for your money!". So sad! Another guy I know, was married to an older woman; they were godfathers to a younger couple and one fine day, he fled with the bride soon after the wedding! They all meet now for a chat over a cup of coffee! Kids included! Now that is something I – for one – couldn't stand to do! I mean I am not that civilized! And speaking about relationship, and getting to funnier issues, this guy comes to the rabbi and says:

-   Oh Rabbi! Can you help me?
-   Maybe I can, my son! What is your problem?
-   I have this wish to live forever!
-   Hmm! Then I think it s best for you to get married!
-   Married? How come? I mean if I get married my wish of living forever will be accomplished? Asks the guy in disbelief.
-   Nope! But your wish will surely disappear!

It is curious how human behavior can alter things and cultural milestones. There are weird laws about human behavior all over the world and it is very interesting to study them - from a safe distance sometimes.

For instance, there is a crazy law in Lebanon about what we use to call zoophilic behavior : it is forbidden to have intercourse with a male animal under the punishment of death penalty, but you can do it if the animal is a female.

Now I'd like to see the opinion of animal rights groups and foundations on this one! Should the owners of poisonous snakes be granted an exception bill? Just in case! What if the alleged animal is a true hermaphrodite, like a snail or something?

This reminded me of a story a guy from the Foreign Legion told me. He joined the French Foreign Legion after our revolution and he spent some 5 years there. He also had gotten French citizenship following his service there. He said:

-   My friend, I am going to tell you a nice story now! Check this out! We were camped in Cartier General de Monclarin in Djibouti, Africa – you know, La 13me Demi-brigade! Close to Camp Lemonier of the Americans!

- Yes, I suppouse I heard about it – I said with precaution!
- Well, we were happy there - -mostly training, nothing serious to do!
- Doesn't look dangerous so far!
- Well, we were also getting bored and the weekends we were having some fun, everyway available way!
- Nothing bad until now!
- One fine day, the major call us in his office and talks to us:
- Ok guys, you have had a strong training and a difficult time. This   makes me glad, but also desperate about the things I get to hear about   you. It is all right to try and relax after so much training but what I just heard about you guys is terryfying!
- What was it? I asked nervously!

The Major winks to us and smiles while saying it very loud:

"Well I heard that you take one particular camel from Legion stables on weekends and use it until morning, when you bring it back! They say that camel ….. is your favorite!

The Major slams his fists into the small tea table in front of him and says.

- I know you are through challenging objectives and need some unsupervised time for yourself – and he winks again.

But…. I was unable to fix all jurisdiction orders, tables and circumstances. so I kept using the old ones. They are ….. more permissive for all of us and – guess what - us, officers, share the same problems with you when we are out here in the desert.

"?......Hmmm, so what do we have to do Sir?" We asked.

"Oh, nothing much he says, lighting a cigarette and looking in some books. Just bring the animal to me this Friday evening! I am curious about the training of this camel"

- "And do it discretely! In my tent at 10 pm."

Some of the guys started laughing or saying something, but I kicked them hard with my boot and I said:

- It is ok Sir! We'll do it!

Next Friday we get the nice 4 years old single hump female camel to his tent and leave it at the entrance, well brushed and equipped, not before preparing the tranquilizer gun just in case.

I got to bed over night, but I had a bad sleep thinking of the poor camel and assessing our past experience with it.

- So what happened next? I was becoming impatient!
- Well, next morning at an early time, they both looked very tired; the camel was chewing some straw stuff as far from him as possible, but the Major looked all beat: tired eyes, one purple, clothes all torn up, with one of his shoulder flaps hanging loose, and his pants barely hanging to the waist, and no boots. He waived us away when he saw us first, but then he sat on a bigger stone next to his tend and yawned!:
- How was your night guys?....As for me, I didn't sleep so well! The darn' camel of yours is savage! Actually, she was useless! I am very disappointed!
- We are sorry to hear that, Sir! She served us very good so far!
- Maybe so! But the moment I touch her … she starts kicking and spitting. How did you…errr! … you know what I mean, how did you use it without getting bitten?
- Sorry Major! Actually, we never tried to make love to the camel; we were just taking a ride with it 3 miles south to a village where there is a brothel!

It looks like in the US state of Georgia, sex toys are forbidden. Shucks!

Thing is it's freakin hard to find any toys at all, because the state leaders strongly believe that any toy can be used as a sex toy! Or a golf ball? OOoooops! The things you can do with a golf ball! Especially if it is a Schlesinger! And the little battery driven train! It is pointed, like one and a half inch wide and it is buzzing like a….. dildo! The worst of all are the balloons! Colored and flavored, capisci??????

They say in North Carolina it is forbidden to wear sunglasses while having sex. Well that would not be a surprise, as most serial highway women killers go those parts and wearing sunglasses was the first idea they had to preserve secrecy over their identity. Secondly, the flashes from the photographers (either paid or paparazzi) can damage your retina while doing your thing, there. This is also encouraging shy women to accept their nudity and their naughty behavior while having sex with all lights on, while you need a little relaxation or while others are taking it on tape.

In Maryland, you cannot buy condoms from a dispenser that doesn't distribute booze as well. This one has simply touched my heart. To think of those politicians that gave some minutes from their life to be in the shoes of ordinary people!

Now having sex is a matter of feeling, financial potency, pure and simple potency or extreme boredom, however, something that will get to your nerves and require a little tension breakup, in order to focus on whatever you have to do and whoever you've got to do it with.

As a civilized person, in your trying to avoid severe contamination with STD or unwanted (and ever after regretted) pregnancy, you will need to procure a condom, sometimes two (for one night if you're young or for a week, otherwise).

So you go to the nearest public toilet or hotel lobby, in trying to find a condom dispenser. Eventually you find one, but you're still missing something.

A nice sip of whiskey or wine before doing it, just to stir up the hormones and the imagination! See what I mean? The law makers already thought about it.

They want you to be fulfilled so you are not aloud to use condoms without drinking something. However, there is a reverse part of the coin here! What if someone needs a drink and every joint is closed except for the darn' dispensers?

You can get the booze, but you need to buy condoms too. This is not necessarily bad, they say! While having your drink, you may get in the mood and the next thing – what do you know? You need them condoms! Or you don't, cause you can solve the problem yourself! Well it is safer with it anyway! You may have shaken hands with a politician! You may leave an opened one in the garbage bin, just to make a good impression to the hotel house cleaner, and keep the rest for a true and epic occasion. I met a guy once who started collecting condoms, you know, like postage stamps! The "piece du resistance" of the collection was a condom supposedly used during Queen Victoria time!

I was very impressed by the size – men were different those days, when they invented steam machines, I tell you no shit! And thinking the "thing" had actually been used, it stirs your imagination; they just washed it up a little and bang on! Bang- bang! By the looks of it, the thing alone was able to satisfy one of them baron ladies even lacking the content. Alternatively, it makes you think that sex and liquor always come together in Maryland, which is not the case. What about the morning sex? Milk doesn't stir you up the same way – I checked! On the contrary! And not everybody in Maryland was born after a party, either!

In Indiana you can be accused of rape if the female traveler in your car wears no shoes and socks. Now that's crazy! Imagine you have to take Aunt Agatha from the church on Sunday and she comes back home with three of her best friends, all born before WW I. During the short trip, they complain about the shoes they wear and how they press against their bunions, so they take off shoes and socks. The police stops you on a routine check just before getting home and finds not one, but four old ladies without shoes and socks, all chatting vividly in your car like sparrows on a telegraph wire in a Sonora train stop. First, the officer will look at you with surprise and respect, but getting a better look inside, his face will get pale and expressionless.

He writes a long paper and hands it over to you. The next day you get called to the precinct, and wonder how long you'll get to stay in, for four rape accounts.

Surprise comes from lawyer assigned to you. He says:

- Relax buster! I cut a deal with the district attorney! Just got out of his office!
- Deal? What deal? You ask, half amazed with hope and half paralyzed with fear!
- Yap! I saved you the day! You were supposed to get 10 years with aggravating circumstances for quadruple rape accusation! That's 2 and a half years for each of the old witches, cause they might have forgotten if they consented. I spoke to them, and given the circumstances, you get only five, for multiple tomb desecration! And no further claim, either!

Oral sex is forbidden in: Alabama, Arizona, Florida, Idaho, Kansas, Louisiana, Massachusetts, Minessota, Missippi, Georgia, North Carolina, South Carolina, Oklahoma, Oregon, Rhode Island, Utah, Virginia, and Washington. Incidentally, these are the states with most oral syphilis cases. This law was sustained by dentists and tooth paste producers, after observing weird flavors demands on the market and dental floss used in horrifying ways we cannot describe while kids are around. Leaving away other states, that possibly explains why New York is so crowded with tourists and people go for vacation in Hawaii. However, I often wondered how they monitor this law. Then it came to me! It is so simple! They can do it in several ways! For instance, when you go to your job, there will be "The Decency Squad" team with probes to take samples from your mouth like for DNA. Hmm, hardly! Another option would be to "bug" you discretely on the assumption that oral sex does not demand necessarily clothes removal. Not likely! The communist style – have the person you were with, defect and confess everything – that's one I would be afraid of, even if it is your word against his! Putting a reactive substance like in pools, to see who's peeing in the water, would work maybe, with a blue color! You would see lots of girls with blueish teeth and some guys too!

In Massachusetts a woman must not be over her partner while having sex.

Like who's gonna find out or why does it matter? Well, I wouldn't be so sure it doesn't. I remember a story during the communist regime, about a local highly positioned hot-shot in the communist party, who was found deceased in a room of the most luxurious hotel downtown, while his family was waiting for him home. Well, I was young at the time, but my imagination served me to understand what happened.

This is not a bad thing those law makers in Massachusetts thought of; what if, according to modern standards, a young woman that spent half her life at Mac's makes love to you shakin' all her 300 pounds on top of you. The medical possibilities of explaining your untimely death are endless, you just pick one:

- Death by suffocation
- Torn liver
- Enteral thrombosis
- Ruptured spleen
- Cardiac congestion
- Panic attack followed by collapse

So we should in fact be thankful to the legislator for issuing a law that protects us even in our most personal moments. However, in the case of a young lady weighing 100-120 pounds and moving cautiously in a heavenly way, your death could not be explained, unless your wife's potential confession.

In New Mexico, women cannot go in public without peeling hairs. Now that is a decent law. Traditionally, growing hairs all over the place is a man's job, therefore not really under tight scrutiny.

It is an attribute of manhood and macho attitude, a message of dominance and possession, a sign of danger to others – "Watch it, this hair covers muscle and stamina – don't make me use it on you – the muscle not the hair! Dude!".

As for the females, towards them it should have the opposite meaning – like "Watch this! This hair covers tons of muscle and stamina! If you are a bit interested, I can use it on you – again, the muscle and stamina, not the hairs!! Even if you are not interested, what do you have to lose? We can have a good time! A glass of Chardonnay, at least? etc."

This is the true reason why you have a weird sensation seeing hairs on a woman in random places.

Remember the "bearded woman" that won the Eurovision music festival some years ago? Her/ his (couldn't decide which) name was Conchita Wurst. Conchita is a regular Spanish / Latino name for a regular honest girl. Wurst, on the other hand, is "sausage" in German. Does that ring a bell? The singer that goes by that name came from Austria and – hold your breath – won first prize! That is for the courage to sing a love song! The aspect was devastating, totally weird. Imagine Mary Antoinette or Queen Victoria with a pitch black beard, all dressed for a palace ball, long vaporous dress and all! The effect was that of a stun gun and worked on thousands of people, who forgot to breathe through their wide open mouths.

It was a hideous moment, when brothers hated sisters and vice versa, men hated women, women hated men (and I briefly hated my wife, until I saw she actually had no beard – on the chin, that is). The sight of that beard was digging its way into our manly conscience and the result had been a questionable "competence" within the next few weeks, if you were straight. Now there is a whole world of difference from getting closer to an unshaved arm pit - especially if it belongs to Cher or baby Lourdes (Madonna's daughter – even if, between "us girls", I'd kill for the mother in this case), and having to use your machete to clear your path down towards the happy grounds of Mount Venus of a natural beauty like in Tarzan's legend. The thickness might be discouraging impenetrable, serving for a better guard than a paid gunman.

There are some communities, however, very much acquainted to the fact; a woman in their society might become undesirable only if and when forgetting to shave her back, while getting to look like a departing buffalo. As a doctor, you become to think who's gonna give birth to offspring with all that testosterone frenzy. Maybe that is how "unisex" perfume came to the market. When is the next step to unisex aftershave?

And finally, a Florida law says it is illegal to have sex with a porcupine. That was something that can silence anyone. Of all animals in the Florida wilderness, freshly joined pythons included, how did they think of a porcupine? I still think it was a wager! I mean if you listen to "Born on a bayou!" you still find nothing about such kinky experience. There is a tribe in Africa where youngsters must prove their manhood – to be ever recognized – if they can put their hand inside a carved log full of killer ants! The more they resist, the more respected they are! But no one in local tribes did think to stick inside the log anything else than the hand. Possibly because hand is no unique organ.

But there is always someone prone to do a stupid thing. The American society has lots of expertise in it. If you get a box with rat poison, they will write on it "Poisonous! Do not eat!" which makes you think there were people who would have really tried it. There are bottles with bleach that have encrypted on them: "Do not drink! Poisonous and harmful!". Maybe you heard about one recent trendy idea American youngsters have for fun! They chew on detergent capsules for automatic laundry washing machines. Some survive, not thanks to their wit but because someone sober manages to be around.

But I had the experience to see an even more interesting case, a case that was not actually made public and there was no law (nor is it now I believe) to describe or rule it. I was working in the ER as an apprentice at the time and I saw one night an older character seated on the margin of a stretcher and weeping his eyes out. I went to comfort him and asked him: "Why do you cry? You lost someone?" He nodded sobbingly and said: "She was my only friend on this Earth!" I said: "Who was your friend?" He replied: "Isobel" I thought the man must have lost his wife and tried again to comfort him: "Look mister! I understand parting was difficult, but she must have gotten to a different and maybe a better world! She may be better off like this!". He looked at me in disbelief and started shouting: "Better of? Do you think after they get you out and roll you on a stick you feel in a better world?" Then started crying again: "How she must have been cold, poor darling!" I was amazed with the details: who would roll a human being on a stick and what was the meaning of out? I took my chances and asked: "Sir I do not want to disturb you even more, but can you tell me what happened?" He was sobbing like a child and he managed to say this: 'I am from the delta" (Danube delta he meant). I got sick some months ago. I went to the doctors they told me I have a parasite in my bowel, a tenia or tape worm!" He blew his nose and carried on: "It was not affecting me deeply so I did not stay for the treatment! I got home, I ate a lot for both of us and soon it was better because I did not feel so lonely: I would talk to her and it was like she would answer to me. I named her Isobel, by the name of my great grand mother's sister!" I looked at him with different eyes now: "So what happened?" I asked. "Nothing much!" he answered. One day I felt very sick so they came and pulled her by the tail and rolled her out my ass hole on a stick. It was a three hour ordeal! I begged them to spare her, but they did not stop until she was out! And took me to the hospital for tests!" I tried to put some reason into him: "Well, at least the sacrifice was not a bad thing after all! You came out parasite free!" Like touched with fresh acid he turned to me and started crying loudly: "Whyyyyy! They had to kill her! They killed my Isobel! My only friend in this world! The only person that cared about me and I shared everything with her……ohhh! I am so sad without her!". Roll over Shakespeare! Romeo was boring and Juliet was predictable! How about real and true love, one that breaks the boundaries of species?

As you can see, sometimes there is a great difference between what we want or choose to say about something and what we really think about it.

DO WE DRINK
TOO MUCH?

We've got accustomed to considering alcohol drinking, in general, as a Biblical sin of the others. Accurately defining it turns out to be a much more difficult and even subtle task, in today's social context.

Let us put it this way: if a mayor has a noon whiskey with his favorite councilors, does that make him a drunk? God forbid!

If a Congress-man has had a heavy lunch with plentiful liquid compensation and then falls asleep during a board meeting, does that make him a drunk? Come on, folks! We can always apply the boss concept line: the boss is not sleeping, he is merely concentrating, planning ahead or having thoughts!

Much better for the Moldavians who simply extricated from their vocabulary the "drunk" or being "drunk" allegation. When they drink, they say they "honor" something or "serve" something. If it so happens that, afterword, you have the "honor" to crash-land in a gutter, it is just a matter of subsequent analysis, which does not harm anyone and becomes irrelevant for our research.

As for the Russians and the Lipova (a Russian related population) from our country, it may be hard to be accurate when deciding if they drink water or vodka, as they use the same jar —size glasses for both. However, I've seen them pretty good with steering boats on the water, but I haven't seen them drinking it, so far.

That reminds me of this Russian Commissar, who getts in a pub with 2 friends and his driver. He asks for 4 jars of vodka. They grab the jars and empty them pronto, while asking for the second round.

Down the hatch goes round number 2, and the Commissar asks for yet another round. The third needs a little more time to go, but down it goes after 5-6 minutes of quality conversation. The Commissar waves again to the waiter, but now he makes the "3" sign with his fingers. The waiter is a little puzzled and approaches: Tavarish Commissar, a patamu shto? (Comrade Commissar, but why so?). The Commissar knocks his forehead with his index and then points out to one of his men, the tiniest of all: Patamu schto on shofer, durak! (because he is the driver, you moron!)

Besides, the name of the favorite spirit in Russia – vodka – comes as a diminutive of water ("vadá"), possibly meaning something like "little / tiny water".

I have thought on countless occasions about the actors impersonating important people in various life stories, characters presented while going and humbly speaking for themselves in AA associations (like when you go there, you stay anonymous for what, five minutes?! All the old household witches, eternally cleaning the hallway of your block with the same broom, all the early-going-to-the-marketplace housewives you meet every day, not to mention your secretary and her 689 Facebook friends, will promptly know your program at the AA association for the next three months before you even go there twice.

The Negro caddy at your golf club will not answer your phone anymore, your mechanic will postpone your car check-up indefinitely and your bank advisor will place the "office out of service" sign, when he sees you at the entrance.

The brutal and rudimentary Captain Caveman- faces around you at the AA association meetings are meant to emphasize your decay and how you've got to have the same basic, gross and unworthy–of-a-sophisticated-mind behavior problems, like the goons around you.

The hero will pass through countless humiliating experiences, before demonstrating that, in fact, he didn't even drink that much and the complaint had been initially filed by his wife in secrecy, as she was cheating on him with his boss and intended to divorce him and take the holyday mountain cabin and his better car, besides half of the house and no kids.

I have also seen in countless movies that Americans are doing this kind of associations for any kind of more or less well diagnosed nervous disorder or "bad" habit, the only palpable results being safely guarded in the associations' bank accounts. I enjoyed a movie where Stephen Seagal (WTF, he is not my favorite actor!) was a police officer, previously charged with aggressive misconduct, who was supposed to go to some sort of association of exceedingly violent people, where they could share their feelings and benefit from psychological advice to calm down.

The mentor of the class was a nice lady with a rare talent – she would succeed to stir you crazy -mad in less than 3 minutes, even if you were a Tibetan monk experiencing a vigil coma or a Hamish on a Sunday afternoon slumber.

To me it is like fishing: you keep quiet on the bank of a pond and patiently place inside the water a small metallic hook with bait on it, hoping that in all that large lake, there will be one stupid – enough fish to chew on it.

Well it is a little bit more complicated, as all the fish are either busy or not hungry, or simply clever enough to avoid your sorry ass trap. I remember a story about a fisherman who was so fond of nature that he would sob about every fish he caught: "Oh my little darling! Poor you, little soul, how come you got caught in my fishing rod?" The fish turns to him, spitting out the hook: "Imagine Einstein, I wanted to kill myself, but you can't get killed with your lousy two-dollar- single –use-Chinese – good-for-nothin'-MF gear!"

All creatures on Earth drink something, starting with plain water. I may have had some doubt with them fish and marine mammals – they gulp so much water anyway, that you can't say they do it on purpose or they simply do it for breathing purposes. I recon their main problem is either not to drink too much of it or maybe find a better way to get rid of the excess, which is also a less obvious operation in their natural habitat. It is like peeing in a large pool so nobody will notice; this is hard to do these days with the chemical stuff they put in the water. With that, peeing in the pool may be an embarrassing experience, as your urine stirs up blue or red clouds the size of a Jumbo Jet trail. Kids start crying, mothers go and drag them out of the pool, old greasy tycoons on surrounding armchairs "tisk, tisk" you!

Like I would like to see them fart in the pool – see who dares smoke out there!

Fish drink like they breathe (or vice versa). However, humans are a distinctive species. Displeased by water in certain moments of their life, the humans started tasting whatever nature provided, with a curiosity matched sometimes even by animals.

I have seen a very interesting film on Discovery, with animals from the savannah crowding to eat the fallen and fermented fruits of a local marula tree. Monkeys were first and –as they used fresh fruit – they couldn't "get high" too quickly. But the elephants preferred the fallen fruit, especially those fermented for a few days, thus being charged with a considerable amount of alcohol. It was amazing to see how much – in a matter of minutes - those elephants were starting to resemble dock-yard workers making their way towards home in the evening,

2-3 steps forward, one behind, making the direction very difficult to assess or to keep. The elephants, bearing the gift of intelligence that places them alongside primates and dolphins, were nuts about this fruit.

Question - Can we honestly blame the "misfit" intellectuals of the Communist regime for their alcoholic addiction?

It is a pity Michael Jackson did not catch this tip – like sipping a shot or two before the concert, instead of getting himself killed over Propofol delivered by his doctor, who was a trustworthy brother. Which reminds me of a story concerning the eternal skirmish between the Romanian and the Hungarian ethnics in Transilvania. They say a Romanian guy called John, getting sick into his dying bed, calls for a notary public to change his name. "What is the nature of the change you desire and why so urgent, Sir?" he is asked. "I want to change my name from John to Istvan (Hungarian for John). "Now why would you do that for?" the lawyer says. The man takes a fierce look, and clinging to his bed with his last energy, he says through his clinched teeth: "Cause I'd rather have one of them dead instead of one of ours".

Almost the same thing happened with two best friends, one Romanian and one Hungarian. One day, John (Romanian) was drunk- stiff and he was sharpening his hunting survival dagger against a rock in front of his house. Istvan (Hungarian) comes by, and seeing the scene, gets curious:

- Hi John! WTF are you doing?
- I am sharpening this knife, you MF!
- I can see that! WTF for?

John, with eyes looking forward towards an empty space:

- Cause I wanna kill a M-F-king hun of your breed!
- Yoy Istenem! (Oh God!) Whatever for?
- Because you and your Hungarian breed killed our late King Michael the Great!
- Hold it, hold it John! Think a little! That happened 450 years ago!
- Yeah, but I only learned about it yesterday!

It is a well- known thing that alcohol does lead to depression. Depression comes with chronic consumption, along with other possible health problems. I have seen many times people that had difficult life problems, triggering their depression along with alcohol abuse. Under such circumstances, alcohol was used merely as an anesthetic to what life was doing to them.

I am not going to promote regular use of alcohol, but if animals can have fun like this, it may not be totally un-natural. Besides, we know that our body produces endogenous alcohol on a daily basis (not much, but anywhere detectable, in the range of 2 ml). Must have been thought useful for something, otherwise Good Old Mighty wouldn't have allowed it! So what if we choose to add some to the already existing quantity?

History probably failed to disclose the story of some primitives who gathered fruit, collected the juice that dripped from it and kept on drinking it until it was fermented. They surprisingly enjoyed it more than the fresh one and tried to make some more, till they understood what the secret of making it was.

The Chief Hunter would order : "I want a Chateau Mango & Banana 200258B.C." and all tribe's men would cheer with drumsticks in their hands: "That was a good year, Boss!". The spirit fabrication secret came later, when some crazy- ass alchemist tried to turn plums into gold over a pot, and the result remained pending but nice flavored, and very much appreciated in the long winter days.

Speaking about depression, it is interesting that you cannot tell it from the beginning, due to the dis-inhibiting action of alcohol. More than that, it is interesting not all people fall to depression. Have you ever seen a depressed Irishman? I've known a lot, many of them sharing the exquisite art of whiskey sipping without getting drunk, and none of them was depressed, or if he was, you couldn't tell!. They just dress in green clothes and they dance.

In my country, I saw old men in their 80s working hard in their household or farm, but only after taking a morning shot of home-made stuff (50 degrees). Home distilleries are very respectable when it comes to refined fruit stuff. Another shot was to welcome lunch and have appetite and 2 shots in the evening for good mood (I mean that already was a good spirit).

And they also smoked plain, sometimes rolling their own cigarettes from the day's newspaper or corn leafs. And they never-ever looked depressed.

My father in law was an accountant all his life, and retirement found him as a respected employee of the largest winery in the country. He taught me a thing or two. As a young law school student, he was abducted by the Communist Security Militia (sort of our local KGB) and deported to another place. He did time in a 25 square feet chamber, together with other three guys, out of which one was always the snitch. All because he was a registered member of a right / Democratic Party, while the Communist regime was struggling to eliminate all democracy and western influence, which they incidentally, succeeded quite well.

He would eat almost nothing, they would beat the shit out of them twice a day and also "enjoyed" some electric- bed "Rambo" treatment because he wouldn't "sing" about his friends.

When he got out he weighed 90 lbs – half the man that got in. He was under strict surveillance, until my wife was born in mid-sixties and he was not allowed to participate at his own wedding.

But guess what? He remained – till the day he met the Maker – one of the funniest and wisest men I ever knew. He would have told you life stories and countless jokes over a bottle of wine and he practically never got drunk, because – he said – "you do not have to drink the wine like a thirsty horse! You have to talk it over and over, not gulp it!"

Once he met with some of his friends – many of whom I knew, and who looked like freshly unburied mummies from Luxor.

They were celebrating something and they overdid it. Their remake of "The Mummy" ended up in the ER of the County Hospital because of gait impairment and stuff, otherwise all were very talkative.

ER personnel – many of which knew me, called my wife and told her that dr.E's father in law is in trouble in the ER. My wife was coming to tell this to me with a rather balanced voice, when she suddenly realized "OMG, your father in law means my father!!!"

He was ok, and he said that shit hit the fan when they were too hurried to drink without eating properly! But they had a very god time. Like I said, I never saw him depressed!

The long life secret of one of the oldest persons in Cuba was quickly buried in the media because she said that whatever kept her alive, were good quality Cuban rum and cigars.

Years before, there was a national company selling vodka in small 150-200 ml UHT boxes with a straw. Drinking from that recipient on the street was known as "cell phone talking".

Depression can be faked by some people, like our former president who was a specialist in arranging whiskey over the rocks; he was so obsessed with this you would say it were ikebana or something. After consuming a number of arrangements like this, the first words that came to his mouth were: "I want to make my country great again".

I participated to a convention of orthopedists (European Congress) in Denmark once. Denmark looks like a country with very sad and depressed people. Maybe their symbol in Copenhagen – the little siren – is luring them into this introspective behavior. Some of them seem weirdos, like some guys I've seen on the city train: one of them was in a terrible hurry, walking towards the front of the train (5 cars ahead) and back like 3-4 times between stations. Every local train seemed to have its own weirdo. Maybe it is because of the weather. One morning I got up in a heavy construction activity noise – some workers repaired the street outside our hotel. I got up and saw it was full light outside and became terrified of the fact that I may get late for the congress works. Must be 9 or 10 I thought, by the looks of it. When I looked at the watch, it was only 5.30 a.m.

Later on, I asked a lady who was complaining of the heat wave (it was like 24 °C in a sunny day), what is the winter like. She made a gloomy face and said- we just have daylight from 9 a.m. to 3 p.m. and it is very cold and a lot of snow. That – I thought – is the answer. On such weather, you just stay in the house and drink yourself to oblivion and try to keep warm. Truth is, everybody in Copenhagen seems to go to bed at 10 pm; hard to find an open pub at this time, even downtown.

But the atmosphere is totally different in the buses and especially in the trains, where everybody drinks. Possibly also in the bohemian area called Christiania, where they say you can meet Mary Jane and it feels like at home.

In dark corners or crowded trains, teenagers dressed in hilarious t-shirts and bizarrely colored jackets, spend their time with a can of beer in the hand and a one liter vodka jar in the middle.

Countless nation ethnics, workers around the city, accompany them in the evening, with the bottles and cans held steadily between their knees. I strongly believe that in this country, the only ones who do not – visibly – drink, are the ever increasing- in- number Muslims.

They say by the end of WW – II, Germany was being occupied by the Russians from the East. A soviet major descends from his car in Jena, in front of the Filetische Museum (Phylogeny Museum), a great natural science exhibition, founded by Friedrich Engels himself.

Being curious and suspecting something wrong in the same time, the major starts wandering through the halls, arriving in a room full of dry insects but also packed with tiny creatures preserved in white alcohol jars. With wide open eyes, he goes to a shelf with some ugly looking critters, placed in cup- size bowls with white alcohol. To the surprise of his body guards, he takes one jar, opens it and removes the little critter from inside, possibly a little locust. Then he approaches two thirsty nostrils to the rim and sniffs carefully. "Vodka" he yells happily and without a second thought, he gorges the whole jar like a thirsty horse would suck dry a bucket of water. "Ahaaa!" He moves towards the next shelf and he grabs a half kilo jar holding inside a little gecko lizard. He removes the lid, picks the gecko out and throws it on the floor, carefully sniffs the content and presently throws it down the hatch to join the preceding one.

Red in his cheeks and all sweat, the major pulls up his cap, raises his Kalashnikov and releases a short burst shattering to pieces the glass ceiling above, yelling viciously: "Harasho! Gde krokodil?" (Ok, where's the crocodile?).

Many specialists are documenting their opinion on drinking in impressive books, either medical or, more frequently, regarding nutrition and metabolism.

Opinions are different: some say a glass of wine / day is welcome. Others say it is not mandatory, but it doesn't harm anyway.

Some cardiologists say red wine is better, others say red wine increases blood pressure. They discuss anyway, such tiny quantities, that some of our citizens would use them for eye / nose drops, compared to what they commonly drink every day. Science doesn't really mingle here with popular practice.

How else can we explain the religious fervor of men in respecting the Biblical demand of drinking 40 glasses of wine for Saint Martyrs day (9th of March for the Orthodox), while totally ignoring important commandments related to stealing, adultery or the sin of worshipping carved face?

Besides, what drink could be better than monastery brandy and the friar's wine? Friar Tuck's skills were not forgotten. I have once visited at Easter time a monastery of monks in Northern Moldavia and I was impressed by the quantity of wine that was "sacrificed" for the event. Some of their too-pious friars were so belly proud, being intensely re-hydrated after the long 40 days of fasting.

Water, after all, has no taste at all. "Tears are the friar's bath!" said one of the younger and good looking friars ; his blue eyes and pony tail hair, together with the grayish long beard and the Hercule-size body were very impressive to younger blonde tourists. He was presently approved by a small rat- profile half hump-back individual carrying some vegetables to the kitchen. One needs to have good taste in order to make good booze.

I suddenly realized that our orthodox religion is very comprehensive when it comes to drinking; we have so many Christian holydays to celebrate, that our ancestral thirst can hardly match the number of non-working holydays. If we would let some guys have their own interpretation of holydays, we'd work some 4-5 days / year, and celebrate for the rest. And judging by this year's government budget, we're almost there!

Now that is a really old habit, as it is not Christianity and the invitation of Good Old Jesus of drinking His blood and eating His flesh that led us to binge partying.

Americans proved to be primitive and underdeveloped as a nation, as they initiated Prohibition very late, in 1920s, whereas we did it 2000 years ago, in ancient Dacia (former Thracian state on the territory).

Overwhelmed by petitions and the lousy presence and performance of men on the battlefield, the All-mighty leader of Dacia, (our ancestors were a special breed of Thracian nation) decided to destroy the visible cause – the vineyards. No sooner said than done! A terrible mistake was initiated – one that the Communist have aggravated with their intensive agriculture – when superior vintage grapes were replaced by hybrid species, with poor quality but more resilient, needing less care and protection. From then on, Romanians got accustomed to "Molan" wine. Molan is a slang term defining bad quality thick red wine, looking like a Deltic locomotive used engine oil, made out of less selected hybrid grapes and helped out with lots of sugar. After regular use, it will put two holes in your body, one in the head, and the other in your stomach.

Super-production was invented. Once you drain the barrel, you put some sugar and water over the squashed grape skins, and within 3 weeks you have the next "vintage" production. It is not as good as the first one, but when all booze is over, by the month of, say late February or early March, works miracles, like gun powder.

Skilled "specialists" can do even the third round, when this second one is over. They put again sugar, water and some yeast over the leftovers, and let it ferment in a distant warehouse, in order to prevent gas intoxication or explosions. They would allow now a longer time for fermentation and decantation, in strong glass recipients, because the plastic ones are not resilient enough and could melt away in contact with the product.

This time they do not drink it, never touch the stuff; they keep it only for guests or get it as a present for the local doctor. It is very important not to get stained with the stuff. There is nothing on the face of the Earth to clean the purple-red "molan" (that is the nickname of the product) stains from fabric, no matter what you try, short of C4. All detergents failed this test, and the IG Farben company in Germany filed a complaint for misleading the chemistry team with alien substances. The only way you can deal with it is the heroic choice: use a pair of scissors and upgrade generously your couture- style or save half a liter of "wine" and dip the whole coat in it. Sometimes the result is a catchy and chic purple color. Once all your wardrobe turns dark purple, you are respected as a "connoisseur".

Although mentioned around many times, I heard the Muslim religion does not specifically forbid alcohol, but this interdiction becomes inherent with every verse. It is a good thing, because drinking a bottle of Jack, and then going out on a sunny day in the desert at 50°C in the shadow is purely suicidal. You might make it to the parking lot, but until you recognize your camel or the animal recognizes you, you're gone.

But Arab people are human after all and once they go to other places they get to "socialize". Once, before the offensive of ISIL, I was invited in Iraq for a Rheumatology conference. One of my friends there – actually ex-colleague from the University we graduated – whom I have known for 34 years, was telling me stories about the other guests.

He showed me a tiny man with the profile of a starving rat; he was very serious and moved like his coat had been dipped in starch before drying stiff. My colleague said: "Do you see this guy? He is the brother of an imam! Professionally he is so and so, but he is very strict with religion. Once we went to France for a convention. After 3 days, when we were supposed to check out of the hotel, our group leader was horrified to find out we had to pay another 450 Euros for minibar drinks. The problem was not over sodas or cokes, but dozens of small bottles of fine red wine. Everybody was looking at everybody and nobody had any clue of who was the culprit responsible for devastating the wine reserve of the hotel. Finally our group leader came with the idea of asking which room was billed and to everybody's stupefaction, it was this rat's room. Of course we cornered him and asked: how can you drink wine like a horse and become a blasphemer of the Coran? He smiled and said he did not realize it was wine; he thought it was a sour grape juice, just good for his throat."

I met recently another guy from the same parts, who managed to build a hospital of his own in our country. He showed me his salt cave for asthma treatment, somewhere in the basement, but he was very proud of his winery next to it, which was the size of a small restaurant and where he would invite his guests.

Now seriously, if you go to Arab countries, holding a freakin' Kalashnikov under your arm, it may be a little embarrassing, but you might get on with it somehow, maybe not in Dubai, though. But if you try to hide a bottle of booze under your arm, you are in a world of shit. Prison is nothing compared to what they might do to you; you'll get crucified alive! In one of my voyages to the Emirates, while visiting a hospital where some friends worked, I had the opportunity to see a patient who was wounded in a traffic accident. He was related to a very important person and he was some sort of VIP himself. His wounds were nothing, compared to the unfortunate possibility of somebody finding out he was drunk- driving. I heard he paid a few thousand just to have this mentioning removed from his file.

The more severe regulations are about drinking – religion left alone – the more people are tempted to drink. Take for instance, drunk driving. You are not allowed to be influenced by alcohol while driving. But this is exactly what drivers passionately do! It is indeed hard to imagine a social category thirstier than drivers. For a professional driver, drinking becomes a physiological necessity, as he is constantly deprived of this pleasure, so he takes bitter revenge whenever he gets free. In time, he slowly starts compensating ahead.

It is already accepted that alcohol may, and certainly will alter perception; after all, that's why the police officer shows you the number of fingers you've got to guess right every time, and walks you around that curved line, with hands stretched forward like a marine holding his assault rifle.

Alteration of perception can go very far, like when John and Mary, both stiff-drunk, were spending a quiet Sunday afternoon on their little farm. Suddenly John points outside and says:

-     Mary, look out the window, there's a horse in our yard!
-     It's a cow! Says Mary, without even turning her head.
-     I say it is a horse!
-     It is a cow, you moron! I see it now!
-     I said the window, woman, not the mirror!

Perception of physical factors can also be distorted because of alcohol:

Two blondes were doing a European tour by car, inside all packed with luggage and tiny bottles of Schnapps and beer cans. Highway patrol stops them while boringly cruising at 20 Km / hour, thousand cars desperately honking behind them.

- Hello Officer! Says the driving blonde – displaying a ruby circled Cheshire cat smile, but with Appaloosa- size plastic teeth!
- Hello M'am! Your license and ID please!
- Here.. you.. are!

The officer takes a suspicious look inside the car and notices the presence of all the booze recipients, apparently full and untouched, along with the quiet and rather suspiciously looking companion of hers. The other woman was pale, her hair was stiff and viciously spread all around her head like from a hurricane powered wind, a scary look lingered on her face, and her eyes looking far away beyond things, while totally speechless and motionless.

- Why are you driving so slow on the highway? He asked.
- Ha,ha, ha! That was a good one, officer! We are on highway E 20, so I'm supposed to go 20 km/hour, right? You can't fool me this time! No Sir!
- Aha! The officer takes notes in his book. "And your friend, she seems ill, is there anything wrong with her?"
- Oh yes, poor thing! The poor darling has been behaving like this ever since we were driving on highway E 190.

Sometimes alcohol can create regrettable confusions, absolutely unwanted in times of crisis.

I heard this story from a friend of mine; his companion in a binge drinking party was very upset, because his wife had told him to give up returning home, if he happens to be drunk. He told the other guy:

- "Do like I do! Undress in front of the door and when she opens up the door throw your clothing inside the house! She won't have the guts to let you wander naked around the hallway of the block!"

Happy with the new idea and satisfied by what seemed to look like an unmistakable solution, his friend got in front of the door, undressed quickly and pushed the ringer button. When the door opened, he threw the clothing in. Then he heard:

- "Mind the gap! Mind the closing doors! Next station is "Bloomingdale Estates Plaza", platform on the right side!" And the door moved away.

Another story about altered perception is the one of the three homeless guys who were enjoying a glass of beer in a joint near a cemetery. One of them lacked an arm, the second one, a leg, but the third one seemed in one piece. Smoke and drunken chat all over the place. Suddenly, door opens and a younger man comes in.

He has blue eyes, long brown hair and beard and he is dressed in a long robe, wearing leather sandals instead of shoes. There is a deep silence in the bar for a few moments. Then, as if after a time lapse, everybody resumed activity. The new comer went to a remote small table, sat down and asked for a beer.

One of the three homeless, the one lacking a hand, turned to the others and, in an excited mood, said:

- Hey guys, look! This is Jesus Christ!

The other two, boldly contemplating the actions of the stranger, turned to him and said:

- Shut up Charley! You're day dreaming again! Can't you see the man walked here from a distant place, maybe another congregation? Just another homeless like us! Keep your moron bill closed!
- Guys, I tell you, it's Him! …..I'm gonna ask!!!

He takes a few steps to the stranger and puts his glass of beer in front of Him:

-       Lord Jesus, because I know it is You, please do me the honor to accept this humble glass of beer as a gift from me! I don't know what else I can give you, because I'm poor, homeless and I can't work because I lost my upper limb.

Jesus smiled to him, raised and gently invited him to sit next to him.

-       I accept your gift, even if it is booze,, as You were the first in this humble inn, to recognize me and you didn't have any obligation to share your beer with me. But tell me what happened with your arm and hand?
-       Oh, God! The man puts on an embarrassed smile, lacking the whole set of front teeth and puts his single hand over his head, like covering it with a giant shovel. "It's an old story; I was working with lumber and I fell to close to the chain-saw".
-       I see! The visitor took a sip from the gift beer, then turned to the man, put a hand on his head and the other on the amputated arm and whispered a few words. Like in a cartoon miracle, the arm started growing longer and longer and then changed shape creating the arm and finally the hand.

The homeless man was astonished; he was looking in disbelief at the newly grown hand and then tried to move fingers. When he saw that the hand obeys command, he started shouting and dancing around like crazy: "I have a new hand! I have my brand new hand, once again! Look guys – two hands! – he was shouting, until he finally sat down, his dirty unshaved cheeks covered with tears.

Meanwhile, the second homeless rose to his "foot" (he had only one), a little shaky because of the beers he already had, but mostly because of his missing left leg. He took his beer mug and limped his way to the stranger:

- Oh, Lord Jesus, I saw what you did with my friend! Allow me, Jesus, to share my beer with you, 'cause it is the only thing I have right now!

Jesus smiles and invites him to his table as he did with the other one. He takes a polite sip from the man's beer and asks him how he lost his leg. The man replies he was the victim of a traffic accident while doing street repairs, as an eighteen wheeler bumped into their site and shattered everything. He was caught against a concrete wall and there was nothing else to do but cut his limb to get him out of there.

Lord Jesus touched his knee and his head and the miracle happened again: his leg grew and the foot developed same size and shape with the other. The man got crazy happy and started dancing barefoot showing everybody his two feet. Oddly enough, he was doing a show moving his toes in both feet, even if the ones in the newly grown one were, as expected, much cleaner.

Amidst the mayhem, the third homeless rose to his feet, took a bottle and smashed it against the table and kept the bigger shard as a dagger in his hand.

- Oh shut up you morons, with your miracles! You make me sick! And you,… hey you, the hippy guy, …I'll carve your face if you even try to touch me, cause I voted for the Democrats! I'm living on allowance and government subsidies!

Another story says that one drunker leaves the pub situated near the cemetery and tries to go home. In order to go home, he would have had to cross the alleys of the cemetery, something not very appealing on a cold December rainy night. He makes his way through anyway, but on a slippery alley he stumbles and falls inside a deep freshly dug tomb. He cries for someone to help him out, but there is no-one to hear, so he decides to wait. After half an hour, another hesitating person comes singing on the same alley. The first one starts crying: Oh, God, I'm so cold! It's freezing down here! Help me! The second one stops singing and, with a curious face, comes near the hole to take a look:

- Hello!...He is trying to fix his buoyance. Is there anybody down there?
- Yeah! It's me! I'm freezing down here! Do something to help me!
- Tisk, tisk, tisk! The second guy looks at him disapprovingly and waves his finger like an old grandpa: "Now, see what you've done? Course you're cold – you moved too much and pushed aside all the ground and became unearthed; keep your feet tight and stop moving. Here, I'll help you!" he says and then pushes the whole earth pile back inside the grave.

Friar Tuck was not the only member of the clergy who did not des-consider tasting God's blood; today's priests do the same. One priest has recently placed a panel at the entrance of the churchyard: "Dear people of our Church, stop stealing, lying, cheating or being lazy; our government does not stand such disloyal competition!".

The world of drunk drivers may be very large, but there are some distinctive types that I want to talk about. Most drunk drivers may fit in one of these descriptions, thus enhancing the value of the classification:

a) Chip & Dale type – sorry- ass clerk, dressed all year around in the same stinking and de-colored suit or jacket that covers his skinny body. He may drink a small beer on his colleague's birthday, and he feels like a tiger already. He has a flushing face, emotion makes him sweat exceedingly, as he drives his ancient Honda Accord as if it were a sixteen-wheel steam locomotive. He has a rictus (tetanus –like smile) whenever he sees a police officer or a police car. Once home, he may need 4-5 clumsy maneuvers to park decently. He will undress in the bathroom, removing socks first and paying attention not to stick them to the ceiling.

b) Uncle Johnny Wrench – solid, placid, with a nose that reminds of a giant bell red pepper or a dwarf colored pumpkin. He hasn't been driving sober ever since Woodstock, but he has a strong liver that enables him to rely upon his motion reflexes even at 1/ 1000 rate. He is not dangerous normally, because he goes to work early in the morning and gets back late at night, when streets are deserted. His temper may become harmful after weddings and parties.

c) Greg Timber – village boy, hard- working, dressed in a coverall day- around, returning with his pick-up filled with building parts needed for extending his barn. He makes one last stop at the gas-station bar and starts playing "Jack and a beer back" with a red-neck from a neighboring village. Greg's IQ sometimes would beat the sugar rate in sodas, so he quickly loses count of the rounds, yet he couldn't care less about that. He gets out smashing the door, head first, and followed mechanically by the rest of his body, in a joint effort to make it to the pick-up truck. Once inside, he feels safe again. He will use the yellow line as a guide home and he will not "pull over for nobody", even if confronted with an eighteen-wheeler. He knows that his dear wife will wait for him on the porch, of course, just to make sure he gets to his bedroom safe.

d) Tony Badass – young, muscular, dressed in latest t-shirt and jeans, driving anything between tuned Mustang to 700 series BMW. His car has 10-12 tail-pipes, 3 turbo-chargers and 5 enormous woofers in the back, which can puff-away panties off the angry blondes riding with him, at the switch of a button. Tony's kind have ugly crashes from time to time, killing themselves and taking other innocent people with them, and nobody knows if it was from the pricks or the shots.

e) Scary Pimp – commonly African American or Negro, dressed like Ken in Ken and the Barbie Dall, unstable in speech and actions like a hamster injected with caffeine and having pepper spray in his eyes. Countless big rubies stand like wounds on his fingers and the 17 golden chains hanging on his neck make the rattling noise of 17 cows chased by a Harley on the street. The pimp sips cognac from a small compartment on his front panel and his victorious look and big smiles can fool no one but the poor girls that choose to work for him. The crazy clown can suddenly turn into a beast that hops his car rear at the stop light and screeches tires to impress audience. You have to be careful with the type; avoid tail collision because he might have a frightened girl all tied up in the trunk.

f) Lord John – grey hair, maybe moustache, tidy and clean, black tie almost all the time. Could be a judge or a Congress Man. Once he opens the car door, be ready to catch him, 'cause he might have just used up all his coordination skills while driving. When he speaks, you have to sniff one option: Porto, Jerez wine or Gentleman Jack (which is so much smoother than simple Jack!). His main victims are mostly neighbor's dogs, fortunately.

The wine has been criticized for decreasing combat attitude. This didn't stop Churchill from giving his RAF pilots a shot of whiskey for courage before missions. But there were days in history when the thing mattered. There's one last story I'll tell you before the end. In our ancient Moldavia, Stephen the Great was a justified ruler and king. He enjoyed white horses, riding the wild horse (he had one wife and countless mistresses), a good cup of wine and he was fierce in battle with his broad sword that could cut a man in two. His sword is a trophy now in the "Topkapi Palace" in Istanbul. He was chased in his childhood by the invading tartars who killed his best friend by hanging him in an old oak tree in the village of Borzesti. Years after,

Stephen the Great did the same to the Han of the tartars, but before that, he got cornered by a tartar mob exactly at the oak tree, after a binge drinking party. He made swift escape by climbing the tree with his trustworthy warriors. As the story goes, the freakin' tartars camped exactly under the tree, so there was no way to go down. Finally, after midnight, tartars fell asleep. One of Stephen's soldiers started talking:

- Oh, Milord! You must understand me! I can't hold it anymore!
- But you will, my son! You have the power to control yourself and you will not drop it until morning when they leave!
- Yes Milord, but I feel it is so heavy! I can't hold it anymore, I'll have to drop it!
- Keep it my son, and I'll give you 10 acres of land in your village! Where are you from?
- Buhaesti Milord! Thank you but it is very difficult for me! I hope you understand. I can barely hold it!
- I understand, my courageous boy! That is the privilege of heroes, they can control their body and their fate!

Hours passed and then again:

- Milord, seriously, I can't keep it anymore! I have to drop it a little!
- Do you realize that could kill us? My son, you were so brave at this time! I'll give you 20 acres of forest near your village!
- Thank you Milord but it is so difficult! I don't know how much I can hold it!

After another few hours, dawn was breaking:

- Milord, Milord! That's it! I can't hold it anymore! It goes down!

-   My little brave boy! Put yourself together and be as brave as you were until now! Hold it for another half hour!
-   Impossible Milord! Can't hold it anymore! I just have to put the darn' horse down!

They say the distribution of survival for drinkers is according to the Gauss bell curve, which means the most dangerous are the extremes: those who drink too much and those who do not drink at all! We are the guys in the middle and we also know one thing for sure – water is precious and irreplaceable, but it doesn't make anybody immortal!

DO WE (MEN) REALLY UNDERSTAND WOMEN?

We are constantly under the pressure of confession, whether it is about an extra beer at the golf club or an innocent glance towards the neighbor's wife, while she is collecting her dried and perfumed laundry from the backyard, wearing her most discrete underwear. Who's we? Us, guys!

Lord gave us the sensibility to appreciate beauty of nature in all its forms, the more curvy, the better, and our conclusion stands proof for our selectiveness – we gladly welcome the other "species" in our life, be it from 19 to 90, mostly because we know we have no alternative.

Did you know that, we men, are actually a natural accident? I'm sure you did not, that is precisely why you do not appreciate man at his right (high!!!) value. Indeed, all individuals of the human species are pre-programed for a 44xx genome – that would be 44 standard chromosomes and two female X-es – which means woman! Somehow, one of the x female chromosomes, deleted one short arm and remained a "y" instead. That is how, thanks to a Divine mutation, man was created! Yes Sir, not the kind of story you heard from the preacher! She seems to have been here first and preceded us into this imperfect world. Obviously, we have no knowledge about the world being perfect before she was made but one can only assume it was so, and we cannot say for sure if the present day imperfections are a direct and regrettable consequence of her creation, but one can only speculate on that.

Even the Holly Book states how good life as in Heaven before she started having a crush on fruit. Or maybe she was already pregnant and had cravings? That would be a poor excuse - for the apple at least - but not necessarily for the rest.

There are many issues to discuss when we approach the main differences between the two cooperating "species" – cooperation which, from our point of view, is getting dangerously close to a survival challenge for ours.

However, it is worth mentioning that regardless the hardships – and remember, there was a bitter time of matriarchate – we managed to pursue our scope in life, sometimes by paying the highest price.

Speaking about this, I am not entirely convinced that matriarchate is totally abolished; on the contrary, I personally observe a recrudescence of its manifestations, from the very discrete to the cruelest. The number of victims is growing day by day and the sacrifice rate is stunning.

Have you ever wondered why women are born more often and generally prevail on Earth – in numbers, of course? I think that it is a sign that at least some of them will find no man to play with, and they should take it as a punishment from God. Instead, they unnecessarily play hard to get – 'cause there is a decent rate of one eligible woman in 10 that is worth fighting for - and that makes our competition more delightful, once you are watching it from a safe distance.

I remember the story of the old Toro Bravo bull who was enjoying a delightfully ruminating afternoon under the shade of a large tree on top of a hill. The young bulls were calling him: "Hey, Señor! Come with us, look! There are many young cows over there, maybe we can get acquainted!" He leaned comfortably to one side and answered – "Muy bien ijos! Very well boys! You go there! I have a good view from here, too!"

Women make no secret of their pluri-valence, making their approach purely scientific and somehow eclectic. We already know there is a mood called ambivalence – one day they love you (or so it may seem!), the next day they hate your guts and they go stabbing you in the back!

Speaking of which I had a nasty surprise with my wife, when she admitted she adores police movies, where the wife cunningly and skillfully kills her husband, well, sometimes simply because he had another girlfriend during high-school. That reminds me of the young lady who asked her lover if she is to be considered jealous. "No dear, he replied, I just wish you gave up the idea of being present on my ID photo! And darling, it is not that I wouldn't want to, but these cruel and misogynist lawful regulations do not allow it!"

I think that I already have the basic ingredients for a theory, enabling me to claim that we, men, are being slightly, but steadily disfavored, and I can still see political maneuvers to manipulate truth the opposite way. The British had the Iron Lady, Germans still have Mrs, Merkel (trying hard to look like iron, but pathetically exposing the red rust she has gotten under her fingernails during her youth adventures in Communist Saxonia Anhalt). Too few had characters like Mother Theresa, but we will rule her out of this discussion as she inspires just respect, love, pity and sacrifice for all mankind. She remains for us an ideal image of a woman, consistent with motherhood sentiment and never-ending love and pity.

Speaking of this, why do you think humanity is called mankind and not womankind? I have tried many times to imagine the perfect relationship between us- men and them - women. It goes like a perfect script for a theater show, in which everyone has his own part to play, and, for the love of God, at least once in a while, he or she gets to respect it!

That may sound perfect, but in reality, the whole thing is a total chimera, because they – women that is - feel the unstoppable need to improve the script.

The oppression suffered in some corners of the world, within the last few centuries, apparently entitles them girls to always yearn for something else than they are supposed to or entitled to, and if they don't, they fake it! So much for predictability!

On the other hand, they have this power to take advantage of our weaknesses and convince us they deserve various things – like a Porsche, a white fur coat, a gold credit card, total freedom or – in other words - our unconditional surrender. We become very weak when it comes to sexy things and we must admit any woman is able to trigger sexiness! Like, any wife has undeniably got something sexy – maybe the hair, if not the hair, then it's the boobs, or the bottom part, or at least her blonde friend from the hairdo parlor…

However, they always try to give the impression that they are the superior component of the pair; and it freakin' works because you – as a normal man – do not feel any itch to get into a stupid competition in front of a more or less comprehensive audience. But audience does enhance their appetite for skirmish.

I once knew a pair of older colleagues; he was a surgeon and she was a GP. We were all invited along with some other friends to a party. I saw him try at least a dozen times to tell a simple joke or a funny story, something, but somehow, she did interrupt him every time he opened his mouth and it was obvious she was doing it on purpose. After about half an hour, he was almost on the edge of doing it, when she suddenly turned and asked him in a harsh voice to stop. Why? - was the question on everybody's lips. "I can say it better" she continued and then she leaned against him, purring like a spoiled cat: "You **<u>know</u>** it, don't you??!!!!". Now why did I sense a note of danger in this question? By the looks of it, all the other men felt it like a cold shiver running down their spine. We all had a shake and grabbed our glasses emptying them in the sepulchral silence.

She takes over saying his joke; as expected, nobody laughs and they are all concentrated to cut the food in front of them as if it were brain surgery. Meanwhile, he is pretending to eat and apparently pays no attention, chewing vigorously on his stake. While recovering from the story – teller spell, she sighs for relief and suddenly questions him with a sweet, but penetrating voice, you know, the kind of voice you can still overhear during the craziest game at the stadium: "Why are you stuffing yourself like this? Why don't you take a break, a deep breath and drink something before you suffocate! Like you never saw better food!" O-o! This was a direct shot towards our gracious landlady hosting the gathering and serving otherwise excellent food. And seconds later: "Trust you to grab the wine, first? Water is not good enough for you anymore? The alcohol will surely kill you, in the first place!"

He then takes a deep breath and confronts her: "Not likely, while you are still around, darling, but you know what they say – it is true that water will help me live, but not forever, either". Some of the men at the table – caught off guard, of course – took the liberty of a short laugh which ended in sudden dry coughs. The rest of us went on quietly, but very satisfied about the perspective of telling this story over the office coffee the next day.

Speaking about embarrassing moments, psychologists say they are numerous in life and very different when assessed in a gender –specific manner. As usual, they have related them to interesting activities of life, like eating, working or having sex. Desmond Morris, a clever ethologist from the UK and a good writer, too, had said in his book called "The bald monkey" that sexual activity in human species has gained a new and rather superficial social touch.

Supposedly we meet on the street, and depending on how we say "Hello", a woman may understand the deeper meaning of this hello and consent to immediately knowing better the person she just met, by proceeding instantly to total sex. Like going on the side-walk and looking at the shops when you suddenly you meet a nice looking lady going the other way:

- Hello Madam! May I say this morning is as beautiful as you are?
- Sure you may! Not very relevant though! Well, if we came to that, let's do it, shall we? We're going to my place or yours? There's also a small cozy hotel on the next street. How about that?
- This morning gets better and better! Excuse my being hasty, but we should finish by 10.30, as I have a meeting at the office!

\-   Oh, never mind, I can finish alone, if needed!

In the Russian outskirts of Moscow, they say loose manners and vice are going hand in hand with hunger. Consequently, when a potential client asks for sexual favors, the dialogue is also bearing a pregnant social touch and goes something like this:

\-   Privet devutchka (girlie)! How do you like it, face to face, rear or blow?
\-   Nu pagady, Diadia (I show you daddy)! As you wish and then we eat!

Specialists say there are some crucially important (and embarrassing) moments in our sex life. For men they are just two and very simple:

1.   First - when they can no longer do it the second time and
2.   Second - When they can no longer do it even the first time.

For women things get more complicated: 1. When they do it the first time 2. When they do it the first time with another one 3. When they ask for the first time to do it 4.When they do it the first time for the money 5. When they start giving money to do it.

However, the embarrassment is not similar during sex life span, and if I may say so, it is not fair at all for us. I mean all they have to do is stay and watch what happens – sometimes smiling, sometimes texting on the phone, whereas us … we have to be high - up to the expectations and very "firm" in our … attitude in order to be very convincing, from the first to the last minute. And the road to Nirvana may take hours, without enjoying refueling pit-stops like formula one drivers.

The odd or peculiar behavior of women transcends from bedtime stories even, but as young kids or boys, we never really pay attention to the symbols hidden deep within, symbols that should ring a bell as big as the one in Notre-Dame.

Take for instance Red Riding Hood. Nice story, little girl getting food and stuff to Granny – family tear shedding story-line. Hungry big bad wolf eats both, hunter kills wolf and releases them from the digestive fate of being turned into wolf poop – Ta-taaa! Happy ending!

What we do not really understand is the drama of the poor wolf. I mean the Red Riding Hood, dressed in a provocative outfit (which is red, capisci?) goes ALONE in the forest (like all girls go alone to the forest from time to time!!). The poor wolf, doing his daily wolfish business in the forest (I mean, that was his job, we could swear he didn't want any trouble with anyone), comes to meet her on a short-cut in the forest. Odd question – why did she take the short-cut? Ha? I'll tell you why, and that is because she had a very good impression about herself – she was smart, elegant, and willing to reduce personal effort in doing a good deed for her beloved granny, so she would have even more personal time, to go to the nearest Mall and search for more trendy red hoods and other red stuff. Well, it's also true she got late, but that happened only because of her sensible personality and her addiction to flowers (with their adequate extension - read perfumes, make-up, brand clothing and stuff!). Fact is they met, and the wolf tried to socialize, by making boring neutral statements – "Nice weather, tuts!"; "What's a nice kid like you doing in a place like this?" and "Nice outfit chica! Does it have a zipper?" And asking convenience questions like, how are you, where are you going, bla – bla stuff.

Now the Red Riding Hood does it – she gave some answers mimicking honesty, but in reality she simply and obviously tried to stir him up. Check this out! "I'm all alone in the woods" she says! All alone – meaning no one will know if you…" harm" me! Like – "Wouldn't you like to?" And there's more - "I'm going to granny; she lives alone, not far from here!" she says! Swell! Granny is alone too, like two females alone in the woods, nearby, at your discretion.

Now if you are a poor, hungry, hard- working wolf in the lousy freakin' forest: what the heck would you do? Submit to the body needs! There he goes to granny's house! In a surprising (for his intellectual capacity) and flickering moment of subtlety, he sweetens his answering voice, so that granny opens door… and he grabs her. Now I must insist that the wolf's behavior was undeniably respectful and strictly professional, directly related to his proverbial hunger, with nothing else altering the correctness of his approach. He didn't try any assault on the old lady, nor did he use dirty talk as foreplay, before eating her.

To everybody's surprise, after eating Granny, his hunger was still active – and that is the part of the story I feel inclined to disbelieve.

Can you imagine how hard it would be for a middle aged, gastritis and colitis diseased wolf, to digest a whole granny, with all her fibrous tissues, hard tendons, dental prosthesis and all? Not to mention the wig, the cane and the rubber slippers.

Nevertheless, the story goes on even creepier. The happy Red Riding Hood – how else could she be, at her age and with her superficial style, since she doesn't know her dearest granny ended up as wolf dinner – strolls freely into the woods, collecting flowers for her beloved grandma, laughing alone stupidly and doing all sort of sissy things when she should have hurried to get there, instead.

When she finally arrives to the cottage, the wolf is comfortably installed in the old lady's bed, industriously digesting granny and possibly wondering if Red Riding Hood is worth even the effort of moving and chewing at all, but there she knocks at the door like destiny! He invites her in, and further on she pretends not to understand what happened by asking even more silly questions: why do you have those big eyes, big paws, big mouth, big tongue, … big..errrrr.., whatever she saw at him, was big. After a painfully long while, she suddenly realizes it is not her granny laying there in bed, but she does not have the time to enjoy this keen reflexive perception, because as soon as she does it, the wolf eats her, too.

Now if she was so ignorant about the interlocutor, she must have still suspected something, or what else was all that asking about?

And correct me if I am wrong, if she suspected – not to say she knew – anything, why all that little- girl inquiry display?

The uneducated wolf – less keen on respectful socializing activities - could have easily taken it for a weird kind of foreplay.

Lucky for her, the wolf's digestive hunger overcame all his other needs, and her only trauma was that she got eaten as well, temporarily that is.

Now the poor wolf, with a full belly and an obvious indigestion – caused by the granny, I'll bet! – decided to take precautions for his later health. According to the doctor's advice, he laid on his right side, with a pillow under his liver area, to avoid nausea and stimulate bile drainage. That was the state he was found in by the hunter, who mercilessly killed the unsuspecting wolf and split him apart, to release the reckless girls (manner of speech!) from their "digestive" prison. Now you will have to look me in the eyes and tell me that the wolf is actually the bad character in this story, and all that happened to him was well – deserved, after all.

Another example of rather peculiar women behavior is the Snow White story. She was indeed unfortunate to lose her mother at an early age, but observe how weak and sensitive is the nature of the fearless hunter, who decided not to kill her, when her step mother ordered it. True is the saying that men are the beautiful and sensitive gender, whereas women are the weak one! However, the girl makes it to the woods, and takes refuge in the "7 dwarf's house".

May I mention that the 7 dwarfs were actually old convinced bachelors, and you may imagine their surprise (read terror!) when they saw the misfortune fallen upon their otherwise quiet home.

Which became no longer quite anymore! For the rest of her life there, she has given us a brief explanation: I go to bed at seven, I get up at seven, so let that be no surprise to anyone! I mean a nice young lady, living <u>alone</u> with 7 men, while not being married to any of them? Sleeping in their beds? Eating their food? I know what you'll say – you'll say "But they were dwarfs!" Well I have news for you! They were not dwarfs, they were little men! And not everything that grows on little men is proportionally little – for example.... the hair! So much had her behavior disturbed the poor dwarfs' life, that Step Mother decided to help them, and tried to kill her twice! The subtle methods she used, like killer comb and poisoned apple, were no match for the smarty Snow White, for at first she was giving the impression she fell for it, but then she relied upon superior female intuition, capable of surviving any enemy attack.

Now we know that was a time when killer drones were not yet available, although I heard rumors the nasty step mother may have thought of something similar. Once the step mother made her K.O., dwarfs got into a worshipping mode like Russians did after WWI with Lenin, and locked her into a crystal coffin, with the intimate hope she will never get out of there, to "fix" their life again.

I'll bet that, in their time, the Russians felt and hoped for the same! This eventuality scared the shit out the poor dwarfs, who lured the local prince to the woods and invited him to a bachelor party, where he got wasted and – among other things related to health insurance and pension increase - he promised to marry the girl in the crystal coffin.

Only the dwarfs and her step mother knew that was no coffin, but a mono-place hyperbaric oxygen therapy chamber built by them – the kind of Michael Jackson used for after-concert revival – and that it would only take a skillful decompression and a kiss to wake her up. Obviously, when the boy showed her his prince I.D., the driver license for his Mustang – along with it his prince gold credit card - she swiftly fell in desperate love with him, and they happily lived ever after.

I mean the dwarfs!

Take for instance another story – the Beauty and the Beast! A little country-side - apparently shy – virgin, called Belle (beautiful in French – thanks for the tip!), accustomed to plant cabbage and to milk the cow – which is still a matter of debate for those inclined to deny her virginity - ambitious to learn how to read and write, unlike her peasant neighbors, is trying to sacrifice herself in the name of saving her notoriously genius - dumb father, from the claws of the Beast!

You should see the latest versions in the 3D cinema: boy isn't she pretty and delicate, but the Beast is a horny- full-of-muscle-horse-powered animal! Oops – did I say horny? I meant horned, that is with horns like a ram or a buffalo or a cheated husband that "fortunately" has no Calcium rate disorder!

The Beast was enjoying his serene life in his castle in the woods, not known to anybody or to the local media, for a fact, surrounded by white, delicate snow and guarded by terrifying wolves. He had hunting, books, music, food and drink, but something was still missing, and – in my opinion - only God knows what!

It was the Devil that kept pushing him, in this case! Instead of working out or doing some other sporting activity, he enjoyed adventure. Making Belle's father a prisoner seemed a normal and less dangerous gesture for a landlord, I'd say even a very generous one, only he was not aware of the hurricane that would follow, for she came to save "daddy". Then, which means too late for his own good, he wished he would have released him before.

Instead of being terrified, the cheeky peasant girl stayed and enjoyed the hospitality of the castle, reading books and having fun with the Beast. It became obvious that getting him under her spell, was her best chance of getting out of her boring village, where the inevitable Gaston, the local "vir fortis", macho, Casanova, "ladies' hero", whatever you want to call him, was becoming more and more daring and demanding.

Now let us be impartial while judging them: on one side is Gaston, army degree, tall, handsome, although a bit vulgar, quite narrow minded and convinced the world begins and ends with their village, in a spot called Gaston, with the Sun spinning around him. On the other hand, we have the Beast, filthy rich, educated but grumpy, ugly as hell, but muscular and massive and full of stamina, and able to give her the life of a princess and undeniable fulfillment in many, (and some very important!) ways.

Now, if you were a sensitive little-girl, who felt her destiny has nothing to do with working cabbage in the fields or milking a stupid cow, which one would you chose? Of course she has chosen the Beast – like they always do! Excuse me for being painfully honest, but us, modest guys without noblesse titles or rich fathers, we have to make a living, too, you know?

But there are so many stories about the eternal female charm and her more or less coherent attitude. Remember Scheherazade, with her 1001 stories? How do you think the poor sheik, hot willing to possess her and kill her after, felt after a 10-20 night delay, not to mention after 3-4 hundred? I think he could barely walk and he was in the same mood as the angry husband that was visiting the zoo with his wife. Suddenly, while passing the apes area, a huge male gorilla – a silverback – grabs wife from behind bars and drags her in.

The bewildered husband hears her hysterical shouting while the ape was departing: "save me, save me, get me out of here!" For a moment the husband looked like trying to jump in over the protective fence, but then he relaxed and shouted: "Relax honey! It will be all right! Now you tell him – like you told me - that you have a headache and you're not in the mood! ......Like you did yesterday,..... it worked for me, remember?"

The woman behavior can be so unexpected and, in the same time, so predictable. Once you screw up with her, you know for sure she's gonna' get you, but what you don't know yet is how and when. It is like wearing a giant bull's eye target on your back and you just wait for the bullet to come! And when it comes, it's not a merciful 22 cal, but rather a naval gun 3 ton shell! Sometime, punishment is physical, like Lorraine Bobbit did. I heard of promises like: "you know what Lorraine Bobbit did to her husband, don't you? Well, he was lucky for she had a sharp knife and it happened quickly, but I am going to use a blunt, toothless rusty blade, and it's going to last forever! And I am going to enjoy every second of it!" Creepy, ain't it?

An old tug boat mechanic told me a story, over a shot of Old Smuggler.

- I was younger and worked on a small passenger ship cruising the Nile; still dealing with the old triple expansion steam puffer, you know?

I knew the machinery – lucky for me I had seen them all as a kid with my father.

- There was this evening cocktail party on the deck, like in Agatha Cristie's book! And they all gathered there, nice tuxedos and black tie for guys, long vaporous dresses for ladies, all drinking and dancing – very nice! I was on my free quart so I pretended to check on the funnel where I had full view to the deck.
- So what happened?

He took time to sip his drink and pushed the glass for another.

- Well, everything went on fine until they got a little "smoky", you know, guys shouting and women laughing loud and horny voices. I guess it's because they didn't eat properly, just some biscuits with fish eggs and some lousy stinkin' clams.

He flushed the drink down like a thirsty Russian tank driver and pushed his glass for refill.

- Then, one English guy with tons of business in Egypt came out with a bottle of French champagne in his hand and said he is in for a wager. Lots of money he said!

He made a break to light a self- rolled cigarette, half wet with spit and puffed vigorously from it. Lucky for us we were in the outside bar.

- The man said: "You all know these waters are infested with crocodiles! I need a volunteer to jump in the water and get back. If he makes it back alive, I will pay 5 thousand pounds here and now! If it so happens he dies in the process, I will fund the grieving family with 2 million pounds!
- So what did they do?

- Well, there was a lot of rumor and shouting and everybody seemed excited, but there was no volunteering on the matter, until….
- Until? I was eager to know what happened, but he stopped to gulp another generous amount of whiskey.
- Hmm, Hmm! Until a big fellow, who was in a more remote corner jumped from the deck splashing water, bridge- high, while everybody cheered.
- Wow! What next?
- Next, about 5-6 crocodiles woke up in the vicinity and hurried towards the guy to have dinner. They surrounded him, but he managed to do a lot of splashing and hitting to keep them away moving like a ton of sardines. He fought the crocodiles that were gangin' up on him for 20 minutes, even killing 2 or 3 of them, then cleared his way to the pilot stair and climbed back on board!
- And got the 5 thousand, right?

He sighed and smiled, throwing the fifth whiskey down the hatch:

- Yap! He did take it all right! But when he climbed back on board he was very upset and yelled to his wife: "I almost died down there! Damn' it woman, why did you have to push me in the drink?"

Such stories may sometimes enable what we could consider as being "a more radical thinking", obviously, to no practical use, after all.

I confess I thought many times I might be thinking too radical. too. Or maybe risk to be taken for a misogynist, which I confess I look like, on certain and isolated occasions! I am on a treatment now. And on a diet, so to speak.

The true fact is that my opinion is not singular! You can stop me from saying the truth, but there are more of us that will carry on the fight for our rights until we are finally…. free! And when I say I am not alone, I mean it. I'll bring forward some of the manly opinions I came across with and I wish they will help for better understanding.

Norman Mailer, for instance, said "you cannot really know a woman until you meet her in Court of Justice". And if there were questions about why the divorce is so expensive – "Because it is worth it! That's why!"

I once heard of a story about a congressman. This guy walks in a dangerous neighborhood and gets mugged: the attacker shouts: "This is a stick up! Give me all your money!" The victim regains some control and a certain posture and says – "You cannot rob me! I am a Congressman! And a Democrat". The thief helps him up and dusts up his boots and clothes, then says with a more harsh voice, placing the gun muzzle between his eyes: "Then give me back my money!"

Speaking of which, Samuel Butler used to say: "The thief lets you choose between money and your life; women want them both!"

Benjamin Franklin said; "Keep your eyes wide open before marriage and half closed after". I mean why would we do that for? What do we need to clearly see (although commonly fail to) before marriage and what is there after, that can hurt us so much that we'd better pretend not to see? I remember having an intimate discussion with then my future wife – sometime before our wedding day – and she said she wants me to be the first man in her life. I guess I wasn't very well understood, until later, when I answered I'll always prefer to be the last man in a woman's life, rather than the first!

Take for instance Oscar Wilde and his allegation about this subject: "First marriage is the triumph of imagination over intelligence; second marriage is the triumph of hope over experience". Why would we be needing imagination to see how wonderful our beloved woman is? Her obvious beauty and charm goes beyond any imagination. Well guys, maybe this is the point when we need wide open eyes! Only our eyes have very limited targets at the time, and none of them is the woman's head or soul. Intelligence? Who needs it for a popular screw? That makes it sound desperate.

Although, it is frequently said that intelligent people can get more satisfaction from sex or love than…others. Our intelligence is mesmerized by the vision of three things like love, love and…..sex. The triangle of passion! Second marriage would be the triumph of hope over experience. See how infinitely romantic we men, are? After we get tormented by one lousy marriage, we still hope the next one will be different, meaning of course, better, simply because there is another woman instead!!! If it weren't for our sensitive sentimentalism, I would say we're either terribly optimistic or hopelessly foolish! Another woman? Yeah! What's the big difference? Hard to give an answer to this. It reminds me about the two married students who were in a Biology University.

They have had a terrible fight over some jealousy issues and arrived to a lecture amphitheater before getting over it, her sitting in front of the room and him, somewhere in the back. A very nice and polite Professor was talking about large mammal mating, like for instance cattle.

- "The bull - Professor says - can mate sometimes a dozen times per day". "Excuse me Professor - she interrupts - I couldn't hear you well, but did you say a dozen times in a single day?".
- "Yes Miss!" – The Professor smiled - "And the next day male is able to do it all over again, without any complain".
- "Excuse me again – Professor - she says standing up and looking towards the back of the amphitheater – I hope everybody back there could hear this!
- "Excuse me Sir – the young husband rises in a back bench – "I agree with you, but tell us, please: is the bull mating with the same cow in each and every of this dozen rounds or every day?"

The Professor smiled again and said: "Oh no, the bull is mating with a different cow every time during the same day! And the next day too!"

- "Yesssss! - the cheerful husband smiles, then adds - "I hope everybody in front heard this!"

Voltaire was less delicate when he said "marriage is the only adventure cowards can afford". Hey, Monsieur Voltaire, s'il vous plait! Where's the adventure part? Now if you come to think of it, sometimes it turns out less boring then "Survival games" or maybe ends in "Sudden Death".

Wodenhouse was even more cynical by saying: "marriage is not a life-extension of love, but a process of mummifying its corpse". Yukiie!

But you know, us manly-men have a weird representation of love, which can display various scenarios: fluffy clouds, where we fly together and embrace, green sunny fields or sunny beaches where we run until she stumbles (we'll never know if it were on purpose!) and anyway, in every scenario the conclusion is we end up making tender or furious love.

Luxurious castles full of Louis XIV furniture and full of sofas awaiting us to consume our love, silver sand tropical paradise beaches where we live a simple naked life, like in "Blue Lagoon" and – good guess – we make love all the time! It must be our romantic imagination pushing us towards the same symbols and gestures, before our brain has a chance to take over. Then comes marriage, like a coronation of all those wonderful moments, and a promise they will never end! Yap!

This Cupid triggered vision of love sure ends the next day of living together; especially when you wake up tired in the morning and you hear her first fart and the pee flow loud and clear in the bathroom. No harm done, it is natural, just wait when that comes into your bed! And you'll love it! Kinky!

The current male behavior is best revealed by this story: two neighbors in Transilvania were going to the church on Sunday morning. One of them asks the other:

- Howdy, neighbor! How come you are alone? Where's your wife Mary? She ain't comin' over?
- Nope! Said the other. She's home restin'. She's got a nasty lower back pain.

- Ouch! How come? Did she raise anything?
- Yeah!.... Her voice!

I once had a wonderful talk with an old sailor; he used to work with my father, who was a Chief Engineer on all kind of ships. He was saying:

- Son, I have seen them all! Had a "wife" in most ports from Cairo to Singapore and trust me, they're all alike. In the beginning they are like candy angels – there's just perfume where they step and you could drink fresh water from their… puss-es. Later on, one of them gets pregnant and grabs ya'. You get to be a father, without knowing when your kid grows and sometimes you need time to remember if it's a girl or a boy. I lost track of that long ago. All I know I ended up married to the dragon you saw yesterday in the kitchen.

I remember I have seen him the day before, as I wanted to ask him for details from his life at sea together with my father. His wife (now I know who the creature was!) came out of the kitchen in a cloud of foul smelling steam and looked like a wet and inflated hysterical kabuki actor, while shouting some orders I failed to understand, but which he obeyed instantly.

- I'll tell you sonny- boy, it ain't worth loving them! You hope for a creature from heaven, curly and perfumed and a voice from angels to wake you up every morning, around noon! Hah! And what you get is a creature from hell that turns itself in a couple of years in a fat restless dragon, having twice the hairs that I grow in a year and a triple chin, farting stronger than a colitic horse and nursing the breath of a dead and deep buried dinosaur. All my dreams of mermaids turned into hideous nightmares and my pecker has gone dry, and sleeps tight like a hidden squid in a coma, ever since.

And he started laughing loudly and poured down the hatch his last beer. I was startled in the beginning, but his wife was great help for my imagining the rest.

Phew, that was a close one, I thought, and then suddenly remembered I was already married.

They say that life in common gets perfect when there are no more secrets: like when taking a leak, farting and shitting becomes family sport, isn't it? It is not anything against the natural or physiological; as an orthopedic surgeon I have seen and heard a lot of things, but try to imagine being in a Jacuzzi tub with her and you smile at each other while she gently farts, like the pelican in the "Search for Nemo" fish movie.

It is not the sound or the bubbles – that's all around and acquainted for, but it is the stink that betrays the weakness of the relationship. The foul rotten egg smell that suddenly surrounds you does no physical harm, except your tendency to give up on your late supper, but it is clearly meant to consolidate the love bonds you have sworn together "for the better or for the worse". So you'd better laugh a little and pretend nothing happened, while gulping fresh air from around and dive to clear your eyes, hoping that the toxic waste bubble did not dissolve itself that quick. Or you can say "nice" – like the male pelican.

Socrates agreed you should marry – and if you have a good wife, you'll be happy (needs clarification!?), if not, you'll become a philosopher. Now, quit laughing! I'm just doing some soul analysis, not philosophy, no matter how analytic I get to be! Kauffman said that "he found happiness only when he got married! But – said he – it was already too late by then!".

We have a local saying here too – "A man is not complete until after he gets married! Then and only then, he is totally finished!".

Mencken H.L. knew things better – he said that bachelors know women better, otherwise they would have ended up married as well!

My favorite quote is from an anonymous – Marriage is the death of passion – if not careful, all of a sudden, you end up sharing your bed with a relative!

I was recently talking to a friend of mine over a glass of wine, and he told me he has discovered the secret of women and he has the best classification of all. Seeing him so satisfied and full of confidence, I urged him to develop the subject, for which I had to order a fresh bottle. He said there are three categories of women: intelligent, beautiful and those with a good soul. He then stopped rather abruptly and put on a large smile, like the Cheshire cat.

I was quite puzzled by the pause and poured him another glass of wine: "Come on! I said, there must be more to it than that! Where's the secret? I already know the three categories. Speak up!

- Well – he grabs the glass and throws it down the hatch like a thirsty Russian tank driver, showing no respect for my Sauvignon – the point is you will never find any of those in the form of pure quality! He looked at me intensely, but I didn't blink. What you get out there, is combinations, brother! Some happy, some sad! Short hysterical laughter - ha,ha!

Feeling things get a little complicated I pretended to relax and poured another wine in his glass. After disposing of it in the same less than gracious way, he decided to enlighten me.

- You see, brother, we have to choose different combinations of those; they're never pure, and maybe it is better this way! He waved his visions away and I didn't have the time to ask why it is better this way. Listen, he said, you get them as follows:

Type a) - Intelligent + beautiful = she's the perfect nasty vicious bitch enjoying to use you; read kill you, if necessary for her; it will be declared a heart attack, as usual;

Type b) - Intelligent + good soul = but hopelessly ugly and increasingly possessive;

Type c) - Good soul + beautiful = but unbelievably stupid - you're just one good person in her life, like many other men before you and probably after you;

There are very rare occasions – and when I say very, very rare, that means so rare, some of us never see them – when you meet one who is intelligent + beautiful + has a good soul, in the same time.

His eyes were shedding a tear in the sunset:

- There she is, the perfect piece, the one you have been dreaming about for so many years,….. but she's already married and inevitably lives with an imbecil, who doesn't deserve her and your admiration and perseverance is hopeless and goes down the drain. Or worse even, you are also already married!

His mobile started ringing like a police car before I could digest all the news and, as he was reading a message, his face darkened. He said: well, it was nice to see you old boy!

- What's the rush?
- Got to get back home; pass by the Grocery and get some stuff! She's waiting for me!

He raised hand to a yellow cab, which stopped presently. I was so upset about this abrupt stage leaving:

- Hey brother! I shouted after him. You didn't tell me!... What type is yours?

At first I thought he didn't hear me while running, but then he jumped in the cab and turned to me:

- She's a solid b, but practicing a-type behavior! - He cried, while closing the cab's door.

I can see you checking the type on the list now; you want to compare her with yours, I'll bet!

The relationship between the two genders is not always idyllic; men in eastern Romania have a traditional reputation in binge drinking and acting rough on women. There was a question about Moldavians: why do they have red eyes after having sex? Answer – because of the pepper spray! Or : what do Moldavians do after having sex? Answer – they go to jail!

However, while totally disapproving such rough conduct related to women, I cannot overlook the hilariously simple traps we men fall for. One of my patients, a nanny all her life and with the wisdom of her seventies, told me once: with men, it is so easy! You can solve all your problems with your breast, no matter how it looks! You put a nipple in their mouth and they will be very still for the next few hours. When they are small, they'll suck the milk from it and fall asleep; when they are grown up, they'll play with it for some time and then fall asleep as well.

Another friend told me how men life is related to tits: phase 1 – suck on them; phase 2 – play with them; phase 3 – grow them.

Confusion may sometimes stir spirits. I red a story about a young girl trying to jump from a bridge. A solid guy from the Hell's Angels rides his bike to the bridge and, passing by the police officer witnessing the scene, goes straight to the frightened creature and tells her: Now isn't it a pity to let such a beauty like yourself to go to waste! At least let me have a good kiss before you go!

And without asking twice, he grabs the girl and hugs her and gives her the biggest wetest, tongue- twisted, kiss ever!

-Now that's what I call a good kiss! Tell me honey, why do you want to kill yourself?

- Because my mom and dad harass me – they do not let me dress like a girl!....

The local reporters noted that the victim finally died of asphyxia, as expected, but failed to specify the cause.

This is sort of annoying, when gender seems to be uncertain psychologically; when it is undecided biologically you've got a visible explanation.

Small kids become aware of their gender by the age of 3, probably by observing the different color of their shoes, blue for boys and pink for girls. They need uninfluenced and abundant information to assess for the rest, not to mention the inherent changes in their bodies and minds.

I am not going to approach this sensitive subject right now; I risk being subjective because my job is thinking pathology first and I'd fail being politically correct over the issue. I remember a story about the first man Adam (called by ancient Sumerian in their legends Adama or Adapa). They say God directed him to a mountain.

- O my Lord! He said – What is that a mountain?
- A mountain, Adam, is a high ground formation, with rocks on top of it, like the one you see there! Go to it!

Adam obeys. Once he gets there, he asks what to do next.

- Now you go look for a cave!
- Oh God, my Lord! What is that a cave?
- The cave Adam, is a big hole in the side of the mountain. Go inside and meet there a woman. She will become your spouse and you will be together and be blessed with children from her.
- As you command, my Lord! But tell me first, what is that a woman?
- A woman Adam, is a human being that looks like you, only a little different! She is smaller than you, with longer hair and she has a child's sweet voice. Go to the cave, make love to her and you will have children. But... Hmm,Hmm! Try not to open up any conversation, for she will make you fail somehow to obey my orders.

Satisfied with the information, Adam reaches the mountain side and finds the cave and goes in.

God smiled; He was so satisfied to see His making come true. Suddenly, Adam emerges from the cave very early, a little hectic and out of breath:

- Oh dear God, my Lord!
- What is it now, Adam?
- God, please enlighten me! What is that a migraine?

They say in Transylvania there are fierce people, trustworthy and hard working. One guy from the area finally decides to get married. He goes to his fiancée and says: now pay attention to what I say, 'cause I ain't gonna' say it twice! Every day I have lunch at 2 o'clock. You can see me coming from far away. If you see me having my hat on the left side, that means I'm hungry and you set the table immediately, with steaming food. If you see me wearing the hat on the right, that means I'm pissed and you instantly prepare my plum brandy jug; my glass should be filled by the time I enter. And if I have my hat on my forehead, that means I'm horny and you should prepare the bedroom and undress, 'cause I come to fool around. Understood?

- Yes darling, she answers! But in return I have a rule of my own! You can also see me from far away in the fields. Regardless the hour, when you see me in front of the house with my hands on my hips and looking angry, you must know it is sex time and you are late, and when I say it is sex time, sex time it is, with or without you!

We often get carried away by stories and gossip and ignore our deepest and most sincere longings. Truth is we feel good when we see people that still live together and love each other after 50 years of marriage. They demonstrate that love as we know it, can turn into something more ideal and less depending on momentary impressions. The secret was revealed by an old fellow who was asked how he managed to have this superb 50 year relationship with his wife. He answered: It is no big deal! All you have to do is to get organized. This means splitting obligations, so everyone has his share to do.

For instance my wife took over all unimportant details of our life, like which house or car to buy, which job to accept, where the kids should go to school or to college, where we go on vacation, and so on. That left for me the important issues of life, like the problem of drought in Somalia, the unemployment rate in Brazil, the hunger in sub-Saharan Africa or the overfishing in Terra-Nova. Guess what – we never had any fight!

Speaking of fishing, while I was a student, I used to hang out with an older colleague of mine. He was also more experienced in life issues and once, as we had a cup of coffee, he told me about how "fishing" for chicks was not always fun to do, as it may seem.

- I was in a downtown restaurant, few months ago! – He said. I ate something and delayed a little my coffee and my mineral water, because two tables down on the same row, there was a hot ginger head, all flavor and stamina. I couldn't help imagining how I would feel in her arms, and even lower than that, when I realized I was actually staring at her. I decided to go away, it seemed as a dead line to me, but suddenly I saw her rising from her chair and coming towards me. I was so stun I wasn't even blinking! She sat next to me and pinched my right cheek (that moment I was regretting I didn't find time to trim my beard). She smiled and said:
- Oh dear, we are all alone tonight and so desperate to get laid, aren't we? Cheeky, cheeky, you need to go home, have a cold shower and sleep over it! It's not gonna' happen tonight, darling! But don't lose hope; someday, someone might be there for you….
- Wait a minute, where can I find you? Can you give me your telephone number?
- It is in a book you'll never get to read, sweety pie!

Then she left, ticking her hills and I could swear I could hear the panty-hose of her thigs gently brushing against one another with a silky friction sound. Her perfume tormented me.

I remained at the table like an idiot, all blushing and with a silly smile on my face, feeling like a clown booed by kids on a birthday! I tell you, these creatures are terrible – they can see right through you!

I was not in a position to reply, but the way he overexposed himself was obvious. One thing I learned and tried to avoid later was not to expose myself. Women have a rare quality – or several if I think better. They want to own your present and for sure your future. The odd thing is when they try to get possession of your past, which obviously is quite hard to accomplish, but not impossible for the skilled ones. I had a good time chatting about this subject but I have to conclude, because my wife called me and she needs me for an important and manly purpose: to correctly cook the Thanksgiving turkey. Cooperation in this one is crucial for my future, as the turkey 's already fried!

A THOUSAND WAYS
TO TRAVEL

Judging from the remains of the oldest humanoids on Earth, many aged more than 3,5 million years, we had back then developed a new way to travel, switching – in technical terms - from 4 x 4 to rear traction, that is hind limb walking, in an ever more vertical position.

We even lost a very "handy" feature – so to speak – the opposable toe, so much used by monkeys when their "upper hands" are busy.

Can you ever imagine the amount of things we could have done with our opposable toe still working like in apes?

I mean you can think about some life facts like, when you come from the mall carrying groceries with your both hands and you find it difficult to open door? You commonly choose to put the bags down and search your pocket for the key. Or you would, but the cups you have in the bag will spill all content out while doing so, or your dog comes in happy to see you back and thumps them over, before you can even blink or the bags simply crack open wide spreading everything in a messy gourmet map.

Any other solution, like having an opposable toe? Simple enough, you put your foot into your pocket (which I must admit requires some serious gym practice time), you grab the keys and unlock the door.

Or when you have your both hands busy cuddling the appetizing shapes of your truly loved girlfriend and you get thirsty for a drink! You cannot abandon your action because of several reasons: you "shouldn't trade" what you have in the palm of your hand for a cup of wine or shouldn't allow this abominable impression to materialize. Another reason is that sometimes, when you let go, the girlfriend runs and doesn't come back soon, the same day or the easy way, so you waste time.

Then you're back to square one and trying to build up your way in again, from scratch (they enjoy this; they say this game turns them on… yeah, after a few months of intense practice). So if you still have them opposable toes, stretch a little and grab the glass of wine from the table with your foot, without interrupting your crucially important activity. You can even share the drink if she doesn't mind the garlic hint left by your sticky socks. Which you may have removed in order to enable full range to the crazy toe.

How about something even more romantic? Simple actions like picking up the handkerchief of a young lady who drops it in your vicinity, just by accident? This is translated like: "Hey, of all the passing by morons I've chosen you and I like you! So f__cking grab it and return it to me politely, so I'll know you like me too!"

You gently pick it up with your left foot and pass it to your left hand, while you use your right hand to raise your hat. A Cheshire cat smile and a blink of your gold tooth will do the rest, I'm sure! Target hit – …..and destroyed!

This reminds me of a story I heard from safari hunters. Young British dude Desmond was full of energy and yearning for adventure, so he registered for a safari in wild Africa. He finally gets there and takes his gear to join the older hunters. One of them, more experienced, tells him: Sunny, if things go on and shit hits the fan, go look for Hank, the vet of the savanna! Desmond did not understand exactly the message, but keeps the information in mind. So there they go into a lion territory and barely escape with their life. Not Desmond, who is severely wounded, having his right arm, right lower limb torn apart and – infamous wound – his genital organ, sliced by the lion.

Desmond, abandoned by group, was desperately trying to get out of the lion territory and somehow he manages to depart from the area. He soon passes out, not before seeing a white haired and bearded man who takes him up and pushes him into a jeep. He wakes up several days later and is pleased to find out he was alive, thanks to Hank, the vet of the savanna.

There were however, some hard to explain issues, but he didn't mind that much about them, as he understood that his life depended on them. Briefly, seems like his torn organs had been replaced with what Hank found available in the field: his right arm was replaced with a chimp's arm, his right leg with an antelope hind limb and his penis was replaced with the tip of an elephant's trunk. He is very upset in the beginning, but seeing the high performance of his newly found limbs, he feels ever more confident. Upon returning home, he makes a stunning press success, especially with his newly found talents: he could swing upon trees with his right arm like a real monkey and soon could leave behind any national champion when running by using his antelope leg.

One cute blonde reporter comes in one day with a more personal question: "Tell me Desmond! I saw your gym performance with your chimp arm, I saw you running with the speed of a train, but how is your love life? How does the elephant trunk serve you?" He takes a sigh and answers: "Actually, I am doing very well! Girls are crazy about me! But I have to avoid going out to picnics! Every time I get into the high grass, the darn thing pics up a bundle of green leafs and tries to stuff it into my ass!"

Now back to traveling! We are mostly used to travel on land! The first locomotion system we used was feet! They carried us from Africa to the Middle East and then west to Europe, where we outsmarted the Neanderthals! They are not entirely extinct – some of us mingled with the good old species. We can still see them if we look carefully, for instance within the bodyguard groups in front of clubs. They have a massive appearance, with shaved heads sometimes, deep buried eyes under prominent ape-like foreheads, with single overgrown eyebrow hanging over the squashed nose that looks like a potato stepped on by a rhino. They have no gap where the backbone should be, as the back side of their head is slowly descending into a mild slope directly to the shoulder blades, eliminating the backbone index angle. The backbone index angle was a referential to tell species apart; not any more these days.

Their look is as intelligent as the one of their ancestors. They commonly take a longer time to understand and process information when spoken to, and to react – as well. They become more keen and responsive at the sight of a 10 dollar bill and might even start to speak, which is something you would hardly expect, considering the appearance. Admit you were equally surprised to see Cesar the chimp speak in the Planet of the Apes.

At that time, the only way of avoiding to use your own feet for walking was getting carried by somebody else. It was risky, as the only way they would do it was when you were wounded or dead and if you were at war with them, that meant you were actually the game / prisoner / next lunch.

The first breakthrough came when we tamed horses, thousands of years ago. The horse – our friend, carrier, bag of pemmican, Bremen singer, confessor and heritage!

The horse chapter reminds me of the Prince Charming story when he was visiting the Fairy Princess, while she had been taken in marriage by the bad ugly despicable Dragon. Please observe that classic stories enjoyed classic manners – even the Despicable Dragon would avoid keeping the princess under his roof without being suitably married to her. What would the old fashioned readers say? He – Prince Charming I mean and please note his way of intruding on an otherwise happy marriage - comes one night and knocks on the front apartment door; "Who is it ?" she asks. "It is me, Prince Charming and I have come to love you dearly!". So she opens the door and they make love (darn' simple with these Vegas wives, isn't it?). Later that night someone else knocks on the door: "Who is it?" she asks again. "It is me, the despicable Dragon! And I come from work and I am so hungry! I can smell a rat…. Hm-hm! a..human Prince here! Let me in so I can destroy him! I'll tear him limb from limb!". "Of course, Darling" she says. "There's nobody else here, but me!" she unnecessarily adds, while starring at Prince Charming who was climbing the window. "My horse will be waiting downstairs and I'll drop on its back!" he said and jumped.

The very next day everything went the same, but outside was raining. They took hours to make love, and when somebody suddenly knocked at the door, she answered: "Coming dear Dragon! It is just me at home!". She helped Prince Charming over the window and then answered the door: "Surprise! Hi, hi, hi! It's me, the horse! Tell Prince Charming it rains outside and I have a back pain from yesterday's stunt, so I went inside the hallway, will you?"

After this painful experience, Prince Charming decides to take precautions – he takes a parachute bag with him. They fruitfully meet again and when somebody knocks: "Coming my dear Dragon, she says!" – by the way - do you observe this "dear" particle added? And the "Darling" show? I mean the difference between the real feelings and the speech! Let that be a lesson to you, whenever you got married or plan to! And for those of you who already did,....you rest in peace!

Prince Charming jumps with his bag from the window and she answers the door. "Hi, hi, hi! Surprise! It's me the horse, again! Tell prince Charming he mistakenly took my oat bag instead of his parachute, please! I hate it when he fails, because he makes cuts on my revenue and the publisher likes him better".

But we have to observe that traveling longer distances, must have been very difficult and tiring, long time ago. The earlier humans might have tried to help each other by carrying wounded companions. And it may have worked until the first smartass pretended to be wounded just to get a free ride. This is how political parties occurred and the idea of state supremacy came to some people. And that of representative democracy!

Fortunately, the horse was tamed in due time. I mean the ox was tame before – or so it seems – but riding an ox gave you little advantage- if any! Small speed and sort of bad image as well! But the horse broke all barriers! Riding the horse in the prairie (a good mustang made 50 / hour) was the supreme manhood and independence statement. In America – and not only – it was hardly matched by carrying an AR-15 gun, on foot. In a school yard – shooting students and teachers like rats in a barrel.

The horse was beneficial in many ways: it would carry you very far, compared to walking distance, it was swift, by all standards of the time, it could drag karts/ chariots full of stuff, it could plough or perform dozens of agricultural activities, it was able to take you home when you were too stupid or too drunk to know the way (or too dead, sometimes), it was used by cowboys to keep herds together and some peoples of Earth – like ancient Mongolians, I think, would even use it as a snack on the way of an invasion. Of course, they would cure the meat for several months first underneath their saddle, just to make sure the horse was dead. When they ate it, it was like ready- made pemmican!

That happened also more recently in countries hit by famine following the war (first or second WW), and Russians did it, Germans did it and others did it. In my country there is a distinctive dry type of salami called "Sibiu", the city where it originates. They say it is made by using horse meat and chicken meat, but the stink betrays its optimal proportion, - one chicken for one horse. I could not eat it until I was 12, but then we went on vacation with our newly bought second hand Russian car. We had to stop in a forest by a lake, as my dad got confused with the national map and the car overheated.

In the good communist habit, the map showed even the roads planned to be built in the next 5 year economy plan, and now I realize we might have tried to use some of those. We slept in the car and I was so hungry that I could eat a horse. And it looks that I did, because all my Mum had to eat in her bag was a couple of this smoked salami sandwiches. And you know what? I started liking it! With "a Jack and a beer back" you can get crazy about it, but I was under-aged at the time. For the Jack and the beer, of course, not for the salami!

The first piece of machinery able to go faster than the horse was the train. The idea that the horse was the real referential resides in the first name the Native Americans gave it – the Iron Horse or the Fire Horse! Anything that moved – so big and so fast – had to be somehow related to a horse.

For a great number of years, the train kept a constant level of comfort – close to none, with the exception of sleep cars. The modern bullet train looks at the inside more like airplanes and goes almost as fast, so you can no longer tell the difference.

I was born in the good old days when many trains were still pulled by steam engines; diesels were becoming more and more important and electrified lines were under construction. The cars were the same like now – there's little difference. You entered your tiny wood compartment, trying to stop the tears from your eyes, tears that came unwillingly because of the smell. There were 2 main seasons to travel. In summer, it was hot! So hot, that only by looking at the artificial leather cover of the seats, your shirt would stick to your skin like mop cloth. The seat was particularly uncomfortable back then: it had a wooden frame where talented rednecks would carve their "Love Mary" or "Anabel". In the middle, there was a small square softer material, covered by artificial leather, where you could cozily install your ischium – if uncovered. The seat, is.

The back of the seat was actually the wall of the compartment (wooden boards) and at head level there was a special head support, again made out of a softer material. If you tried to lean your head against it you had to stick your back to the wall and bend the head with your chin down, like being crucified. First class had some 3 armchairs on one side of the compartment and nothing else. Those were at least softer and cozier. Oh, I forgot to mention mice. They hung over at first class only. The third class was a wooden wagon with wooden benches, where anything you touched was wood hard; all the iron was beneath and making a lot of noise. No comfort for skinny dudes, who would rattle their bones to destination! But third class was later abolished, because "we lived in a non-discriminative communist society".

First class was for rail-way professionals or for top party staff. The rest of us smart - dicks could enjoy the cozy second class, if we could get a seat.

So you enter the compartment and search among the crowd the seat that bears your number. The number of people in the compartment is at least double the regular capacity and soon we get to understand why. The aggressive fat guy with a moustache, holding 3 live agitated hens in his right hand and a piglet plus a 20 liter wine canister in his left hand, finally realizes he indeed picked the right compartment, judging by numbers, but in the wrong car! And – can you believe it, the wrong train! Now he is desperately trying to pull the emergency lever to stop the train.

Another woman - with 5-6 bags apparently stuffed with bed covers and rugs, all soaked in Naphtali - has the same blunt revelation, short of the train confusion. Which brings me to the younger dark guy, staying very quiet and relaxed on my seat. I show him the ticket and he finally decides to raise, not before putting a face, like: here I go, a simple and honest working class citizen of this lousy nation, trying to get back from far away to my poor family, and I get humiliated by these rich, good- for- nothing, profit- thirsty individuals, who can afford buying seats in a train that belongs to us, the democratic people.

I had no idea at the time that he was actually an impostor who was hired in 3 major state enterprises and ran away with the salary money of two of them, but I strongly suspected him to be a bad ass. Not that it made any difference.

I make my way swimming through luggage piles, and finally sit down, when we are already almost halfway to destination. I kind of regret this immediately because of two possible situations: due to the heat, everybody wants the window pane down, so there is a terrible draft, like all the air goes to my head and ears and the smoke of the locomotive makes its way in, darkening our faces relentlessly. If this sounds bad, then imagine that conversely, everybody is afraid of draft and they close both the window and the compartment door, until you feel you are inhaling a hot- spiced soup. This soup is filled with dust and with various aromas, from the armpit of the fat madam near you, to the slimy socks of the guy who just takes off his shoes in front of you and raises his no 56' hooves in your lap. He does it on purpose, with a sigh of satisfaction and a smile on his battered- canister unshaved face, reminding me of a horse's wounded- knee.

In winter, there are also two possibilities: either it is very hot or very cold. It may be very hot, because you are in a car closer to the steam locomotive and enjoy primary hot steam, and everybody is puffing and sweating patiently and with determination, with fixed looks in their eyes like a cat caught in the washing machine, to resist until the targeted station. Conversely, it may be cold like the Ice Age, with the window pane dripped in frozen crystals, all people inside breathing as superficially as possible to avoid inhaling the cold air until we get out of Narnia. Any fart in there is not at all welcome, but somehow promptly forgiven, as it brings hot gas able to redeem transparency to the window pane. Hopefully, nobody smokes inside because a fire or an explosion would be most annoying inside the crowded car!

The heat makes me loose contact with reality and I fall into a heavy slumber. I dream that the locomotive has inside some of the hamster wheels and we take turns in running inside them, to power the locomotive. From time to time I get sprinkled by the outside rain, that helps me spin the wheel faster, then I get actually woken up by drops of wine dripping from the canister located above me, and fallen to the side. The red country wine has no match when coloring things and modern detergent factories spent billions in trying to remove such persistent stains. I can tell you this – the best way to deal with it is ask for 1-2 liters of same wine and dip your clothes in it, so all of it takes an even color. Or use a pair of scissors. I tried to move aside, out of the reach of the wine source.

The comfort inside was nothing when compared to the toilet. Once you decide you really – really need it, you have to painfully make your way to the toilet along the corridor of the car. Plenty of people without seats, yet full of luggage like leaving bombarded Syria, seem to viciously try to stop you: you get stung with Bulgarian umbrellas, knocked down by tons of wooden bags, covering the floor with hard, stinky, slimy or wet content, some of them giving way to unsuspected depth, full of surprisingly smelling substances, which you have to avoid like land-mines; bumpy characters, unable to suck-back their stomach while you pass- by, will viciously press you against the opposite wall, visibly enjoying it, especially if you happen to be a young lady, adding a convenience burp or a loud fart to the already crowded atmosphere.

All sorts of more or less imaginable obstacles will be there ahead of you, but then, when a man has to go, he has to go! The Hexatlon games seem child's play compared to this. Upon reaching the toilet corner, you can see that the door is wide open, and the whole place is filled with bags, on top of which there sits – half asleep – a deaf old lady dressed like a witch, resembling Sid - the sloth's Granny in "Ice Age" or Granny from the "Croogs".

You somehow make her understand she sits in an area quite sensitive to others and after about 20 minutes of playing mime, she finally realizes your natural unstoppable desire and mobilizes her nearby standing family with a long cane, to take action and move the bags. In order to make room, they need to carry some of the bags in the next car, opening the sliding connective door towards a dark passing bridge-way, full of smoke and roaring noise, rendering everyone there speechless. They look – of course – very unhappy about your intrusion, much like a feeding Grizzly bear surprised by your trying to take the salmon out of its mouth. With your left hand. And no red hat or scarf for the occasion.

You ultimately get inside the toilet, hoping to finally have some privacy, but the darn' door doesn't close. I mean it sort of closes, but instantly opens up wide every time the train shakes sideways. So you actually have to hold it with one hand, hoping your other hand will be skillful enough to help yourself in whatever you have to do.

Bad idea! – your hand feels some brown, half dried traces of creamy substance, set against the door knob by someone with a very particular sense of humor. Clinching your teeth, you resist the natural temptation of releasing the knob, while yelling and finally jumping down from the speeding train, off the bridge to the river 300 feet down.

The toilet bowl is metallic, dirty, without any seat and shaking furiously with the whole car. If you are a man, getting a good aim and holding it while you pee, would be pure marksmanship and it would be like trying to hit a 2 000 feet away moving land target with a 50 caliber machine gun from a speeding Humvee hopping up and down on a field road. Or maybe like being a sniper trying to hit a rabbit one mile away, while both of you are running during an earthquake.

If you are a lady, trying to get a good aim while "hovering" the seat, the train shaking wildly, is like trying to couple a Soyuz shuttle to a Chinese space station slot, while re-entering atmosphere. Or doing lap dance to a drilling rig. Imagine doing that while you hold the "brownie" stained door knob, or the door will open, offering the clear view of your bottom to everyone on the hallway. Not that they are not interested, unless very asleep; what I want to say is they do not really expect it, but when opportunity like this comes your way, you don't argue, right? So needless to say, one way or another you get to be the center of public attention. And appreciation.

Let us imagine you somehow do the annoying thing you came there - so painfully - to do. There is no water and no soap – and the dry rusty signs on the bowls and sink show there hasn't been any (water) in the past few years. If you accidentally kept the paper you used for blowing your nose, you will manage to wipe out the essential parts, well sort of, but you cannot disinfect your hands. You will get back to your seat minutes before getting down from the train and someone will find it appropriate to candidly offer you a piece of melting chocolate, which you will gracefully decline "because you just had some" and you show him your "brownie" stained hands.

I still think it was anyway better than the new motorized commuter trains they mistakenly assigned for intercity travel. Cleaner, nicer, using Diesel on electrified lines thanks to a logic we may never understand, almost always on time, but with no toilets at all. After numerous complaints and manifestations of protest – many of which hard to eliminate, because of the smell and the traces- they gave up and assigned them back to commuter lines. The idea belonged to a socialist minister of transportation, who, according to socialist thinking – considers everyone else below his intellectual level, which we would actually need to dig for. And he hated hedgehogs. And 2 layer toilet paper. And anchovies.

The bus travel inside the city beats them all. Once you get up you must prepare for the adventure of your life. When I was a kid, we used to take a trolley-bus to the seaside resort next to our city. They were so crowded, people would take the ride on the stairs. When we finally were getting there (doing some 7-8 Km in almost one hour), we felt like out of a sauna and were thirsty like an Irish fish in the dry desert.

It goes beyond normal imagination what connotations simple body- contact can deliver under the circumstances. An old story was about a man who yelled at a young lady to pass on the ticket to his wife in front. She answered with a bored face: Hey pops'! You can drop the Miss thing! I ain't a Miss anymore since three bus stops ago! There was another story about a guy who woke up in the ER. The paramedic asked him: No offence Sir, but what happened to you! You look like you tried to dodge an eighteen wheeler on the highway! And failed!

The man blinked in disbelief and said with feeble voice: I was in the elevator and wanted to go up to my office at the second floor, when this lady comes in. She had these huuuge tits — absolutely titanic! – biggest ones I ever saw! I was still staring at them when she said: "Push one!!". I couldn't help it!

The bus is also exposing you to unwanted dialogue. Let me see, you currently have to choose between an over-exhausted genitor woman, possibly Mexican, chewing on a garlic gum – if that is possible – and nervously shaking all her three chins, while hanging tight to her food bags and a chirpy dressed young colored person (possibly – no, probably male!). He… hope I am not wrong – is wearing a sport's shirt – unable to conveniently hide his armpit hairdo, a tiny pink bikini which is tightly stretched over a pair of lily colored panties. Crocodile high heel shoes will complete the picture and the missing front tooth enables him to - from time to time - exhale some cinnamon flavor from his chewing gum. The hands – large enough to sustain inertial flight – are safe guarding a purse called "Chanel" – probably a good fake. Now that's classy! You hate to disturb the young …errrr…..miss, but the next one is a fat garage assistant with a green shirt, much too thick for the warm season and he proves it by perspiring a lot. His large trousers - apparently designed for two persons at a time, or just one person while riding a mule – stay on him simply because they are connected to his shoulders by elastic braces. He seems very satisfied with the room left inside the pants, as he can take a few steps to and fro without anybody noticing it.

The eternal pick-pockets is present, dressed as a honorable clerk in his grey suit and black tie – like who goes inside a bus in July dressed like for a wedding?

The also unmistakable guardian vulture of the block smiles at you from a back seat: the odd looking grey old Miss Marple with eyes like an army radar and ears like a submarine sonar, always on!

You suddenly realize you already saw her when getting out of your block in the morning. You also saw her looking at the shop windows like some half an hour ago in a different part of the city and now HERE she is, riding with you the same bus.

I'll bet you she will be the first thing you see when you get home, like cleaning with a broom in front of her apartment. Scary shit!

I would feel tempted to say – but of course, she managed to be riding it home (the broom that is) and she had just jumped down from it when she saw you, like a Japanese test pilot from his Hayabusa! No! I'll not fall for that! Instead, I'll just observe that there are people – and I saw such old neighbor ladies – that have a distinctive talent of being in several places in the same time. I called mine "Old Mrs. Ubiquity".

I have been – once in a while – in the position to take a flight to more distant places. Oh, the airplane! This eternal miracle and scary story!

Whenever I need to get someplace by plane, I unwillingly discover a lot of (bad) news in the area. Weeks before, a plane of our national airlines had to abort takeoff or landing because of something happening THERE. And days before, a plane full of military personnel from a distant African country ditched in the jungle moments after take-off because of heavy rainfall. Of course you get annoyed by such news; only later on you find out that your airline plane aborted takeoff as there was a lady screaming because she saw a mouse under her chair. And they had to wait until the poor mouse was disembarked. It doesn't seem dangerous or out of the ordinary, if you consider Delta Airlines and their disembarking passengers for a lot less. Again, later on you discover that the African plane took off from a country where there was no rain – or they actually were in the dry season, and it came down together with a ground-to-air missile shot by the second in command General Sesokko Mokono – who later took responsibility for downing the plane in which the late President was accompanied by military staff obedient to him. Clear sky! I took a trip to Austria for a medical convention. Nothing dangerous so far. It was time to leave now. I go to the airport, when the time comes, leaving always in advance and getting there kind' a late. I stay in line for getting rid of my cargo luggage – many colored people before me. Some with amusing faces, some not. I get to the front, where a bored young lady takes my papers and seconds later asks me: where do you go?

I reply : I just gave you my reservation, it says destination, time and everything, but she answers bluntly: why, you do not know where you want to fly? I'm just checking!

"Ok, all right, miss!" I say my story and then place my bag on the counter (where there is a scale). I look at the electronic display and take a sudden decision to break it before showing the true weight of my luggage, but it turns out to be much smaller than the limit. I take the other belongings – the cabin luggage – and go to check point area. A streaming crowd takes dynamic positions on that grid and makes it hard to choose the right lane. Fortunately, there is always an employee who diverts you on the longer queue at the right moment, so you take your bag and start slaloming your way to the check-point. While you approach you have to throw away your liquid content baggage: the beer in your hand sadly goes the same way. You grab a plastic crate – not before putting on a fight over it with 2-3 Russian female tourist retirees, and place all your stuff inside. The last – complying with the demands – your belt. You wait before the electronic gate holding your pants with one hand, while trying to minimize the damage to your external looks with the other, when you get called through the gate.

I have nothing metallic on me, but the darn' bell rings. The massive guardian in front of me rises an eyebrow (little discomfort) and waves to me – take of your shoes and pass again!. I take off my shoes and place them in another plastic crate, hoping the smell coming out of them will not trigger any alarm and I pass again. Bell rings!

I get called closer and they start to check me physically and with a small gadget that chirps from time to time. Getting with it to my behind pocket, it starts chirping like a dozen parrots. It turns out I have forgotten a key in my back pocket. Sorry guys! I do not get to smile my way out, when the solid guy comes back to me, and, with a less polite hold on my arm, he drives me back to the conveyer: "Is this your bag?" he asks. "Yes, of course!". "Then you'll have to hand me the knife!" he says, in a cold voice." Knife? Good Heavens, What knife?" I start thinking how could a knife get into my bag, imagining large butcher shop knives all lined up on the bottom of my shoulder bag and me cutting the heads of the pilots. "Here!" he indicates my bathroom bag, which lately became to me some sort of survival kit. I hold there card pins, important medication, some flash memory sticks, pens and a lot of miscellaneous stuff. I was looking at him in disbelief, not remembering what I would do with a knife in there. "Take your time!". He smiles back to the other guy, the one looking in the machine: "this time we've got him nailed!" says his smile. I lose patience and turn the bag upside down and somewhere from the bottom of the bag, there comes out "the knife". It was the smallest version of a Swiss –knife, having a nail cutter and a beer opener on it and yes – a blade - some 4 cm long. He shows me that the blade is long enough to be dangerous when stabbing someone with it. I was thinking that a person his size would barely notice such sting, unless given to the eye, but he looks very serious and my mind is made up. "Ok. That was a gift from my mother. I forgot it in there a long time ago! I am sorry! You can keep it!"

He throws it away over his shoulder onto a huge pile of similar stuff placed in a crate. Forgive me Mum! I am sure you can see from heaven he did not mean wrong. His eyes avoid looking at me again, but his chest is up, like saying: "we just prevented an act of terrorism, people! Nothing extraordinary! It's all in a day's work!".

He claps his elastic braces on the shoulders and then points at me to a colleague on the other side. I am staying there like the French deportee Papillon on the selection corridor at French Guyana prison camp, holding my pants with one hand, trying to arrange my shirt that has gone out and, generally speaking, trying to raise less interest and pity on the crowded airport.

The other colleague comes to me; he wears rubber gloves and for a brief moment, I fear he is going to do THAT right there, across the counter. Instinctively I drag my trousers higher and decide to deny any access to my rear region, whatever the cost. However, he doesn't seem interested in that, as he takes a small sponge and tells me to raise shirt. He rubs the sponge around my neck, chest, belly and hands, doing the already known routine for explosive detection. WTF? Do they think that if I had a bigger clipper, I am in for bombs now? I ask the guy how did I become suspect, but he smiles and tells me it's procedure, nothing personal. I reclaim my belongings and once I put my belt on, I regain some of my dignity.

I stroll around the travel shops trying to regain my spirits and try to find some small gifts for family. You know, the kind of stuff like key holder, magnet toy, small sweet boxes, but it turns out those are the most expensive and I retreat to a nearby seat, not before getting a small bottle of apricot schnapps – a gift for me!

We go to the plane. Smiling people everywhere. The flight attendant comes along the corridor and smiles to us; actually she holds a cricket in her hand and she is counting. I manage to get more comfortable and buckle up. Then suddenly, we receive the bad news – we need to go back to the waiting room, because of technical issues.

We remember once again about flights that never made it back. Thoughts come to your mind: "maybe this is a SIGN! Maybe this is THE SIGN that you have to quit and take the next flight or the train! Or just walk away!" says a worried little green spirit on your right shoulder. "Hi, hi, hi, ha…aa!" laughs with a hysterical voice the little red devil on your left shoulder – "What's the matter buster, chicken already?". However, after 2 hours of waiting in a separate waiting room, we come to find out we are going to leave in 30 minutes. We also find out which was the technical problem they encountered: one of the 3 toilets didn't flush properly. Of course, there was another minor issue, as one of the crew observed there was a difference between the programmed takeoff weight of the plane and the real weight, given by the fact that refueling was ordered in liters and was actually accomplished in lb.

OMG- I thought, the fuel would have been enough for just half way back – and then all the way down!

We were further advised - to our own comfort - that the plane would use only half of the ordered quantity on the flight back, but they completed the ordered fuel quantity anyway.

Well, we get in the plane again. Inexplicably, it took 15 min until everyone finds his seat again. While we take off, a nasty small toddler starts crying. I mean almost anyone has kids and they cry from time to time – although they say it is never without a reason. I am a physician and supposed to be tolerant to any kind of natural manifestation. But this kid was unlike others.

He was crying hysterically, possibly trying to get his mother's attention and it looks like it worked with anybody else, but her!. She seemed tired, bored and asleep and she was slumbering, while "shush-ing" him from time to time and shaking him to sleep. What sleep? The little guy was yelling like being cut with a chainsaw and his crying was louder than taking off throttled engines. One of the attendants tried to take him and comfort him by hugging him dearly; he started yelling even louder, and she dropped him in his mother's lap a.s.a.p., like it were a ticking bomb! When the flight attendant came near to me, I told her that it might have worked if the kid were, like, 20 years older! "I'm not sure he would have cried at that age!"- She answered back to me, with a presumptuous smile! "That is correct!" I answered. You didn't see me crying, although we had reasons to! But I could sure use a hug anyway!" She laughed and when she passed with the coffee, the busty attendant stopped by me and asked me if I want some more milk. Capisci? I said no, but I appreciate the offer! Oh, I forgot about the baby! Well, the baby yelled like rabid his bottom out for another quarter of an hour, until his neighbor – likely same age – got stirred up and started howling like a shadowing wolf. I thought it is going to end like in Robinson Crusoe, but apparently paradoxically, when the second started yelling, the first one stopped to listen and fell asleep, deeply satisfied that someone else took over.

However, the second one was easier to calm down with a pacifier. So simple and so effective? I still suspect that pacifier has been generously dipped in whiskey. His mother had a whole bottle of it in front of her.

Well, you know how cozy the airplane economy seats are. You stay straight, like tied to a tourniquet pole by the Inquisition, hands in front on your knees and keep the aspirin tight between your knees. I'm joking here with the aspirin; it reminded me about the questions with Radio Erevan: "Can the aspirin be used as a woman contraceptive?" And the answer was: "Yes, but only when you squeeze it tight between your knees!". So that is the position, and when you are tired you can recline your seat backwards. In theory, maybe. The person in front of you is doing it first thing after takeoff, but when you try to do it, at some point, the person behind you will protest vigorously.

Then they bring you the food parcel. You start unwrapping it, and you cannot but observe that there is more care about how you collect and pack the garbage after you finish, than is there respect for the food inside. One piece of bread is recognizable – fluffy and sweet. And small. A small trey/ casserole holds in it some warm food. Hard to say what it is made of; looks like some odd veggies in a stew and some pieces of meat, which you push gently with the fork to make sure they are dead and don't move like maggots. Small salad wrapped in a separate plastic – it all looks like astronaut food – the kind you take a gulp and throw the pack. The fork is small so you have to dig gently and aim right in your mouth, as the plane inevitably enters "an area of turbulence". Half of the food and the precious sip of water in a plastic cup lands in your lap.

You manage to eat the rest in- between two consecutive shakes of the plane and delicately start wrapping up the garbage and prepare it for collection, while still sipping on your glass of wine. Why? I mean why not? After all that happened I feel entitled to some sort of anesthesia. After all, it is not Propofol, right?

I still need to go to the bathroom, before the plain gets to destination. I am waiting after an older lady, while on the other side, people come and go very efficiently. I remember the joke about how the Irish started dancing – in front of occupied toilets of the bar! No offence intended. After some Irish whiskey you get lured anyway! Finally she is out! And air is in! Please, make more air! Open the door or the windows! Some depressurization please! I mean somebody should tell her that something died – not very recently - in her stomach, but I suspect she knows it too well, because she has been hunting it all her lifetime, whatever that was and how big it was, and she ate it all!

I pretend to mess with the folding door, hoping to get some more fresh air and then I lock myself in. A crazy thought tells me: how about claiming this spot to yourself to the end of the flight? I do not know if you ever noticed how particularly small these toilet cabins are on a plane? Even so, Chinese medium currier flights suggested to have them removed and replaced with 4-5 more seats. That will be a big smelly and greasy mistake. You can't stand straight, because the round cabin ceiling goes down on a slope. So you keep your chin in your chest while doing whatever you do. Still have to hold on to something, if there is turbulence outside. I once grabbed by mistake the flush lever; OMG! The sound of being sucked out of the plane and thrown in the minus fifty degrees cold darkness beneath – possibly the ocean – makes you freeze and renders you unable to produce anything within the next 24 hours.

I got scared as I did not expect it the first time. Are they really throwing poop away from the plane? I asked a guy when I was a novice in flight transportation. He said: not so much lately; they still use the sucking pressure of the environment, but collect stuff in a tank, which is removed on arrival and replaced with an empty one. Some media news suggest not all aircraft are that modern. At least judging by the lesions of the innocent passing-under victims.

The worst thing when we landed was hearing the applause. I mean, what is the extraordinary thing about it? It happens so rare for a plane to land safely? Is it an exception? Is this the only pilot that can do it? It reminded me of a story about two blind pilots, who made their way to the cockpit using white sticks. Every person on board smiled at the good joke, but they set the plane in motion and somehow made it to the end of the runway. After a second, the plane swings forward accelerating. Meanwhile in the cockpit:

- Anytime now, Jim!
- Yeah! Throttle more!

Engine roar increases and plane speeds up towards the other end of the runway, but although speeding fast, the airplane does not give any sign of preparing to take off. Meanwhile, terrified passengers see how the end of the runway comes closer and closer.

In the cockpit:

- Ready Jim?
- Anytime now, Dick!

From the cabin, a sudden terrified howling chorus of the passengers peaks into the cockpit.

- Now! Pull up! Pull up, Jim!
- Yeah, right! Answers Jim pulling up the nose of the plane and retracting landing gear.
- Wanna' know something Dick?
- What?
- One of these days, those stupid morons in the back will shout too late and we're going to ditch it!

I then remembered the comforting words of a blonde flight attendant from "Newton" air-ways: "Do not be alarmed! Whatever it happens, and when I say whatever, I mean whatever - we're gonna get back to the ground anyway!"

DO WE DRINK
TOO MUCH?

We've got accustomed to considering alcohol drinking, in general, as a Biblical sin **of the others!**

Accurately defining it turns out to be a much more difficult and even subtle task, in today's social context.

Let us put it this way: if a mayor has a noon whiskey with his favorite councilors, does that make him a drunk? God forbid!

If a Congress-man has had a heavy lunch with plentiful liquid compensation and then falls asleep during a board meeting, does that make him a drunk? Come on, folks! We can always apply the boss concept line: the boss is not sleeping, he is merely concentrating, planning ahead or having some thoughts!

Much better for the Moldavians who simply extricated from their vocabulary the "drunk" or being "drunk" allegation. When they drink, they say they "honor" something or "serve" something. If it so happens that, afterword, you have the "honor" to crash-land in a gutter, it is just a matter of subsequent analysis, which does not harm anyone and becomes irrelevant for our present research.

As for the Russians and the Lipovas (a Russian related population) from our country, it may be hard to be accurate when deciding if they drink water or vodka, as they use the same jar –size glasses for both. However, I've seen them pretty good with steering boats on the water, but I haven't seen them drinking it, so far.

That reminds me of this Russian Commissar, who getts in a pub with 2 friends and his driver. He asks for 4 jars of vodka. They grab the jars and empty them pronto, while asking for the second round.

Down the hatch goes round number 2, and the Commissar asks for yet another round. The third needs a little more time to go, but down it goes after 5-6 minutes of quality conversation.

The Commissar waves again to the waiter, but now he makes the "3" sign with his fingers. The waiter is a little puzzled and approaches: Tavarish Commissar, a patamu shto? (Comrade Commissar, but why so?). The Commissar knocks his forehead with his index and then points out to one of his men, the tiniest of all: Patamu schto on shofer, durak! (Because he is the driver, you moron!)

Besides, the name of the favorite spirit in Russia – vodka – comes as a diminutive of water ("vadá"), possibly meaning something like "little / tiny water".

I have thought on countless occasions about the actors impersonating important people in various life stories, characters presented while going and humbly speaking for themselves in AA associations (like when you go there, you stay anonymous for what, five minutes?! All the old household witches, eternally cleaning the hallway of your block with the same broom, all the early-going-to-the-marketplace housewives you meet every day, not to mention your secretary and her 689 Facebook friends, will promptly know your program at the AA association for the next three months before you even go there twice.

The Negro caddy at your golf club will not answer your phone anymore, your mechanic will postpone your car check-up indefinitely and your bank advisor will place the "office out of service" sign, when he sees you at the entrance.

The brutal and rudimentary Captain Caveman- faces around you at the AA association meetings are meant to emphasize your decay and how you've got to have the same basic, gross and unworthy–of-a-sophisticated-mind behavior problems, like the goons around you.

The hero will pass through countless humiliating experiences, before demonstrating that, in fact, he didn't even drink that much. It was just a momentary crisis, and his wife in secrecy had initially filed the complaint, as she was cheating on him with his boss. She intended to divorce him and take the holyday mountain cabin and his better car, besides half of the house but no kids.

I have also seen in countless movies that Americans are doing this kind of associations for any kind of more or less well diagnosed nervous disorder or "bad" habit, the only palpable results being safely guarded in the associations' bank accounts. I enjoyed a movie where Stephen Seagal (OMG, no, he is not my favorite actor!) was a police officer, previously charged with aggressive misconduct, who was supposed to go to some sort of association of exceedingly violent people, where they could share their feelings and benefit from psychological advice to calm down.

The mentor of the class was a nice lady with a rare talent – she would succeed to stir you crazy in less than 3 minutes, even if you were a Tibetan monk experiencing a vigil coma or a Hamish on a Sunday afternoon slumber.

To me it is like fishing: you keep quiet on the bank of a pond and patiently place inside the water a small metallic hook with bait on it, hoping that in all that large lake, there will be one stupid – enough fish to chew on it.

Well it is a little bit more complicated, as all the fish are either busy or not hungry, or simply clever enough to avoid your sorry ass trap. I remember a story about a fisherman who was so fond of nature that he would sob about every fish he caught: "Oh my little darling! Poor you, little soul, how come you got caught in my fishing rod?" The fish turns to him, spitting out the hook: "Imagine Einstein, I wanted to kill myself, but you can't get killed with your lousy two-dollar- single –use-Chinese – good-for-nothin'-MF gear!"

All creatures on Earth drink something, starting with plain water. I may have had some doubt with them fish and marine mammals – they gulp so much water anyway, that you can't say they do it on purpose or they simply do it for breathing purposes – the fish at least. I recon their main problem is either not to drink too much of it or maybe find a better way to get rid of the excess, which is also a less obvious maneuver in their natural habitat. It is like peeing in a large pool so nobody will notice; this is hard to do these days with the chemical stuff they put in the water. With that, peeing in the pool may be an embarrassing experience, as your urine stirs up blue or red clouds the size of a Jumbo Jet trail. Kids start crying, mothers go and drag them out of the pool, old greasy tycoons on surrounding armchairs "tisk, tisk" you!

Like I would like to see them fart in the pool – see who dares smoke out there!

Fish drink like they breathe (or vice versa). However, humans are a distinctive species. Displeased by water in certain moments of their life, the humans started tasting whatever nature provided, with a curiosity matched sometimes even by animals.

I have seen a very interesting film on Discovery, with animals from the savannah crowding to eat the fallen and fermented fruits of a local marula tree. Monkeys were first and –as they used fresh fruit – they couldn't "get high" too quickly. But the elephants preferred the fallen fruit, especially those fermented for a few days, thus being charged with a considerable amount of alcohol. It was amazing to see how much – in a matter of minutes - those elephants were starting to resemble dock-yard workers making their way towards home on Friday evening,

2-3 steps forward, one behind, making the direction very difficult to assess or to keep. The elephants, bearing the gift of intelligence that places them alongside primates and dolphins, were nuts about this fruit.

Question - Can we honestly blame the "misfit" intellectuals of the Communist regime for their alcoholic addiction?

It is a pity Michael Jackson did not catch this tip – like sipping a shot or two before the concert, instead of getting himself killed over Propofol delivered by his doctor, who was a trustworthy brother. Which reminds me of a story concerning the eternal skirmish between the Romanian and the Hungarian ethnics in Transilvania. They say a Romanian guy called John, getting sick into his dying bed, calls for a notary public to change his name. "What is the nature of the change you desire and why so urgent, Sir?" he is asked. "I want to change my name from John to Istvan (Hungarian for John). "Now why would you do that for?" the lawyer says. The man takes a fierce look, and clinging to his bed with his last energy, he says through his clinched teeth: "Cause I'd rather have one of them dead instead of one of ours".

Almost the same thing happened with two best friends, one Romanian and one Hungarian. One day, John (Romanian) was drunk- stiff and he was sharpening his hunting / survival dagger against a rock in front of his house. Istvan (Hungarian) comes by, and seeing the scene, gets curious:

- Hi John! WTF are you doing?
- I am sharpening this knife, you MF!
- I can see that! WTF for?

John, with eyes looking forward towards an empty space:

- Cause I wanna kill a M-F-king hun of your breed!
- Yoy Istenem! (Oh God!) Whatever for?
- Because you and your Hungarian breed killed our late King Michael the Great!
- Hold it, hold it John! Think a little! That happened 450 years ago!
- Yeah, but I only learned about it yesterday!

It is a well- known thing that alcohol does lead to depression. Depression comes with chronic consumption, along with other possible health problems. I have seen many times people that had difficult life problems, triggering their depression along with alcohol abuse. Under such circumstances, alcohol was used merely as an anesthetic to what life was doing to them.

I am not going to promote regular use of alcohol, but if animals can have fun like this, it may not be totally un-natural. Besides, we know that our body produces endogenous alcohol on a daily basis (not much, but anywhere detectable, in the range of 2 or more ml).

Must have been thought useful for something, otherwise Good Old Mighty wouldn't have allowed it! So what if we choose to add some to the already existing quantity?

History probably failed to disclose the story of some primitives who gathered fruit, collected the juice that dripped from it and kept on drinking it until it was fermented. They surprisingly enjoyed it more than the fresh one and tried to make some more, till they understood what the secret of making it was.

The Chief Hunter would order : "I want a Chateau Mango & Banana 200258B.C." and all tribe's men would cheer with drumsticks in their hands: "That was a good year, Boss!". The spirit fabrication secret came later, when some crazy- ass alchemist tried to turn plums into gold over a pot, and the result remained pending but nice flavored, and very much appreciated in the long winter days.

Speaking about depression, it is interesting that you cannot tell it from the beginning, due to the dis-inhibiting action of alcohol. More than that, it is interesting not all people fall to depression. Have you ever seen a depressed Irishman? I've known a lot, many of them sharing the exquisite art of whiskey sipping without getting drunk, and none of them was depressed, or if he was, you couldn't tell!. They just dress in their green clothes and they dance.

In my country, I saw old men in their 80s working hard in their household or farm, but only after taking a morning shot of home-made stuff (50 degrees). Home distilleries are very respectable when it comes to refined fruit stuff. Another shot was to welcome lunch and have appetite and 2 shots in the evening for good mood (I mean that already was a good spirit).

And they also smoked plain, sometimes rolling their own cigarettes from the day's newspaper or corn leafs. And they never-ever looked depressed.

My father in law was an accountant all his life, and retirement found him as a respected employee of the largest winery in the country. He taught me a thing or two. As a young law school student, he was abducted by the Communist Security Militia (sort of our local KGB) and deported to another place. He did time in a 25 square feet chamber, together with other three guys, out of which one was always the snitch. All because he was a registered member of a right / Democratic Party, while the Communist regime was struggling to eliminate all democracy and western influence, which they, incidentally, succeeded quite well.

He would eat almost nothing, they would beat the shit out of them twice a day and also "enjoyed" some electric- bed "Rambo" treatment because he wouldn't "sing" about his friends.

When he got out he weighed 90 lbs – half the man that got in. He was under strict surveillance, until my wife was born (in mid-sixties) and he was not allowed to participate at his own wedding at the time.

But guess what? He remained – till the day he met the Maker – one of the funniest and wisest men I ever knew. He would have told you life stories and countless jokes over a bottle of wine and he practically never got drunk, because – he said – "you do not drink the wine like a thirsty horse! You have to talk it over and over, not gulp it like a hyppo!"

Once he met with some of his older friends – many of whom I knew, and who looked like freshly unburied mummies from Luxor.

They were celebrating something and they overdid it. Their version remake of "The Mummy" ended up in the ER of the County Hospital because of gait impairment and stuff; otherwise, all were very talkative.

ER personnel – many of which knew me, called my wife and told her that dr.E's father in law is in trouble in the ER. My wife was coming to tell this to me with a rather balanced voice, when she suddenly realized "OMG, your father in law means my father!!!"

He was ok, and he said that shit hit the fan when they were too hurried to drink without eating properly! But they had a very god time. Like I said, I never saw him depressed!

The long life secret of one of the oldest persons in Cuba was quickly buried in the media because she said that whatever kept her alive, were good quality Cuban rum and cigars.

Years before, there was a national company selling vodka in small 150-200 ml UHT boxes with a straw. Drinking from that recipient on the street was known as "cell phone talking".

Depression can be faked by some people, like our former president who was a specialist in arranging whiskey over the rocks; he was so obsessed with this, you would say it were ikebana or something. After consuming a number of arrangements like this, the first words that came to his mouth were: "I want to make my country great again".

I participated to a convention of orthopedists (European Congress) in Denmark once. Denmark looks like a country with very sad and depressed people. Maybe their symbol in Copenhagen – the little siren – is luring them into this introspective behavior. Some of them seem weirdos, like some guys I've seen on the city train: one of them was in a terrible hurry, walking towards the front of the train (5 cars ahead) and back like 3-4 times between stations. Every local train seemed to have its own weirdo. Maybe it is because of the weather. One morning I got up in a heavy construction activity noise – some workers repaired the street outside our hotel. I got up and saw it was full light outside and became terrified of the fact that I may get late for the congress works. Must be 9 or 10 I thought, by the looks of it. When I looked at the watch, it was only 5.30 a.m.

Later on, I asked a lady who was complaining of the heat wave (it was like 24 °C in a sunny spring day!), what is the winter like. She made a gloomy face and said- we just have daylight from 9 a.m. to 3 p.m. and it is very cold and a lot of snow. That – I thought – is the answer! On such weather, you just stay in the house and drink yourself to oblivion and try to keep warm. Truth is, everybody in Copenhagen seems to go to bed at 10 pm; hard to find an open pub at this time, even downtown.

But the atmosphere is totally different in the buses and especially in the trains, where everybody drinks. Possibly also in the bohemian area called Christiania, where they say you can meet Mary Jane and it feels like at home.

In dark corners or crowded trains, teenagers dressed in hilarious t-shirts and bizarrely colored jackets, spend their time with a can of beer in the hand and a one liter vodka jar in the middle.

Countless nation ethnics, workers around the city, accompany them in the evening, with the bottles and cans held steadily between their knees. I strongly believe that in this country, the only ones who do not – visibly – drink, are the ever increasing- in- number Muslims.

They say by the end of WW – II, Germany was being occupied by the Russians from the East. A soviet major descends from his car in Jena, in front of the Filetische Museum (Phylogeny Museum), a great natural science exhibition, founded by Friedrich Engels himself.

Being curious and suspecting something wrong in the same time, the major starts wandering through the halls, arriving in a room full of dry insects but also packed with tiny creatures preserved in white alcohol jars. With wide open eyes, he goes to a shelf with some ugly looking critters, placed in cup- size bowls with white alcohol. To the surprise of his body guards, he takes one jar, opens it and removes the little critter from inside, possibly a little locust. Then he approaches two thirsty nostrils to the rim and sniffs carefully. "Vodka" he yells happily and without a second thought, he gorges the whole jar like a thirsty horse would suck dry a bucket of water. "Ahaaa!" He moves towards the next shelf and he grabs a half kilo jar holding inside a little gecko lizard. He removes the lid, picks the gecko out with two disgusted fingers and throws it on the floor, carefully sniffs the content and presently throws it down the hatch to join the preceding one.

Red in his cheeks and all sweat, the major pulls up his cap, raises his Kalashnikov and releases a short burst shattering to pieces the glass ceiling above, yelling viciously: "Harasho! Gde krokodil?" (Ok, where's the crocodile?).

Many specialists are documenting their opinion on drinking in impressive books, either medical or, more frequently, regarding nutrition and metabolism. Opinions are different: some say a glass of wine / day is welcome. Others say it is not mandatory, but it doesn't harm anyway.

Some cardiologists say red wine is better, others say red wine increases blood pressure. They discuss anyway, such tiny quantities, that some of our citizens would use them for eye / nose drops, compared to what they commonly drink every day. Science doesn't really mingle here with popular practice.

How else can we explain the religious fervor of men in respecting the Biblical demand of drinking 40 glasses of wine for Saint Martyrs day (9th of March for the Orthodox), while totally ignoring important commandments related to stealing, adultery or the sin of worshipping carved face?

Besides, what drink could be better than monastery brandy and the friar's wine? Friar Tuck's skills were not forgotten. I have once visited at Easter time a monastery of monks in Northern Moldavia and I was impressed by the quantity of wine that was "sacrificed" for the event. Some of their too-pious friars were so belly proud, being intensely re-hydrated after the long 40 days of fasting.

Water, after all, has no taste at all. "Tears are the friar's bath!" said one of the younger and good looking friars ; his blue eyes and pony tail hair, together with the grayish long beard and the Hercule-size body were very impressive to younger blonde tourists. He was presently approved by a small rat- profile half hump-back individual carrying some vegetables to the kitchen. One needs to have good taste in order to make good booze.

I suddenly realized that our orthodox religion is very comprehensive when it comes to drinking; we have so many Christian holydays to celebrate, that our ancestral thirst can hardly match the number of non-working holydays. If we would let some guys have their own interpretation of holydays, we'd work some 4-5 days / year, and celebrate for the rest. And judging by this year's government budget, we're almost there!

Now that is a really old habit, as it is not Christianity and the invitation of Good Old Jesus of drinking His blood and eating His flesh that led us to binge partying.

Americans proved to be primitive and underdeveloped as a nation, as they initiated Prohibition very late, in 1920s, whereas we did it 2000 years ago, in ancient Dacia (former Thracian state on the territory). Overwhelmed by petitions and the lousy presence and performance of men on the battlefield, the All-mighty leader of Dacia, (our ancestors were a special breed of Thracian nation) decided to destroy the visible cause – the vineyards. No sooner said than done! A terrible mistake was initiated – one that the Communist have aggravated with their intensive agriculture – when superior vintage grapes were replaced by hybrid species, with poor quality but more resilient, needing less care and protection. From then on, Romanians got accustomed to "Molan" wine. Molan is a slang term defining bad quality thick red wine, looking like a Deltic locomotive used engine oil, made out of less selected hybrid grapes and helped out with lots of sugar. After regular use, it will put two holes in your body, one in the head, and the other in your stomach.

Super-production was invented. Once you drain the barrel, you put some sugar and water over the squashed grape skins, and within 3 weeks you have the next "vintage" production. It is not as good as the first one, but when all booze is over, by the month of, say late February or early March, works miracles, like gun powder.

Skilled "specialists" can do even the third round, when this second one is over. They put again sugar, water and some yeast over the leftovers, and let it ferment in a distant warehouse, in order to prevent gas intoxication or explosions. They would allow now a longer time for fermentation and decantation, in strong glass recipients, because the plastic ones are not resilient enough and could melt away in contact with the product.

This time they do not drink it, never touch the stuff; they keep it only for guests or get it as a present for the local doctor. It is very important not to get stained with the stuff. There is nothing on the face of the Earth to clean the purple-red "molan" (that is the nickname of the product) stains from fabric, no matter what you try, short of C4. All detergents failed this test, and the IG Farben company in Germany filed a complaint for misleading the chemistry team with alien substances. The only way you can deal with it is the heroic choice: use a pair of scissors and upgrade generously your couture- style or save half a liter of "wine" and dip the whole coat in it. Sometimes the result is a catchy and chic purple color. Once all your wardrobe turns dark purple, you are respected as a "connoisseur".

Although mentioned around many times, I heard the Muslim religion does not specifically forbid alcohol, but this interdiction becomes inherent with every verse. It is a good thing, because drinking a bottle of Jack, and then going out on a sunny day in the desert at 50°C in the shadow is purely suicidal. You might make it to the parking lot, but until you recognize your camel or the animal recognizes you, you're dead.

But Arab people are human after all and once they go to other places they get to "socialize". Once, before the offensive of ISIL, I was invited in Iraq for a Rheumatology conference. One of my friends there – actually ex-colleague from the University we graduated – whom I have known for 34 years, was telling me stories about the other guests.

He showed me a tiny man with the profile of a starving rat; he was very serious and moved like his coat had been dipped in starch before drying stiff. My colleague said: "Do you see this guy? He is the brother of an imam! Professionally he is so and so, but he is very strict with religion. Once we went to France for a convention. After 3 days, when we were supposed to check out of the hotel, our group leader was horrified to find out we had to pay another 450 Euros for minibar drinks. The problem was not over sodas or cokes, but dozens of small bottles of fine red wine. Everybody was looking at everybody and nobody had any clue of who was the culprit responsible for devastating the wine reserve of the hotel. Finally our group leader came with the idea of asking which room was billed and to everybody's stupefaction, it was this rat's room. Of course we cornered him and asked: how can you drink wine like a horse and become a blasphemer of the Coran? He smiled and said he did not realize it was wine; he thought it was a sour grape juice, just good for his throat."

I met recently another guy from the same parts, who managed to build a hospital of his own. He showed me his salt cave for asthma treatment, somewhere in the basement, but he was very proud of his winery next to it, which was the size of a small restaurant and where he would invite his guests.

Now seriously, if you go to Arab countries, holding a freakin' Kalashnikov under your arm, it may be a little embarrassing, but you might get on with it somehow, maybe not in Dubai, though. But if you try to hide a bottle of booze under your arm, you are in a world of shit. Prison is nothing compared to what they might do to you;

you'll get crucified alive! In one of my voyages to the Emirates, while visiting a hospital where some friends worked, I had the opportunity to see a patient who was wounded in a traffic accident. He was related to a very important person and he was some sort of VIP himself. His wounds were nothing, compared to the unfortunate possibility of somebody finding out he was drunk- driving. I heard he paid a few thousand bucks just to have this mentioning removed from his file.

The more severe regulations are about drinking – religion left alone – the more people are tempted to drink. Take for instance, drunk driving. You are not allowed to be influenced by alcohol while driving. But this is exactly what drivers passionately do! It is indeed hard to imagine a social category thirstier than drivers. For a professional driver, drinking becomes a physiological necessity, as he is constantly deprived of this pleasure, so he takes bitter revenge whenever he gets free. In time, he slowly starts compensating ahead.

It is already accepted that alcohol may, and certainly will alter perception; after all, that's why the police officer shows you the number of fingers you've got to guess right every time, and walks you around that curved line, with hands stretched forward like a marine holding his assault rifle.

Alteration of perception can go very far, like when John and Mary, both stiff drunk, were spending a quiet Sunday afternoon on their little farm. Suddenly John points outside and says:

- Mary, look out the window, there's a horse in our yard!
- It's a cow! Says Mary, without even turning her head.
- I say it is a horse!
- It is a cow, you moron! I see it now!
- I said the window, woman, not the mirror!

Perception of physical factors can also be distorted because of alcohol:

Two blondes were doing a European tour by car, inside all packed with luggage and tiny bottles of Schnapps and beer cans. Highway patrol stops them while boringly cruising at 20 Km / hour, thousand cars desperately honking behind them.

- Hello Officer! Says the driving blonde – displaying a ruby circled Cheshire cat smile, but with Appaloosa- size plastic teeth!
- Hello M'am! Your license and ID please!
- Here.. you.. are!

The officer takes a suspicious look inside the car and notices the presence of all the booze recipients, apparently full, along with the quiet and rather suspiciously looking companion of hers. The the other woman was pale, her hair was stiff and viciously spread all around her head, a scary look on her face, and her eyes looking nowhere, while totally speechless and motionless, like posing at Madame Toussaud's.

- Why are you driving so slow on the highway? He asked.
- Ha,ha, ha! That was a good one, officer! We are on highway E 20, so I'm supposed to go 20 km/hour, right? You can't fool me this way! No Sir!
- Aha! The officer takes notes in his book. "And your friend, she seems ill, is there anything wrong with her?"
- Oh yes, poor thing! She has been behaving like this ever since we were driving on highway E 190.

Sometimes alcohol can create regrettable confusions, absolutely unwanted in times of crisis.

I heard this story from a friend of mine; his companion in a binge drinking party was very upset, because his wife had told him to give up returning home, if he happens to be drunk. He told the other guy:

- "Do like I do! Undress in front of the door and when she opens up throw your clothing inside the house! She won't have the guts to let you wander naked around the hallway of the block!"

Happy with the new idea and satisfied by what seemed to look like an unmistakable solution, his friend got in front of the door, undressed quickly and pushed the ringer button. When the door opened, he threw the clothing. Then he heard:

- "Mind the gap! Mind the closing doors! Next station is "Bloomingdale Estates Plaza", platform on the right side!"

Another story about altered perception is the one of the three homeless guys who were enjoying a glass of beer in a joint near a cemetery. One of them lacked an arm, the second one, a leg, but the third one seemed in one piece. Smoke and drunken chat all over the place. Suddenly, door opens and a younger man comes in.

He has blue eyes, long brown hair and beard and he is dressed in a long robe, wearing leather sandals instead of shoes. There is a deep silence in the bar for a few moments. Then, as if after a time lapse, everybody resumed activity. The new comer went to a remote small table, sat down and asked for a beer.

One of the three homeless, the one lacking a hand, turned to the others and, in an excited mood, said:

- Hey guys, look! This is Jesus Christ!

The other two, boldly contemplating the actions of the stranger, turned to him and said:

- Shut up Charley! You're day dreaming again! Can't you see the man walked here from a distant place, maybe another congregation? Just another homeless like us! Keep your moron bill closed!
- Guys, I tell you, it's Him! …..I'm gonna ask!!!

He takes a few steps to the stranger and puts his glass of beer in front of Him:

- Lord Jesus, because I know it is You, please do me the honor to accept this humble glass of beer as a gift from me! I don't know what else I can give you, because I'm poor, homeless and I can't work because I lost my upper limb.

Jesus smiled to him, raised and gently invited him to sit next to him.

- I accept your gift, even if it is booze,, as You were the first in this humble inn, to recognize me and you didn't have any obligation to share your beer with me. But tell me what happened with your arm and hand?
- Oh, God! The man puts on an embarrassed smile, lacking the whole set of front teeth and puts his single hand over his head, like covering it with a giant shovel. "It's an old story; I was working with lumber and I stumbled and fell to close to the chain-saw".
- I see! The visitor took a sip from the gift beer, then turned to the man, put a hand on his head and the other on the amputated arm and whispered a few words. Like in a cartoon miracle, the arm started growing longer and longer and then changed shape creating the forearm and finally the hand.

The homeless man was astonished; he was looking in disbelief at the newly grown hand and then tried to move fingers. When he saw that the hand obeys command, he started shouting and dancing around like crazy: "I have a new hand! I have my brand new hand, once again! Look guys – two hands! – he was shouting, until he finally sat down, his dirty unshaved cheeks covered with tears.

Meanwhile, the second homeless rose to his "foot" (he had only one), a little shaky because of the beers he already had, but mostly because of his missing left leg. He took his beer mug and limped his way to the stranger:

- Oh, Lord Jesus, I saw what you did with my friend! Allow me, Jesus, to share my beer with you, 'cause it is the only thing I have right now!

Jesus smiles and invites him to his table as he did with the other one. He takes a polite sip from the man's beer and asks him how he lost his leg. The man replies he was the victim of a traffic accident while doing street repairs, as an eighteen wheeler bumped into their site and shattered everything. He was caught against a concrete wall and there was nothing else to do but cut off his shattered limb to get him out of there.

Lord Jesus touched his knee and his head and the miracle happened again: his leg grew and the foot developed same size and shape with the other. The man got crazy happy and started dancing barefoot showing everybody his two feet. Oddly enough, he was doing a show moving his toes in both feet, even if the ones in the newly grown one were, as expected, much cleaner.

Amidst the mayhem, the third homeless rose to his feet, took a bottle and smashed it against the table and kept the bigger shard as a dagger in his hand.

- Oh shut TF up you morons, with your miracles! You make me sick! And you,… hey you,… the hippy guy, …I'll carve your face if you even try to touch me, cause I'm living on allowance and government subsidies! I'm a liberal!

Another story I heard says that this drunker leaves the pub situated near the cemetery and tries to go home. In order to go home, he would have had to cross the alleys of the cemetery, something not very appealing on a cold December rainy night.

He makes his way through anyway, but on a slippery alley he stumbles and falls inside a deep, freshly dug tomb. He cries for someone to help him out, but there was no-one to hear, so he decides to wait.

After half an hour, another hesitating person comes singing on the same alley. The first one starts crying:

- Oh, God, I'm so cold! It's freezing down here! Help me!

The second one stops singing and, with a curious face, comes near the hole to take a look:

- Hello!...He is trying to fix his buoyance. Is there… anybody down there?
- Yeah! It's me! I'm freezing down here! Do something to help me!
- Tisk, tisk, tisk! The second guy looks at him disapprovingly and waves his finger like an old grandpa:
- Now, see what you've done? 'Course you're cold – you moved too much and pushed aside all the ground and became unearthed; keep your feet tight and stop moving. Here, I'll help you!- he says and then pushes the whole earth pile back inside the grave on top of him.

Friar Tuck was not the only member of the clergy who did not des-consider tasting God's blood; today's priests do the same. One priest has recently placed a panel at the entrance of the churchyard: "Dear people of our Church, stop stealing, lying, cheating or being lazy; our government does not stand such disloyal competition!".

The world of drunk drivers may be very large, but there are some distinctive types that I want to talk about. Most drunk drivers may fit in one of these descriptions, thus enhancing the value of the classification:

g) Chip & Dale type – sorry- ass clerk, dressed all year around in the same stinking and de-colored suit or jacket that covers his skinny body. He may drink a small beer on his colleague's birthday, and he already feels like a tiger. He has a flushing Pinocchio face, emotion makes him sweat exceedingly, as he solemnly drives his ancient Honda Accord as if it were a sixteen-wheel steam locomotive. He has a rictus (read tetanus –like smile) whenever he sees a police officer or a police car. Once home, he may need 4-5 clumsy maneuvers to park. He will undress in the bathroom, removing socks first and paying attention not to stick them to the ceiling.

h) Uncle Johnny Wrench – solid, placid, with a nose that reminds of a giant bell red pepper or a dwarf colored pumpkin. He hasn't been driving sober ever since Woodstock, but he has a strong liver that enables him to rely upon his motion reflexes even at 1,8 / 1000 rate. He is not dangerous normally, because he goes to work early in the morning and gets back late at night, when streets are deserted. His temper may become harmful after weddings and parties, and he calms down when busy repairing his car, which needs solid repairs every week, because it is his first car and he has it since Woodstock, remember?.

i) Greg Timber – village boy, hard- working, dressed in a coverall day- around, returning with his pick-up filled with building parts needed for extending his barn. He makes one last stop at the gas-station bar and starts playing "Jack and a beer back" with a red-neck from a neighboring village. When sober - Greg's IQ sometimes would beat the sugar rate in sodas, so he quickly loses count of the rounds, yet he couldn't care less about that. He gets out smashing the door, head first, and followed mechanically by the rest of his body, in a joint effort to make it to the pick-up truck. Once inside, he feels safe again. He will use the yellow line as a guide home and he will not "pull over for nobody", even if confronted with an eighteen-wheeler. He knows that his dear wife will wait for him on the porch, of course, just to make sure he gets to his bedroom safe, saving explanations for the next day. Or maybe the other day.

j)   Tony Badass – young, muscular, dressed in latest t-shirt and holed jeans, driving anything between tuned Mustang to 700 series BMW. His car has 10-12 tail-pipes, 3 turbo-chargers and 5 enormous woofers in the back, which can puff-away panties off the angry blondes riding with him, at the switch of a button. Tony's kind have ugly crashes from time to time, killing themselves and taking other innocent people with them, and nobody knows if it was from the pricks or the shots.

k)   Scary Pimp – commonly African American or Negro, dressed like Ken in Ken and the Barbie Dall, unstable in speech and actions like a hamster injected with caffeine and having pepper spray in his eyes. Countless big rubies stand like wounds on his fingers and the 17 golden chains hanging on his neck make the rattling noise of 17 cows chased by a badly tuned Harley on the street. The pimp sips cognac from a small flask hidden in his glove compartment and his victorious look and big smiles can fool no one but the poor girls that choose to work for him. The crazy clown can suddenly turn into a beast that hops his car rear at the stop light and screeches tires to impress audience. You have to be careful with the type; avoid tail collision because he might have a frightened girl all tied up and gagged in the trunk.

l)   Lord John – grey hair, maybe moustache, tidy and clean like Lawrence Olivier in his good days, black tie almost all the time. Could be a judge or a Congress Man. Once he opens the car door, be ready to catch him, 'cause he might have used up all his coordination skills while driving. When he speaks, you have to sniff one option: Porto, Jerez wine or Gentleman Jack (which is so much smoother than simple Jack!). His main victims are mostly neighbor's dogs, fortunately.

There are plenty of occasions to victimize yourself and divert attention when you drink. For example, a guy I know was complaining once:

- You know, I'm beginning to dislike my drinking friends from the club! I mean these guys literally drink their minds out! They are unable to act responsibly! You know what they did last night?
- What? - I was curious what he had to say and hoping to see a sign of sobering up!
- They are a bunch of good for nothing drunken morons! They dropped me twice on the staircase while carrying me home!

The booze has been criticized for decreasing combat attitude. This didn't stop Churchill from giving his RAF pilots a shot of whiskey for courage before missions. But there were days in history when the thing mattered.

There's one more story I'd like to tell you. In our ancient Moldavia, Stephen the Great was a justified ruler and king. He enjoyed white horses, commonly riding the "wild horse" (he had one wife and countless mistresses), a good cup of wine (followed by many others to keep company) and he was fierce in battle with his broad sword that could cut a man in two in one swing, they say, pretty much like Samurai swords. His sword is a trophy now in the "Topkapi Palace" museum – former Sultan palace - in Istanbul.

He was chased in his childhood by the invading tartars – partners to Turkish invaders - who killed his best friend by hanging him in an old oak tree in the village of Borzesti.

Years after, Stephen the Great did the same to the Han of the tartars, but before that, while in his youth, he got cornered by a tartar mob exactly at the oak tree, after a binge drinking party.

He made swift escape by climbing the tree with his trustworthy warriors. As the story goes, the freakin' tartars camped exactly under the tree, so there was no way to go down. Finally, after midnight, tartars finish chewing on their horse pastrami and fall asleep. One of Stephen's soldiers started talking:

- Oh, Milord! You must understand me! I can't hold it anymore!
- But you will, my dear boy! You have the power to control yourself and you will not drop it until morning when they leave!
- Yes Milord, but I feel it is so painful and like, heavy! I can't hold it anymore, I'll have to drop it!
- Keep it, my son, and I'll give you 10 acres of land in your village! Where are you from?
- Buhaesti Milord! Thank you but it is very difficult for me! I hope you understand. I can barely hold it!
- I understand, my courageous boy! That is the sole privilege of heroes, they can control their body and their fate!

Hours passed and then again:

- Milord, seriously, I can't keep it anymore! I have to drop it a little!
- Do you realize that could kill us? My son, you were so brave at this time! I'll give you 20 acres of forest near your village!
- Thank you Milord but it is so difficult! I don't know how much I can hold it!

After another few hours, dawn was breaking:

- Milord, Milord! That's it! I can't hold it anymore! It goes down!
- My little brave boy! Put yourself together and be as brave as you were until now! Hold it for another half hour!

- Impossible Milord! Can't hold it anymore! I just have to put the darn' horse down!

They say the distribution of survival for drinkers is according to the Gauss bell curve, which means the most dangerous are the extremes: those who drink too much and those who do not drink at all! We are the guys in the middle and we also know one thing for sure – water is precious and irreplaceable, but it doesn't make anybody immortal!

ADVERTISING, A SPICY INGREDIENT OF OUR LIFE

The list of the things that we would definitely buy, even if we do not see / hear any advertising about on the TV / radio is dramatically short, and even so, since you are determined to buy the stuff anyway, there's bound to be someone somewhere, to tell you which of your wanted stuff is better, tastier or cheaper.

The general perception is that you – the average American / or European consumer – will fall for one of these three arguments.

That means - for instance - you are perhaps one of the quality maniacs, always determined to buy best quality, or what is presented to you as best quality, even if it looks all the same – which kinda' makes you a moron.

Alternatively, you are the obese eat-it-all-around type of consumer, who is judging life by tasting everything around him like a dog or a todller and mistakenly decides better for tastier, which makes you a sensorial moron once again.

The third variety is not placing you in a better light, as poking around for cheap stuff means you are a really incapable moron, unable to make a decent buck and buy yourself a better life, like the rest of us dudes do.

Maybe this is the problem – somewhere, someone takes pleasure in considering us a tribe of dizzy and disoriented moronic monkeys, unable to decide when and what to eat, drink or do, the only thing credited for doing by themselves being fur growing.

I was puzzled more than one time by this approach and I have taken advertising very seriously ever since I realized they have a precise psychological approach, looking for my hidden weakness and subliminally inducing the need for unnecessary stuff. Good for their business – bad for my budget!

I once had some friends from France as guests for a few days, just a few years after the Revolution of 1989. I was puzzled by their behavior, I mean being in a country where everything seems so cheap, you don't freeze in your tracks to count the bucks in your pocket in front of a gift shop, right? Wrong! They took me all over the commercial areas in the city and tested hundreds of things, clothing and all! In the evening I was exhausted, felt miserable and asked: why didn't you buy anything? Was it all so bad? Oh.no! They answered smiling! We just noted down the things we were craving for, then confronted them with interesting things we would really need, and now we discuss and decide which of them we should buy. And so they did! The next day they said: we want to go to these 3-4 shops and buy these 3-4 items! Totally irrelevant from my point of view and seeing my dissatisfaction they added: Ok. We would - like anybody else- enjoy to buy a lot of things, but you know we already have a lot of quality things in France and even if we are a little better situated economically than others, it doesn't mean we have to throw money down the drain, like buying stuff we already have or do not really need! Full stop! No comment! Lesson finished! I realized I could never be like them or – maybe it would be very difficult for me! Or God only knows, I may get to the point I have no choice but do the same. Fate decided otherwise: my wife and my older son are deeply involved in the shopping activities and concerned with mixing styles and colors. I couldn't care less about that, like I don't run around naked, but I put something decent on and I need a clean blanket for the night. I may be wrong though, because, somehow, in the bitter end, I get to pay for all fashion adventures in the house. I remember about a question women had to answer before getting married: which are their favorite animals? The correct answer was: mink around the neck, polar fox as a coat, a Jaguar in the garage, a tiger in bed and an ox to do odd house jobs and pay for everything. I am checking if my horns get growing in the bathroom mirror every morning when I shave; no sign yet, although I have no calcium shortage. Sometimes my ears get donkey- long, but I never get to baa, though!

The advertising system was meant to fight and subdue modest people and it was brought to perfection in almost every detail.

Psychological behavior and reactions were studied and pertinent / quantified responses were obtained from responsible authorities. They know when you are hungry and thirsty and they come up with suggestions for great eats or something to drink, not necessarily cheap; they know when you are tired and they place at your feet different corridors towards ideal all-inclusive vacation havens; they know when your kids go to school and suggest adequate sandwiches, roller blades and jeans for your daughter; they know when your neighbor goes to Washington on business so they happen to send you for testing the best night vision binoculars to spy on his wife; they know what is your favorite ice cream flavor, they know when you are bloated and send you the miracle pill to fart bloating off, they know when you run so they recommend the purest water and the best jogging shoes in the county, they know when you have sleepless nights and advertise the best sleeping pills, and they f---ing know when you're horny and recommend the exact condom flavor your wife likes. Not married? No problem, someone will come to your home to help you test them, because it is written on the label they are not edible. These things are like old shoes, once you get your toes in, the hills still stay out and sometimes, especially if you buy them fresh new from China, you'll feel like Cinderella's step sister when trying to put on the crystal shoe. Only you can't afford to cut any part of it to fit in. You know why the Jewish are the bravest men on Earth, someone asked? Because they have the guts to cut it long before they can see how big it is going to grow.

In Communist Romania there was a story about condoms; they were made at the same rubber factory as the kid's teats or pacifiers, in the city of Timisoara. The dictator once paid an official visit and went to the teat sector and heard a pleasant noise like "fluuuuush –

bang!). He asked about the meaning of the noise and the workers were eager to answer: fluuuush is the noise of inflating the teat or pacifier and bang is the perforator that pierces a hole through it to let the milk pass. The Dictator then moved to the condom sector (one he disliked because it was undermining his previous order of forbidding abortion or contraception in order to increase natality). The noise he was hearing was rather different, as it went like : fluuuush, fluuuush, fluuuush, bang, fluuuush, fluuuush, bang, fluuuuush, fluuuush, flluuush, bang. He asked about this new sequence of sounds and the production manager said: the fluuuush sound happens when the condom is inflated. "Ok, the Dictator said, what is the bang now and then doing?" The Manager was a little embarrassed and admitted: this is modern marketing, Sir! The bang from time to time is meant to indirectly and randomly sustain the production of teats and pacifiers!

The Communism was indeed a Nirvana of advertising going wrong. As a teenager in the seventies, I remember how, in the local supermarket, the milk sector was filled with peeled tomatoes and tomato sauce cans. My conservation instinct and keen observation spirit instructed me to avoid asking why. Looks like everyone else knew and was not at all curious to know why there was no milk in the milk sector. I ended up being convinced that if I ask such question my mother's son would end up learning the answer the hard way in a very remote place, guarded. Poor mum! She wouldn't even dare to talk about these things at the time!

But this reminded me of a story about a western international coalition that grabbed hold of the blueprints of the latest Russian supersonic fighter – I guess it was the Mig 25 – Foxbat at the time. They all took turns in trying to build it according to plans – Japanese, American, German, but all failed in the meaning that whatever they did, the final product stubbornly became a T-60 tank! A patriotic Romanian team of engineers was asked then to complete the project and they spent almost a week before going out, spitting and cursing. They went back in the shop and one week later they unveiled the project – a fine looking supersonic plane! A group of foreign reporters rushed in and asked them: how come you've done it? Everybody else built a tank!

The master locksmith smiled, lit up a plain cigarette and told them: well, in the beginning it was all the same for us! We've got a tank all right, but we did not give up and then we switched the blueprint upside down and left to right and simply adjusted it here and there with a grinder!

If you want to understand the mechanism of modern advertising, you need to look when it is "detergent time". You - my friend, are the unbelievable moron using THIS BAD product, something disgustingly placed in a white or grey slimy box, carrying no label, and your detergent never washes your laundry properly, that's why you always look like wearing inherited clothes, that's why you always scare people on the street and carelessly bust all your job interviews. But HERE it is, THE PRODUCT – OUR PRODUCT - which is thousand times better, in a nice little box (which for morons like you it means you do not need much of it to wash perfectly), with nice colored drawings and pictures showing morons like you how to use it (and adding it is not edible and should not be used for other purposes, for instance spicing food with it or washing your pet monkey or camel with it). It is so perfumed – here, can you feel it? A lubricous lazy blonde (looking like she never washed her panties in her whole life, as she could always afford to buy new ones every day or every time the old ones had to go down) explains how easy it is to use.

You just put it into the washing machine (which – like in toy story - smiles happy, because you are using its preferred brand of detergent and anti-calcar) along with your really dirty laundry – God only knows where you've been with your stinking clothes - and relax the whole rest of the day. By the way, did you notice that, when accidentally splashed with the MARVEL PRODUCT on the face, Gorbachew lost his forehead mark? All you need to do when the machine stops is dress up for the occasion.

Now the lady turns angry: she is asking you in a cold, polite voice, how can you outlive the unbearable shame of having used the other inadequate detergent, when the PRODUCT she recommends was at hand all this time? What kind of a blind fool were you to ignore it? What will your neighbors say? What kind of poor excuse have you thought of? You have to reconsider your behavior and your choices are numbered: although she would personally be in favor for allowing you to commit a honorable suicide – the clean seppuku could be an option - she cannot overlook the fact that you could still become a normal human being again, full of success and satisfaction in your miserable sorry- ass life, but only, and only, if you buy - and start using immediately – the detergent she tells you about. Let that be a bitter, but well deserved lesson to you!

You think that was a close shave? Well, I got news for you, buster! It wasn't!

"Let us take a good look at you!" – a pair of academic-like, boring elderly couple staring at you from the TV screen. "Ok, now turn to one side!" You start feeling like invited to the police precinct three blocks away and somewhere in the deep layers of your conscience, there is a reaction of resistance. "Hey, I've done nothing!" you suddenly realize, but still carry on staring at the screen to see what more the pair has to say. That reminds me, fox, of a hot summer – I guess it was in July – a deep dark steamy night, when I let my wife sleep with our little daughter. I could thus enjoy the chill of the whole other sleeping room for myself with wide open windows. I may have slept for a while when a sudden "booom – booom" – boot-like knocks in our iron-gate woke me up trembling! WTF… ? Who the F… is trying to bring my gate down? I looked on the window and asked "Who's there?" "Police" they said. Commotion! If the police bangs at your door at night, you must have done something! "Come downstairs – we need to talk! Please open the door!" My first reaction was to hide somewhere in the basement, asking myself what I may have done and trying to remember my possible crimes within the last few weeks. I could not recall any name of killed or buried persons in the basement. While doing so, I realized I have actually done no crime, so there must be some misunderstanding. Yes, that was it! A terrible misunderstanding! The boot banging in the gate was a discrete reminder that the most urgent thing to do was opening it before it collapsed. I grabbed my sleepers and my pants and went out to open gate. There were two of them, one of them smiling superiorly, apparently (loosely) detached, and the other was the intellectual who started talking (I can imagine it took a while until they decided their roles). The one who knew how to talk asked me with a candid voice: do you know what time it is? I was startled at first, and presently managed to cut off my natural reaction which demanded me to grab his throat and yell to his ears "Yes moron, thanks to you I know what time it is and I can tell you for sure I haven't slept enough!". Instead, I politely answered that it made no difference anymore, once I was confronted with the (hopefully!) rare pleasure of spending some quality time with them – err, both of them. Then the smiling one turned to me and pointed with a disgusted finger (I couldn't help noticing a slight shadow under the fingernail) towards my wife's car in front of the gate. "Is this your car?" I took a better look and admitted that it wasn't mine but it definitely belonged to my wife, last time I checked. It was then like a convulsive disease that shook them both – they both took one step aside, each of them, and pointed to the car, gasping air like chocking over a plastic bag: "And how can you leave your car like this at night?" While they kept shouting to me, trembling and foaming like a well shaken beer can, I took a closer look, this time eyes opened. Yap! Gee! That was something hard to conceive even for me, not to mention them! The right front door had the window completely lowered and my wife's purse/ bag was reluctantly occupying the right seat, in full view! ID papers and cards inside! But I can swear the car was locked!

At this moment it was difficult to calm them down and the only argument I could bring to convince them not to book her was the sad and tired look on my face: "Now you see what my life is all about? You think this is an isolated incident? Ha! You know, yada - yada, the "Do I really deserve this?" or "What have I done to deserve this?" kind of conversation?. They finally left, not before saying that this was their weirdest night on the job, ever, short of maybe seeing an UFO. They argued that most likely, thieves saw the bag there, but were afraid to take it because they feared it was a frame-up or maybe the bag was booby-trapped. That -I thought- might have been possible. If now you are anxious to ask what my wife said – I have bad news for you. Not only she said nothing, but even relapsed some weeks later (however, I managed then to "contain" that situation in due time).

But let as get back to the story – so the boring elderly couple kept on staring at me until I gave in to the reflex of checking the front slit of my trousers, to see and feel if zipper is closed and everything in due place. Then they sat down and started asking me: if I get enough sleep at night, if I always remember what I need to remember and if I feel rested the next day or not. As I had in mind only worrying answers to all their questions, I took a seat and watched on. They kept talking, like they found the fountain of youth, the answer to their prayers, the solution to all their worries, the one and only thing that grunted them a new era of youth and good health. That is what we call the "charging technique" – the more curious and desperate you become to know the answer, the more they circle it like vultures attracted to a nice fat juicy corpse, and stubbornly delay revealing its location. Well, I thought, if it worked for them at least 10%, there must be some move on my behalf, also. Finally, I found out how all my problems could disappear in thin air, on one condition only. Believe it or not, it is yet another pill. But not the ordinary sour pill that melts in your mouth without purpose, or at most, succeed in decreasing your fever. No Sir! This is a totally different thing. THIS is a special pill! A miracle pill! The Wonder-pill of all times! THIS is the Mother Pill (Father pill for Germans) of all the pills in the long history of pills and that can be SCIENTIFICALLY PROVEN by expert pill scientists and numerous clinical pill trials that took place right under our nose. The fact that we did not hear about those trials is only because of the jealous competitors who had been desperately trying to compromise THIS PILL to the benefit of their SYRUP (see the other channel in 5 minutes or so!). This pill – OUR pill – provides a special kind of inner peace and a deeeeep and comforting sleeeeep second to none – another grey haired lady says in a soft voice while walking with the interviewer in quiet place like a park or something. "Only those who appreciate the restful sensation that our pill provides can act like connoisseur (as in wine tasting) and we should ask those with experience before taking the pill". It was only then I realized she was being interviewed on the alleys of a cemetery! So much for the restful sensation! But wait, there's more to it! The PILL also improves your memory! The example is a tiny old man dressed in green clothes like forest spirits on St. Patrick 's Day, who – at first - seemed hard to be convinced to talk. When he finally did, I understood why – he lacked all his teeth, with the exception of his wisdom molars, because they were too deep in for his dentist to remove. However, they did not help much with spelling. Once started, the little leprechaun could not be stopped, spitting and sassing all sort of nonsense; the best I could understand is that he remembered how Robin Hood got a scar on his right cheek while shaving. Once the goblin was out, in came a tall and handsome clerk type of sharp dressed gentleman, who said he worked as a NSA agent appointed with supervising foreign influence over internal economic and political affairs of the US.

He said he has taken the pill for some time now and he was very satisfied with the results. "What was your best time since you have taken the pill? - asked the reporter. "Oh I don't know, he said, maybe the month of November last year, during the elections. I slept undisturbed like a baby the whole month through. "Where did you get your pills?" "I don't know, I think someone brought them from Russia, or something!".

Have you seen the late coffee advertising? Like the boy who collects steam from the fresh coffee pot inside a jar, and then opens it to the sky and lets the aroma go up in haven until Santa smells it and dives in for a coffee (toys included)?

I've just seen a better one. The guy who slams the alarm clock to the wall, then – eyes closed – sleep - walks out of the balcony on top of a furniture truck and gradually makes it to the streets and enters the first courtyard in his way, gets to the porch and sits down in front of a fresh cup of steaming coffee on the table. The landlady, seated next, gives an embarrassed smile when husband comes out to have his coffee and finds out a total stranger in pyjamas sipping on his coffee. It is only then that the guy realizes where he is and probably excuses for his behavior or maybe tries to, while the other one is banging him with his eye against the corner of the table or cuts his throat ISIS style with the nearest knife in the kitchen. However, the advertising stops short of that. OMG! If coffee can have such power – and this one does! – what will happen with other stimulating factors? Speaking about coffee, I remembered a story about a guy who fractured his mandible in a fight and became unable to chew on his food. Decision was made to provide any type of semi-solid food he wished, on the condition it would be administered by enema. He agreed, so a waiter asked him if a soup would be convenient for appetizer. He nodded and the soup went down – or should I say, up! He made some faces and when asked if everything is ok, he complained the soup was a little too hot. Next, in came some small meatballs with olive sauce, which he found all right and vanilla ice-cream was the desert request. Will you have a coffee now Sir? The waiter asked, and the man nodded. The guy brought the coffee and poured it in the tube. At his moment, the patient started having like convulsions and breathing heavily and mumbled something. "What's that? I can't understand what you say!" – the waiter got closer. "It's too sour!" said the patient between clinched teeth. "Put in some sugar for Christ's sake!"

Speaking about special coffee, I learned one of the most expensive in the world is the coffee grinded from beans previously digested by a small animal in Sumatra, called the palm civet cat. The Kopi Luwak coffee is the best in the world, they say, or otherwise it wouldn't cost 20 times the regular cup (more than 100 bucks/ cup).

Now, I am not a great coffee lover, nor am I obsessed with the bio stuff, but I was wondering what would be the best way to advertise for this coffee. I know – the price is a powerful magnet, but you have to provide for that price. I keep imagining various alternatives. For instance, two ladies on an exotic porch in the Philippines, enjoying breakfast. One of them calls the butler and asks for 2 cups of good coffee. "Certainly madam", the man departs facing them, "Right away". He then turns back and whistles twice "Lulubelle!"- he cries! "Lulubelle! Oh Lulubelle!" he shouts, passing by the intrigued guest. "Sorry madam, he says, It may take a little longer with the coffee!", "Hey Lulubelle, you blundering flee bag, where the hell are you?" he mumbles in a lower voice.

Finally, Lulubelle, the palm civet cat drops from the small roof of a kiosk and maliciously walks to him. "Go to the poop pot right now, and don't make me "milk" you – says the nervous butler. Lulubelle goes to the sand box and drops the necessary quantity for 2 coffees. The butler victoriously collects the goodies and goes right to the kitchen to wash and clean the beans. Roasting and grinding was done in a minute and he proudly presents the ladies two cups of the best coffee in the world. The host takes one and takes a long and a bit noisy sip. The other woman looks at the civet cat, hanging comfortably on the handlebar of the porch and staring at her, like wondering: "hey gadis / wanita (girl or woman in Malay dialect - we don't know if she is married!) Let me see if you are so stupid enough to drink that shit!

The guest lady turns around like having a shiver and smiles to the butler: Thank you, but I already had one before getting here! Then, with a sadistic glitter in her eyes, she continues: but you can have it on me! Bottoms up!

Another option would be to try and sell a Kopi Luwak coffee machine. It would look quite normal for a coffee machine or expresso maker, but the only odd thing would be the pouring orifice, which – in order to look more appetizing – will be shaped as a civet cat ass, and pulling the tail will release a dose of coffee.

I also thought of a civet cat revolution, with the animals invading a building and opening coffee shop. On the entrance wall there will be a poster: "Screw Starbucks! Drink your own pee!" or, like the ancient advertising for Kent cigarettes went: "Come for the flavor! You'll stay for the taste". They will expose a board that says: "We ~~make~~ do the best coffee!"

Or imagining a Sumatra guy coming home from the night shift and suddenly, while entering the house, he feels the smell of fresh coffee penetrating to his tired brain. Waves and waves of coffee aroma lured him to the kitchen, where he was already imagining a giant coffee jar warming up for his rhino morning coffee thirst. Actually, in the kitchen there was his wife, holding and cuddling a civet cat in her arms, and she gave him a plate with 2 old dry sandwiches: "You;ll have to excuse Lulubelle, she must have had an indigestion. Poor darling has been farting all night! Do you want me to make some coffee?"

Another story comes to my mind about a very sick old fellow. He was not a star or a tycoon, he was just a regular guy who did things his way (like in Frank Sinatra's song!) and at a certain moment he gets very old and very sick. As he lays in bed upstairs, something definitely divine wakes him up from his diseased slumber and that was the aroma of his preferred chocolate chips cookies. The smell was coming from the kitchen and was overwhelming, penetrating all fibers of his soul. His preferred cookie smell was connected to all important moments of his life, good or bad. Instinctively, he tries to jump out of bed, actually falling down from it and pathetically starts crawling like an 8 months old toddler on the hallway and down the stairs. He spent almost ten minutes to climb down every stair, without having any major injury. Meanwhile, smell got stronger and, as he was going down, he started seeing the inner view of the kitchen, where hundreds and hundreds of chocolate chip cookies were made and his wife would place dozens more in the oven, like working delirious.

All tables and chairs were busy holding cookie trays, but on the central table there was a maddening display of the best good looking, well filled and aromatic cookies. The sick guy somehow crawls through the double door and gets near the table, already salivating and feeling once again the healthy deep hunger he was used to as a boy. Unseen by his wife, he grabs the table cloth and slowly drags himself up to reach for a cookie and exactly when he was ready to grab a big juicy cookie, his wife presently turned around and slapped him on the hand with a paddle: "Tat, tat, tat! "- She says. "Don't touch them! Those are for the funeral!"

One of the cruelest advertising items I have seen is dedicated to baldness. The film is horrific – maybe we could academically call it ….err.. Inspirational.

A Viking – strong and courageous like a bulldozer, lands his boat and furiously leads his comrades towards victory. In the aftermath of the battle, the conqueror sits tired on a log and – as it had gotten warmer – gets rid of his horned helmet, only to reveal a huge bald skull. Another character is a woman – older I guess. Actually, my opinion is that she had been freshly unburied for the occasion; she looked bad anyway, and, on top of it all, a few rare long hairs broke the boring landscape of her bald skull. Now the first message is clear: you, average income moron consumer, are getting old! Yes, do not pretend you are not; we can see it, we actually count on it to sell you old people stuff, XXL diapers included. Anyway, even if you are not THAT old, how would you like to get to look like these disgusting creatures? No discussion about stress, about hormonal issues or impaired vascularization of the skull skin, plus genetic factors, it is all written on your forehead and you are as blamable for losing your hair as you would be for losing your wallet at the mall.

What you need to do is use THIS PRODUCT – it is all natural, made from a scientifically designed mixture from 14 herbs, snail shell, chicken bill, lama spit, camel milk, the luxury version containing hairs from Cher's armpit and / or Tom Hardy's beard, depending on your gender. I strongly advise you not to take these things the easy way, because if you do use the product with other than the adequate formula, side effects may occur.

I heard about the story of a lady who was growing bald and was desperate about it. Her doctor recommended lots of creams and potions, pills and hormone busters, but nothing worked. Finally he takes a small bottle with a dark liquid in it and gives it to the woman saying: "Be careful about this; I made it by the indications of a tribe's wizard in Africa!" Just two drops a day and only 5 days a week, or you'll have side-effects. Ok?" She takes the bottle with trembling hands and thanks the doctor. "Remember, come for a check-up every 2 months or so!" After a few days the doctor forgets about her, but in a couple of weeks, in comes a busty woman with a haystack of hair on her head, barely missing the upper door frame. "Hello, hello!" "Have a seat, Madam!" She smiles and answers" Don't you recognize me?" Suddenly he realizes who she is but now he is busy concealing his shock: "Hey!!!!! Look at you! I didn't know the African drops could be so effective!". She smiles back "Oh, but they are! Obviously, I had to be a little more creative about the dosage! I took a spoonful every day and today my "coiffeur" refused to do my hair. He said he will have to charge me 4 times the price. Oh doctor! You do not know how happy I am!" and she squeezed a tear. Puzzled but willing to take full control of the situation, the doctor asked: "You took such large doses! Were there any side effects?" She wipes tear with handkerchief and admits: "Oh yes, you were right about side effects. In fact I experienced one," "What was it?" the doctor anxiously asked. "Oh. Nothing much though!" she replied. "I grew hair on my body too! On my neck, breast, back, belly, down to...." "Down to what?" doctor askes. "All the way down to my penis!" she answers, blushing.

Sports and recreational activities have been intensely approached by advertising activity. You are overweight, right? Then you're the next victim. Overweight, exceeding cholesterol, increased blood pressure, type II diabetes, metabolic syndrome, and complications like heart attack, clotted arteries and strokes, it's all there in the text. Once they get you really scared, here comes the deal: you have to use this ointment and you get slim. No diet, no working out, no sweat – just have that cream spread on your skin, especially in the fatty areas. Simple enough for any regular overweight moron! And considering you don't have to keep a diet and work out! Hey, maybe I can even eat more than usual and put more ointment on my belly and I'll stay the same.

You'll say I am a wicked or cruel person, right? It is not my fault, it is my childhood! I looked too much to cartoons and read bad stories. As a young boy I saw Tarzan always strolling naked in the jungle, Cinderella went to parties and came home after midnight, Aladdin was a thief and Pinocchio, a liar, Snow White lived in the forest with seven men, Batman was driving 200 mph, Popeye smoked and had a tattoo! It's too late for me to change now! Besides, I could easily shed 25 pounds myself, if I come to think of it, only it is not that easy.

However, the label does not explain how does the ointment work so then we go on to listening to a whole lecture about belly fat, which is squeezing the pancreas and we have to loosen it. Once free from the toxic "embrace", the pancreas will start working like Swiss rail-road clocks.

A new approach is that of the work out. They advertise a gym device, which, as an orthopedist, I really appreciate and I bought one. It is called ab-generator and biomechanically makes sense. But the way they do it is a riot. Forget about tiring work out and effort, about diet constriction and care. Be yourself - the all mighty moron you ever dreamt of being – and if you work 5 min / day (!!!!) you get the six-pack you longed for in a matter of weeks, you put down 30-50 pounds and decrease your waist by 30 inches! Now – in order to demonstrate all this, they invite you to watch - let us call her - Adriana Doe, their "sympathetic" presenter. Hello Adriana! I was looking up for a long, slender Adriana that would make my wife jealous! Instead, there she comes, cousin to Square-pants Spongebob, a short thick female creature, with tits so tiny that compel her to suck even more her belly in order to have a decent profile look. She is clearly overweight and sort of wide framed! Even from the profile, her abdomen looks like needing tons of ab-generation. Maybe next generation. But the truth is, to say it all, she is sort of sympathetic and I reckon that's why she got into this business. However, it is not her "good looks" that convinced me to buy the product and use it.

Her companion was present in many other films with gym equipment, but it looks he didn't get proper use of any of them. He is still constitutionally robust – to use a euphemism - and beer-belly like, no matter how much he sucks it in – sometimes so much, he can barely speak and looks like choking! You know, a slender guy who worked out to get muscle mass looks very different from a fat guy who worked out to get thinner and you can always tell the difference, and there will always be a difference because they are constitutionally different. As for working with the machine, I only lost 2 kilograms ever since, but I am proud of it.

The set background is filled with 5-6 sports people working out with the machine. Wait till you see those guys and girls! Wow and double wow! Compared to them, Adriana is a fat hump-whale short on somatho-trope hormone. Her companion, a sorry – ass walrus with a broken fang.

Those guys never – ever had any belly fat – they are so young they didn't have the time to grow it! And the way they use the machine – if you would let them do it for you, boy, you would lose fast kilos every day! Especially the girl team impressed me – if my wife would let me hang around with them, I'd become "The Rock"'s or Stallone's worst nightmare. I am satisfied with the result anyway and generally, if you get at least a quarter of what they promise, you are very fortunate.

I will not go deeper in travel advertising, about dream hotels nobody heard of, about air travel with companies so polite they never kick you out of your flight and your booked seat, about restaurants that give you the best of this or that, about shoes that walk by themselves (all you had to do is stay inside them, and you'll get very far, if you can handle it), about resorts where there are no hotels bought by Russians or blown up by ISIL, about hospitals in Dubai which are not ruined by the Indian HR mafia.

Not my purpose, but I want to point out that it all has a meaning, and that meaning is emptying your wallet. I know a good example to have you cured, as I remember a story about a secret top billionaire meeting (not the Illuminati but close to that) that started peacefully over a cup of coffee. There were some important people there: one African dictator, a rich Arab prince, an American, a Russian and among others, Itzhak, a Jewish businessperson. The American rose up and said: "Guys, I did well, in fact I did so well that I intend to buy Boeing, their new military 1,2 billion contract acknowledged by Trump included.

The Arab prince was anything but patient: "My friends, I bought 300 billion worth weaponry from Trump and the 12 billion arms sold for Qatar is also mine, actually. I still feel so wealthy I could buy Microsoft.

The African dictator rose up with a glass of absinth in his hand and said- "I already made an offer to Apple, but I still wait for an answer from General Motors and Shell".

The Russian declared he is interested in Lockheed Martin and Texaco.

The silent one, the Jewish guy, went to the small bar, poured a little coffee in his cup and said to the others: "Relax guys, I'm not selling anything! Yet!"

THE WAY WE DRESS

Mankind has a few million years old history. During all this time, we realized 2 basic things: first, that living outdoor was no sport, in some seasons, and second, sort of avoided to stay naked, regardless the weather and the place.

Consequently, hair was our first and cheapest wardrobe piece.

In the beginning this was a simple job – you just had to let it grow all over you. No shaving, no dye! Ask a chimp!

Just some grooming once in a while, preferable done by inferior members of the tribe, and even better, by females (see National Geographic film about chimp habits!).

We might have happily lived like this ever after, if it weren't for the Ice Age. And that time, it was no squirrel or peanut to blame! When drizzle came and wind started blowing and stubbornly penetrating any crevasse or natural hole of our body, we painfully noticed that hair, no matter how long, thick or wide spread, was a poor defense against blizzard. Especially when wet or after falling.

Well, at that time our imagination was not so broad, so that when empirical observation pointed out with irrefutable arguments that our fur is not sufficient, the only – otherwise predictable - idea we could come up with, was getting more of it. Since harvesting "hairdo" from other tribesmen and apply it to your body was hard to accomplish technically, nor was it clear which was the best way to convince them to give it up, we started covering ourselves with other animal's skin and fur.

Many scientists have pointed out ever-since that covering our body with foreign materials, such as animal skin and fur, led – as a later developing consequence - to the falling down of our own natural hair cover, as it had been rendered useless in the process. Perhaps this is what led – in a cascade of consequences – to the need of covering our body at all times, not to mention that some more or less representative excrescences of our denuded body would become painfully remarkable. We like to make our females laugh, but not when they see us naked.

We thus lost gradually most hair on our body; some of it remained in what we consider normal areas, like head, and maybe the face in males.

However, a smaller part of it (in some people the proportion is impressive), still populates rather intriguing places, where it does not seem to be really needed or maybe even gets disliked, so we shave it off.

There must be – and I am sure I can come up with it, if I make some research – a perfectly valid explanation for the presence and/or even the persistence of these vestiges of Neanderthalian wardrobe, possibly related to heat exchange, salt and sweat dispersion and even entertaining an "aura" of spicy pheromones.

Naturally, we feel vexed when a solid guy apparently lost his head hairs, but still grows pony tails in his armpits and hosts a wool carpet on his buffalo back, thick enough to clean your shoes on in rainy days or to have your pet slumbering on in front of the fireplace.

That is not all - let me also say this: nature can place it sometimes in unexpected areas. Why would an older woman need hairs on her face or around her nipples? Yet it still stubbornly grows, betraying despicable and most unwanted (in a woman!) levels of testosterone! What's that? Oh, yes, pardon the expression – I am aware that older women do not actually exist, they are either very young, young, still young or charmingly mature!

What is the use of the armpit hairs, displayed with genuine relaxation by rednecks and sometimes exhibited with extreme pride by women, as well? Fancy for the acrid smell that makes your eyes cry, every time your loved one hugs you? Wait till it comes in mixed with a cheap anti-perspiring spray – you may never forget it and start hating your car's windows.

In male population that would be considered a masculine attribute – with a touch of classic tolerance and a hint of kinky sensorial approach. The impact of a gracious woman lifting her arm, and letting "explode" - from underneath the vaporous fabric of her dress - a vigorous black sturdy brush of rough hairs, like Alien from the astronaut belly, may be unprecedented!

Gracious? Kinky? Weird? Maybe all in one? Please have someone tell Lourdes (Madonna's daughter, remember?) that whatever was trendy 3 million years ago for Lucy – the tiny female prehistoric hominid - had changed a little meanwhile! And if you talk to her, tell her I said Hi to her Mum and asked about Madonna's number!

I would like to avoid any comment on other places, where hairs grow excessively, and we must carefully consider trimming it in order to preserve a decent look. Hard to understand its necessity in those places and sometimes hard to deal with. Shaving it off – on the other hand – may stand comfortable proof for the absence of insects and parasites, some of which commonly populating those areas.

Stylish haircut and dying of woman pubic hair is now competing total shave. Total shave has its advantages, as parasites like crabs do not find support, but it might lead you to the conclusion that such "haircut" may be a professional requirement, so you may not appreciate it in your future spouse, for instance. However, classics would advise for leaving there a small amount, sort of a "third eyebrow", not that it has any covering effect (and by all means it shouldn't!), but it just leaves the chance for a "wink". I am inclined to agree with nature and God's will and if that means a women deserves hairs on her nose and a beard, not to mention the chest, than she must be repenting for foul deeds and sins to her husband.

When I was in college, a friend of mine in the same class told me he got emotionally aroused when our history teacher was coming into the classroom. To clarify things, our older (to be retired then) teacher, was the ugliest person wearing a female name I knew. In our classification she stood for "teacher-zilla" and was nicknamed "Adolf Hitler" - I'll bet you wonder why, but try to use your imagination!

She had a short-cut, sticky, hard-to-describe reddish color hairdo, those bushy joined eyebrows of a criminal - as described by Lombroso - the constitution of a well fed Bulgarian wrestler and where she stepped no grass grew anymore, like in Chernobyl.

Her thick moustache and beard were a challenge to those of Michael the Brave, our former king of Valachia, as he was pictured in fierce battle. When compared to her, in the older paintings, Vlad Dracula, the Impaler, looked more like Red Riding Hood in the school theater! I always thought my colleague had a peculiar taste in women (poor euphemism!) and at the moment I promised myself I'll try to meet his future wife, when the time comes. I may have forgotten about the incident meanwhile; besides, he did not invite me to his wedding! I later read about the "fascination for ugliness" that haunts us from time to time. Haunts is a good word! J.F. Franz Rosencrantz, a German philosopher of Konigsberg, wrote about the "esthetics of ugliness". I am no fan, but I've came to the age when I am able to respect the beauty of soul in ugly persons, even women that is! However, this is rare, because when you are really ugly, people find a million ways to remind it to you, so you never come to forget it. The result is that sometimes you get to be mean, thus fitting to your physical appearance!

Even brighter minds could not resist the exposure temptation; Churchill himself, while being under the charm of whiskey replied to a Lady who told him he is drunk: "I may be drunk, Miss, but in the morning I'll be sober, and you will still be ugly". So it greatly depends how you put things.

Well, fact is we gradually replaced personal hairs with covering items we commonly call clothes. However, not all people were always happy with that. Nope! Sometimes, we feel that walking freely and naked represents a statement for liberty and paradoxical spiritual elevation, besides airing all hidden corners of our body.

It only depends on when and where you want to do it. And who sees you! And who pays bale!

Another hard to describe tendency is shaving your body hairs. Men shaving their face- that's already common now and stands for a marker of conformism, cleanliness and orderly life, like in the military. We can skip exceptions like beard trimming and undecided manly appearance of the Italian style "Barba da 4 giorni" – that would be "the 4 day beard", catchy for the "lumber-style" dressed machos.

While extremely beneficial for many women, especially those suffering from ovary poly-cystoids- body shaving is hard to understand in men, unless related to Sasquatch and needing a new ID card photo. There is an impressive arsenal of electrical and chemical weapons meant to definitely and permanently terminate the hairs that stubbornly grow on women feet – and all around sometimes! And if you are a man, you know – unless you find it kinky, of course! - how …errrr..uncomfortable, the feeling of being tickled by her unshaved legs can be. As I was saying, while so beneficial in women, body shaving is so difficult to understand in men!

Modern male pattern requires a freshly shaven torso, with slimy humid skin, like a hoard of snails patrolled it! That's yukee! We all remember old beliefs that men lacking body hair do not have enough testosterone. Now how could you tell for sure on a freshly shaved one? Maybe he is having enough steroids, but they came in with a fungus infection?

There are sites on the internet with such guys offering view to their hairless bodies, some of them young enough to be dragged by the ears to the principal, others lacking a real job. Such pictures might be successful in the "Dear Diary!" of a 15 y.o., feeling miserable because she is overweight and has a dental correction device which makes her spit while she talks and renders her unable to say "excess" without drooling and making it sound like from the bottom of a sink. Oh, yes, and she has stinky breath, so she has a hard time kissing boys! That's because of the ketchup on the burgers and the onions inside. And the developing hiatal hernia! If I would look at those pictures in a clinic lab or secretariat, people next to me would pull chairs away from me and take long disapproving looks - "tisk, tisk!"!

Long time ago, one of my colleagues in secondary grammar school was repeating the year. We were in the 6th grade and he was already a well-developed young man. His body had already grown mature areas of hairs on his chest and lower limbs. When summer came, he started skipping sports classes, although he was very fond of football.

Once we switched to summer equipment we saw the reason. One fine day he came in line with us and somehow he looked weird to us. Then we understood why; he had been shaving his both lower limbs and his chest totally and he was standing bashful like a stray cat on a bench or a featherless crow on a fence. I think the latter describes the situation better, as he was darker than us.

More than that, he had at least 10-12 fresh skin cuts on each leg and almost the same number on his chest, like he had been using for shaving a discarded potato peeling knife or his grand-pa's gardening shovel! It was a riot because there was a stunning difference between his former woolly-mammoth appearance and the way he looked now, like the bald ghost of himself. Soon enough, for his birthday party he received 23 canisters of after-shave! 17 of them were the same label, called "Adam".

I find it intriguing that we still meet people who, indulgently and meticulously grow hairs in their nose and ears, sometimes even the eyebrows. While this is not covering any shameful part of their body (quite questionable when it comes to some people's nose, say in Ireland, for instance), it contradicts many times with the co-existence of a bald head and lack of hairs elsewhere. I have seen bald people with enough hair in their eyebrows to cover the entire head, if they only had the means – and the powerful wish - to spread it evenly.

The assumptions that growing such hair is a mandatory "tribute" we have to pay to aging, or that trimming it is proof for superficial / light/ trivial manners, are both dead wrong. Sometimes the result is stunning! Each nostril barely holds a bunch of thick grey elastic hairs in the shape and the full length of a paint-brush. I cannot stop imagining what happens when the man gets a serious flue! It would be impossible to bring food to your mouth, without touching it against your dripping double paint-brush, long enough to suck or chew, if you put your mind to it.

On the other hand, the nostril hair brushes would be a valuable indicator of your mood: while having them hanging loose to the mouth could mean depression and despair, their getting curly and aroused may suggest a more cheerful or even lubricous attitude.

With the ears, it is totally different! The initial noble task of those hairs was to prevent penetration of insects (such danger being less frequent these days), but the huge bush overgrown there (sometimes apparently representing most of that person's hair, any region included!), I think it could represent a hard obstacle to be penetrated by anything at all, including bacteria. I also assume that, in correlation with exceeding local wax production, not many things could further penetrate in there, ever again, starting with fresh air and normal sounds, and finishing with soap or the family ear specialist.

There are stories about the barber who brought the hearing back to some older people, but I refuse to think it could be that easy, can it?

One subtle development of this trend is growing sideburns as big as needed in order to engulf the entire "Hircus" (goat in Latin) "beard" – that would be the ear-hairs, so no-one would find reasons to complain! Their happy owner will look from the back like an overgrown koala grandpa, sick with unexpected and exuberant mumps, or like the small critters who fought the "Empire strikes back" on planet Tatooine (or something!), led by Luke Skywalker, and what's more, successfully using spears and arrows against the laser-guns of the Imperial forces. And they won, by the way, because they were able to find and destroy the defending field generator! Yes!

Clothes have also developed because of our need for diversity. I mean it would have been so boring to see everybody look the same – disregarding skin color and other attributes that come with it - growing the same bunch / bush of hairs here and there, when our modern clothing is so complex, that it now serves as additional means for expressing our attitude and sometimes, even mood.

Our attitude is frequently controversial when it comes to fashion; we try to copy the same clothes pattern and even the color from a model, and then still expect to look different from one-another, demanding well-balanced and personalized consideration, as well as denying any possible resemblance to other dudes (we are superior to, capisci?) and still being trendy. Like when a star has 5000 fans, dressing the same and desperately trying to look the same, they are all going to look different to others, …….like flies they do.

When I was young – that is young enough to be interested in both fashion and girls (Hey. I'm still interested in girls!) – there was a trendy fashion about trousers.

They were tight on the hips, so tight you could see every muscle fiber, along with all the other neighboring things, just like in a James Brown stage costume, but with a large belt and a huge Texas style buckle, able to hold a wagon, centered in the pubic area (that hurt when seated, like the Bowie knife would sting the thigh of a greenhorn when seated - Karl May used to say in his book Winnetou), and very – and when I say very – that means Very large panty cuffs. I have seen people walking with trousers that measured more than 35 inches at the cuffs. Looking like the mini-sized Vostok Russian rocket engines or an opera singer in Cho-Cho-San.

Sure took special skills to walk with those trousers without stumbling, the bouncing movement being something in-between old time cowboy and tired samurai, both suffering from hemoroidal thrombosis, needing to keep his lower limbs spread all the time, to air the inflamed area!

Another subtle advantage was that very large cuffs were draping all around those not always first class shoes, especially in the countryside, and they were large enough to retain the invasive aromas vaporizing from the sticky over- worn socks, thus preventing them from reaching to sensitive noses.

Long hair was mandatory, in spite of communist regulations and stretch shirts were necessary to complete the picture. The result was that – in their quest for personal good looks – the boys ended up looking all the same, like sparrows on the telegraph wire of a remote countryside train station where the train stops only twice a week.

Now take a bunch of these 12 guys dressed in this same manner. Let us assume you are the loving girlfriend of one of them (not implying you were not!) and you all of a sudden feel like kissing Him! I'll bet you would have a rough time trying to pick your sweetheart from the lot, especially at night time. That was one lottery ticket you had to assume. You may have needed all your subtle Sherlock talents and your sensorial skills (including smell and taste) to pick the right one and you even succeeded. Who knows? ….Yeah! I know what you really think now! You hate you were so accurate at the moment! Maybe, you might have picked better then, if you'd only had taken the decision to …errr….conveniently mistake, am I right? – and abominable **Him** doesn't even appreciate this! Not even now, after all these years! Well, let me tell you something, my dear: do not feel sorry, cause after all these years, they are now so much alike, that you could sleep with each of them for a month and still be unable to tell them apart, if it weren't for farting and snoring, which bring more color to the intimate life at this age!

Shortly after the 1989 Revolution, some friends from France visited us. They told me about one of their observations – otherwise absolutely correct – but which still startled me, because I could see it for myself, while being unable to clearly reveal it. It was as if it were in the blind corner of the eye!

All people in our country, especially those past 40s or 50s, were dressed in dark colored clothes – black, brown, dark blue and grey. The gloomy appearance was not related to the fact that, from wedding to retirement, all you had to do was simply adjust sizes, never minding the couture or color, nor was it related to the fact that some people kept their favorite dark clothing very tidy, so it would be very practical and at hand, for the meticulously prepared simple funeral!

I think it actually had to do with the terrible cold we endured during communism, without heating and electricity most of the winter. So we put on thick and dark colored clothing to keep us warm. However, do not consider the other explanations as being totally inappropriate!

The working class, however, was alternating the Prusian blue of the secret militia troops (equivalent to and inspired by the omnipresent Russian KGB) and the brown of common thick fabric, displaying all pastel nuances (and should I say aromas, as well) of the deep "situation" we were in!

We, the younger people, on the other hand, had the courage to display sometimes colors that would make us look alive. The common use of blue-jeans (eternal injury to the pride of the communist regime, determined to convince us to buy the cheap Vietnamese Dang surrogate!) and colored shirts, went to a real frenzy after Woodstock and after we discovered engraved / printed T-shirts.

However, simple white T-shirts and socks were avoided, partly because they were too visible in the distance and at night, and also because they reminded people about American prisons, where they were very trendy. Many would associate those with prison and inmate life, where wearing long hair and bending down for your soap would be listed as extreme sports.

Like the story I heard about Jimmy, who asked his mother: "Hey Mum! I heard you were a student when I was born! Back then, you really wanted a boy or a girl?" "Oh Jimmy! Says his Ma with a bored voice – We were on a trip hiking in the mountains and I just wanted to tie my shoelaces!"

Materials were not a problem during communism: women fashion went into a stall when it discovered calico in the 50s. As for men, cotton stuff from communist Vietnam and the Khaki shirts made in our country and refused by the Popular Army of Baghdad (Saddam's guard!) made the most of our preferences. At the time (1970-1980), our communist dictator was a close friend to Saddam, then a prominent member of the Baas Arab Socialist Party, and helped him in the war against Iran, we heard.

Sometimes, lucky sailors would bring Romanian shoes and Romanian wool fabric, previously exported to UK. We were amazed that our country could produce such good quality stuff, yet never really questioned why we cannot actually buy them at home (!?).

Suedette /moleskin was used in more comfortable garments like home coats/ robes and, above all, pyjamas, the large number of models from the latter, being possibly meant to get you acquainted to wearing stripes, as a discrete remainder of what can happen to you if you did not behave and didn't keep your mouth shut.

One good question on Radio Erevan was: "Is it true that following the Chernobyl accident, many people lost their teeth?" The answer was: "Yes, but only those that didn't keep their mouth shut!".

Wool braid was pretty much praised; they were doing hats, caps, coats, shirts, trousers, slippers, pullovers, even socks and gloves out of it, short of condoms, 'cause they'd probably give an itch or two.

Knitting wool was becoming a national sport, as everybody was terrified about the next winter to come, when you had just 4 hours of electricity and 2 hours of central heating, every day.

So when you came back to your block at the cover of night, with a piece of cheese or meat for your family hidden under your arm, it might have been possible to encounter a strange procession of wooly/hairy monsters going up or down the stairs, with lit candles in their hands, and it would take some time to discover that they were not on a ritual sacrifice procession, but actually were the Joneses from the third floor, coming home from a visit to their grandparents or Harry and his neighbors, recovering from notorious parties in their secret distillery in the block basement. Or maybe your wife and kids coming from grandma's cheese pie reunion. However, you were supposed to take care and avoid de-conspiring your pray to the neighbors. You could grill your meat only after carefully closing all windows (especially kitchen), or else, the family upstairs would go crazy and call the secret police (Security), to find out where you got the meat from (no shop at the time would sell fresh meat and animals grown in countryside were requisitioned by communist government).

Cotton was a luxury product; sometimes found in the cotton wool packages so much cherished by women "in those days of the month", it would be found in endless piles of pants and body tops. Even the army had them. Generally, they were made in China, Vietnam or the former Cambodia (or the happy Democratic Republic of Kampuchea – much to the Russian taste). They were in so trendy that families would make them presents for the newly wed or leave them as heritage for the younger generation, while they got back to the use of bot/bell pepper style panties, made out of softer blanket cover. The Kampuchean cotton pants had the signature of Pol Pot and were bad omen for teachers or those wearing glasses.

Another industrial marvel was the discovery of synthetic fibers. They did anything out of them from spandex pants to overcoats. Enthusiasm dropped a little after some guys blew themselves up while filling their car's gas tank because of electrostatic discharges while moving around them gas pumps.

Incidentally, the investigation was more likely directed toward finding out where the guys took the gas from, as it was currently rationalized to 3 gallons/month/ car. The modern aspect, indestructible colors and elasticity, made plastic fabric friendly to lots of rednecks in the countryside. As a doctor I saw many of them wearing this plastic pants – in many occasions bathing pants, like Speedo style, close to body. That was for them the maximal stallion cool- stage, sort of "being ready for it" all the time. No matter what/ when circumstances left you undressed – medical, accidents, fire, storm, you HAD THEM ON YOU, so you enjoyed some sort of unquestionable immunity and consequently, superiority. Your aspect was undeniably active, meaning you were ready for it and, perhaps, you even sort of anticipated it, capisci? The only problem with synthetic, spandex and plastic stuff is that you get hot in them, you perspire and your skin cannot breathe. And your testicles may boil within, leaving you without …popsicles.

The result is in many occasions an undecided color mixture of the over-worn pants, completed by sticky /slimy appearance and an odor that would bring tears and redeyes to any young and otherwise healthy skunk.

We were lucky the fireplace was no common facility in apartments, or people trying to warm up would have ended up engulfed in flames. Imagine you had a problem with a stubborn young lady all dressed in plastic fibers! All you had to do was just bring her near the fireplace for a little while and, within minutes, she would willingly and rapidly undress on her own! What would follow next shouldn't surprise anyone, right?

Have you seen the latex or spandex costumes? I know they are mostly visible on the stage and in xxx rated films, but have you really seen them? Or tried them, for a change? They cover and copy body shape to any lubricous detail, they are not expensive and display gadgets that enable you to do a lot of basic things, like an astronaut. A particular trend is dressing like this for sex meetings, as such garments are packed with a surprising number of secret openings, pockets and detachable appendix holes. However, no matter how horny, eager, hurried or kinky you may get, try to avoid using them in public places, like the park or the subway. Not that you might get technically hurt – plastic and rubber are both waterproof or conversely, good electricity insulators – but you risk a slight misinterpretation of your actions there. I remember about the story of a very talented reporter – must have told you about him. He was always deployed in the best place to take an interview or witness something that constantly made breaking- news. One day he ended up being savagely raped because he was so fast and early to get to the crime scene that he arrived there before the victim did.

Consequently, my advice is not to expose yourself in such "inviting" clothing, unless it happens within the right environment, whatever that may be.

The type of clothes you wear brings a lot of information about the person wearing it. As a young man, I did an exercise of thinking about that, having minimal information available; character – anyone; location – like, for instance, the beach – Black Sea seaside, Mamaia resort – very popular.

I went there very early, I grabbed my binoculars and I made the following observations.

Around 7 – 7,30 the first guy showed up. Sticky and savage longer hair, quite muscular, cheese- white body but red on his neck and forearms, typical for outside agricultural working class, wearing a pair of huge black fabric shorts with wide sleeves, displaying around his thighs some wide open areas of mysterious darkness, where only occasional flies would venture, without the certainty of getting out again. He takes his old towel next to the water, then grabs a thick bar of house made soap and goes to the knee deep water, determined to combine pleasure with practical activities. He splashes sea water on his body and starts frantically to rub his skin with the soap bar. He takes a break, turns the bar around and becomes even more industrious. However, he soon puts on a baffled and amazed face, seeing that the soap does no produce foam, as he expected, after all the frantically spent energy. His lips mumble something – I can only imagine he has an interior conversation about his mother in law that provided the bad quality soap, which does not work in salty water – then gives up washing and goes back to his towel.

By now it is 9 o'clock and, punctual as a Swiss watch, the government employed clerk makes his entrance, with family. His wife, with a sordid sticky hairdo and the wasted remains of an unsuccessful makeup on her face, wearing a common housewife body swimsuit in despicable grey & yellow colors, drags with her the family umbrella, 3 bags with towels, beach toys and the food for all the 3 kids, aged between 2 and 9, left behind and who start crying because they are afraid of the water they see for the first time. The last one is the 2 years old, literally dragged by the collar of his shirt like the family dog, leaving a long double trail with his bottom in the sand, crying from time to time when he gets a sting from an occasional sea shell that comes his way.

Father is a skinny, medium height creature, with dark hair correctly cut, but full of dandruff that gets more visible above the ears – oh no! Sorry! That was grey hair! He is slim, but with a little beer belly (his soft spot!), muscle shape of a chess player and all white. He wears a slim panty swimsuit made out of a thick blanket like fabric, which successfully covers any expected "asymmetry" in his lower body line, and it is raised almost to his chin, superiorly, so that the chord knot that prevents the pants from falling is the size and in the position of a bow tie. He is wearing thick glasses and he carries the family beach volley ball – a huge ball painted in the national colors which would be taken by the wind countless times and will drop upon the beer or the sandwich of the nearest neighbor. The clerk goes to the water line, spreads his spider legs, then rolls up his panty sleeves, to allow the sun light touch the base of his thighs – same size as my forearms, in a gesture that happens only a few times a year.

He puts his hands on his hips and starts gazing towards the people swimming in the distance, hoping to see a shark fin or something that would make his morning less boring. He takes a longer glance towards two young ladies dressed in very economical bathing suits, actually lacking their bra as they come out of the water. Can't imagine what he thinks, but he takes a rapid glance back to his wife, to see if she saw him focusing attention elsewhere than the randomly wet and democratic landscape.

That reminded me about the story of a guy who is asked by his son: Dad, what is the first thing you do if you see a beautiful woman? Dad answered: I first look at your mother and make sure she didn't notice.

Well, by now it is 11 am and the lazy people come to the beach, to enjoy the infrared rays that would give them sunburns and the danger of melanoma.

The man I talk about a is an older dude, thick, but not exceedingly fat, coming straight from the hotel on the beach side and smelling top quality after-shave lotion.

Little hair – if any, on his head; what's left is carefully combed and that does not let his baseball cap ruin the general impression. The bathing suit is tiny – Speedo style – but clearly expensive and imported.

He already has a slight tan and is in for more. Possibly an exec or a highly ranked politician. A much – and when I say much, that means some 30 years - younger lady follows him, dressed in a tiny bra and an even tinier bikini, slowly bouncing her tush and divinely shaking her super- fat tits, while all the other men on the beach gaze at her drooling. If she is his wife, then I want to be her lover! That reminds me of another story about an older guy who asked his gym trainer: can you tell me what device should I work most so I can be more successful with ladies? The trainer answered: Try the ATM! And another story about two guys having a walk together. One of them says:

- Hey, dude! Do you see those two nice looking ladies in front of us?
- Yap! I do!
- Well, the one on the left is my wife and the one on the right is my mistress!
- No shit! For me it is exactly the other way around!

The thick guy places his towel on the sand and leans down with a satisfied grunt, like a sea lion. She takes time placing baggage around their umbrella, bending and tossing until all the men on the beach focus on her and then she lays next to him. She produces a bottle of tan moisturizer and starts spreading it to his hairy back. Gently and slowly, careful not to skip any inch of it, to and fro, to and fro… Is she his secretary, his associate or his laboratory helper? Who cares, if she is so yummmy good! All the other guys on the beach have eyes wide open with small pupils, like intoxicated with insect killer, and they stay on their belly in order to avoid the embarrassing natural reaction of appreciation that could be seen by their wives and everyone else from a quarter of a mile. A few of them instantly get sentenced to take a cold bath with the kids. The others pretend to fall asleep immediately and dream on with eyes closed.

Another hard to look aspect is piercing. I mean I can "enjoy it" as seen on actor pirates; even Spanish style ear rings may look "manly' on them, combined with the wooden leg, the hook and the eye cloth. By the way, a Spanish friend – an orthopedic surgeon from the Puerto Real clinic near Cadiz, told me a story about a pirate who fell from his ship into a time vortex and landed at the door of a modern luxury mansion near Ibiza, where they were having a masked ball! The old buccaneer was mesmerized by the light and the noisy strange music coming from black boxes all around. The host meets him at the entrance and gets ecstatic about the costume:

- You are so extraordinary! Your hair is sticky and smells salty, your coat is dirty and your sword is as genuine as it can be! ….And look, your wooden leg is perfect and your hook looks terrifying….. and even your finger nails have dirt underneath,,, Marvelous disguise!

The host, a young man with a feminine allure and gestures, takes him by the hand and pulls him in front of the others:

- My friends and comrades! I want to present you the winner of our masked ball tonight! Meet Mr. - sorry, I didn't catch your name, Mr. ….. ?
- Jessup! Mad-dog Jessup! That's me name!
- Well people– I hereby give you Mad-dog Jessup, our winner tonight! Let's drink to him!
- Huray! Huray! This is for Jessup – everybody yelled!

Jessup, blinking his only good eye because of the strong light, set sail towards a punch basin, took a huge flower vase, threw the content towards the orchestra and sunk the vase in punch until almost full. He then raised it for everybody to cheer and drank half of the content like a thirsty camel in the desert, to everybody's delight. The host took over the mike and asked him:

- Most welcome, my dear friend; you are a great talent making things seem so realistic! What do you do in your every day life?

Jassup was busy emptying the vase and hardly noticed him until the end; he wiped his mouth and beard with the stained sleeve of his coat and answered:

- I…..every day, I… I am a pirate, that's what I am! And everybody was laughing desperately.
- Ok,ok! Tell us how you got your wooden leg?
- Just a moment – and Jessup pointed out towards his empty vase, putting out a smile and displaying 3 or 4 lonely broken yellow teeth. Some guy from the audience rushed to him and filled his vase with another gallon of punch.
- Well – he starts after a few gulps – we was boarding another ship – British I guess! When we came near, I jumped for boarding but my rope broke and I fell with my leg between

the ships, where it got squashed! They had to cut it off, but I got 2 gallons of Jamaica rum on that, by Neptune's beard, har, har, har!! He laughed proudly!

- Oh, how wonderful – the host broke in – but now you have to tell us what happened with your left hand, which became this fearsome hook?

Jessup emptied half of the vase gain, wiped beard and mouth and spoke:

- Well, that's another attack! We was attackin' a French cannon ship – guess they had some 50 cannons or so – full of high hat and fat wig turkeys, all in shiny freakin' uniforms. They got scared like rats when we boarded them! We was fighting like hell and I got further aft fighting one of their subs. Another one came from his back and while I made a go to him, I saw the other swing his sword and chopped off my hand! Blundering fool! Thunders and rum to his grave! It hurt so much and I was so mad, I killed them both. But the hand was off to the fishes and I had to screw myself a hook instead! That's how I got it! Hey – you! – the dick-less buddy with small pants and long hairs, fill this jar for me, cutie pie!
- Ok Jessup, the last question – I promise – is about your eye patch! How did you lose your eye?
- Me eye? Hmm….. Well, here I was down from my ship. We've gotten on our treasure island and safely buried our treasure. Can't remember the place anyway, he said carefully. I was tired after all that diggin' and the drinkin' after and laid down under a palm tree full of birds to take a nap.
- Doesn't sound too dangerous so far!......
- Yeah, I thought so too! But then one of the freakin' birds pooed to my left eye!
- Still not dangerous, I guess…. How exactly did you lose an eye over bird poop?

- Well, you see… it was right after I lost me hand and I wasn't exactly handy with me hook, yet!

Cruel aspects of the fashion take their toll, as well. The piercing fashion hits consistently lately. We can see in every location advantages and shortcomings. Remember the ear-ring fixed to the nose? On the middle it looks rather piggish so it was mostly presented to one nostril. You can see fine ones, like in slender young ladies or vigorous ones in back-street boys, so thick and strong you could pull Santa's sleigh with it – and your nose would become red like Rudolph's.

I cannot stop thinking how do these people wipe their nose when they catch a cold.

How about the tongue one? Oh Come on! I know all of you, boys and girls, at a certain moment, watched xxx rated movies. Maybe you still do – which is good for style enrichment, but let us think of the pleasure it can bring. I mean whatever you eat has a metallic taste and gets stuck in your mouth like a boat rope. Think like having oral sex with someone having this metal thing on her tongue? Better stick it into a hole with barb-wire, it'll scratch less! You can't lick your ice-cream without making noise like a Dutch cow! But it is does a world of good at the dentist's. "Hello madam, if you don't stick your tongue out I'll grab it by the ring and hook it to the front window pane!"

How about the metal piercing of the nipples? Kinky! I wonder how you make the distinction between pain and pleasure when you get those pooled vigorously! What if they came out together with the silicon bags and all? Suppose such lady gives birth to a baby (not likely but still possible in theory). The little thing will cut lips trying to suck on those nipples. You could have the same fate while trying to…. practice.

But imagine how handy they become when you are single on a crowded bus or subway and you have your hands full of bags. How comfortable it must get to be when you suddenly realize you have where to hang your skates, your salami, your potato bag, your umbrella or your purse, thus freeing your hands to be able to pay ticket or hang to the bars.

The way we dress seems to tell a lot about us, but the discussion would be incomplete without mentioning the fashion channels. You know, the ones women look at, while being at the office from 9 to 5 and men watch after midnight, when bathing suits fashion is presented.

These channels are somehow the expression of total behavioral freedom: anything is permitted – in fashion that is! Any material, any fabric, any style, any cut and any association of material or color is aloud and the more weird and fantastic they look, the more approved they get on the stage. However, I have rarely seen articles/clothes of crazy imagination make their way from the catwalk to the wardrobe, with the exception of some VIP s and celebrities who, if dressed normally, would go unnoticed on the streets. No autograph, no attention, no cameras, no money and then depression and lots of pills, till the curtain falls.

The frustrating idea is that someone who thinks he or she is an artist, starts cutting clothes - occasionally for the first time in their life - and then get a bunch of rich friends to arrange a presentation. With a few not-so-expensive reporters and the help of a tabloid, the event gets the proportion of a general election and you are bound to find a few eccentrics (to use an euphemism) ready to invest in the weirdo's garments. And they make tons of money with that and create an entire zoo of characters, who are carefully "nursed" by media, like white rhino babies. Those characters are gold value for holyday times when nothing happens, but they become a bottomless fountain of unhappy statements, they drunk-drive and get caught in the process, get married and divorce several times a year, go to rehab clinics and get exotic pets like cobras, tigers, poisonous sea snails or pythons. There's no God- blessed day without some spicy news about these well- known nobodies and their hang-abouts.

A whole world of people gather and participate – most of all, those practicing modelling. Being a model is a rough life. You could wear anything you like with the money you make, but you are not allowed to wear anything else than the company's products (which you sometimes hate or represent a poor coverage for the season!). You could eat anything your heart craves after, from camel steak to boiled

Chinese worms, but you are not allowed to eat anything at all. You are watered with tons of green tea and lemon and from time to time you are given pills to vomit even that.

You can exercise – and if you are a nice young lady your exercise will mostly be entertaining old rich goons (read screw them!) – all the rest is for TV shows. Just when you are so skinny and sick you think of quitting, you meet the right body measure standard and you're good to go. Going is tough; you need to start learning how to walk again and the result is as painful as it was when you did it the first time, when you were 1 year old. You have to cross your legs while walking, like with roller blades, something easier to do for women, as they have a wider pelvis and this feature has to be emphasized over the parts above and below. For male models, however, walking seems by far the toughest task to accomplish without stumbling, especially with the kind of clothes and shoes they are forced to wear. Sometimes they look like stepping over venomous snakes or tip-toeing on red hot charcoal, other times they seem to have stepped on a pin and go sideways like a car with a flat tire or a frog with a sting in the ear.

Take for instance this young man with a Capone - style hat. Not really matching his fluffy blond haircut, but his general look is completed by black tie and a long coat like the clerics in the "Equilibrium" movie. It may seem ok down to this part, but then you observe that he wears no trousers and he has a pair of rubber "Croco" beach sleepers in his feet, making his gait somehow wobbly, if the slippers are wet. His face bears the expression and the look of a freshly drowned cat and his slightly opened mouth, together with the hands that keep annoying him, as he finds no place to hang them, lead to a confused appearance, suggesting among other biological setbacks a microscopic IQ.

By all means, he seems generously witted when compared to the next appearance – a confused young man with fair complexion and a dazzled look, slightly enhanced by his cross-eye condition. He wears a vaporous pink scarf, over a waist coat that has seen better days on an even smaller person. He can barely button it at the top button and his belly is left uncovered partially by the exceedingly large shirt, half of it out of his pants. His trousers have holes in the knees and the whole outfit seems worn by a stuntman run over by an eighteen wheeler and who did several takes with it. I wonder how the young man would feel dressed like that in the foyer of a theater; I can bet he is bound to make a fistful of quarters and maybe even 10-12 dollar bills.

Well this one was a classic when compared to the next one. The next male model has a devastatingly modern haircut, which could be only obtained if you have water, 2 nails and a 110 volt source around. He is also using red lipstick, so his tiny mouth, hidden under a thick brown moustache, looks like a squirrel's ass after falling on a stingy pine tree branch. He has a melon hat and a "papillon" and shirt cuffs with golden cufflinks, but the shirt and all the rest is missing, and he is barefoot, as well. Yap! The man is otherwise completely naked!

He is holding his "family jewelry" with one hand, as the other is busy hiding his rear part, you know, the one that made some of his colleagues crave for.

What an inspiration! What talent and what fabric quality! This fashion creator is blinding us with his /her talent! The model represents the quintessence of masculine readiness – you have your hat, your neck-tie and cough-links for distinguished looks, otherwise you're ready to "go for it" anytime. The charm of such costume is irresistible and success will unmistakably come this way, if you are patient enough. Some 5 years as patient as you can be in a mental institute, could rid you of your passion for fashion.

The previous performance is doubled by an entire chorus of young ladies that follow in displaying new and interesting clothes, while every reporter is busy doing HD of the event and inside stories.

The first model comes in; you can tell almost immediately the model is a woman, if it were only for the hairdo. If curled with real hair, it would take about 10 meters of it, and the only competent contestant in this matter is the Guinness Book awarded Vietnamese man who refused to cut his hair for more than 2 decades, until his hair reached 32 feet in length and over 40 pounds in weight.

An overwhelming variety of accessories, from auto antennas, spare parts, paper clips, to can openers, shoe laces, screw drivers, large sticks and metal buckles, anyway and anything fit to hold the whole haystack together. Alternatively, natural hair is hidden under a bunch of fluffy colored wool balls put together in the shape of a wig and reinforced with flower garments that turn it into a genuine ikebana arrangement.

I have also seen short hair bundles, hysterically colored and tied or stuck to the skull, all effort being done in order to draw your attention from the clothes which actually represent the main attraction – or should do so!

A variation was the completely shaved head, along with eyebrows and ear hairs; the little-green-alien-from-Asgard- look, making gender establishing a matter of debate, if you lack DNA testing.

The face is a perfect arena for fashion display. Commonly heavily painted in various colors, the girls' faces match the dress-up of a successful airplane carrier and the paint is embarrassingly thick, even for a Kabuki theater.

The spots and stripes on their face are so aggressive, they would scare to death even a Cherokee chief, looking for a skilled squaw to remake his long feather "hairdo".

However, from all make up types, we can distinguish some which are more often employed.

For example, there is this "sepulchral" style. Face darkened by enormous dark rings around the white eyes, with prominent cheeks and an overall skull appearance. With extremely skinny models the effect is devastatingly realistic; all you need is throwing a couple of fistful of freshly dug earth on the catwalk while they clank their bones to and fro, and you can take a double for the "Adams family" album.

The "brigand" (mugger) style comes with a painted face mask, displaying a dark stripe at eyes level, in contrast to the light color of the face, with a faint resemblance to Zorro or the Locust Boy. When together, the girls look like a pack of joyful raccoons, set out to check all the dumpsters in the neighborhood or a female congregation of Ninja Turtles.

The maniacal face is achieved by using different colors, the important thing is to use red and yellow excessively, because they are known to raise blood pressure and peculiar ideas, as Van Gogh would say.

Senseless vivid moves, slightly disarticulated, will complete the insanity appearance that justifies the rest of the outfit.

We can encounter a serious problem with these male and female models; sometimes, it is practically impossible to determine correctly their gender, because of the makeup and the clothing. I had plenty of surprises watching such fashion shows: fluffy angelic blondes who later proved to be boys and female models who wore false beards or moustaches, impersonating men. Upon my presence there, I wouldn't have had the heart to tell them how considerably those accessories improved their general look.

But enough about the face! Let us assume we have established the model is a woman. While testing winter or autumn clothing, we have no nasty surprises in general, but when we get to summer, it is a wholly different story.

For summer, the definition of a simple dress may be a cement sack with three holes. It may be improved with some rope pieces, some fountain chain segments and some razor blades (careful with those when you attach them to a neckless!). The rest of the body is unforgivingly visible and it is thousands of miles away from the Rubensian voluptuous shapes we adore in women, more or less.

Gone is the roundness of the romantic shoulder, gone is the amplitude of the pelvic challis of motherhood, gone are the voluptuous hips awaiting the embrace of loving arms, gone are the tiny feet and the gracious hands writing flowers into thin air!

All we get now is a scary display of bony square shoulders, like when suffering from a double scapula-humeral dislocation, with disgustingly visible rib cages and protruding bones that remind us of the Nazi concentration camps, all stepping crisscross, in order to cover for the inappropriate parenthesis between the emaciated bony legs.

When they fall down on the catwalk – which happens more often than you'd think, because of the strange outfit and the bizarre shoes they wear - the noise is not a decent thud, but a spine-chilling rattling of empty bones.

The show is a success! Who else besides these poor creatures would let themselves dressed in a cement sack with chain pieces garments? It is interesting that these girls are not assigned to make the show for bathing suit presentation (or else we have Scary Movie 5); the bathing suit fashion is presented by classic beauties (90/60/90cm), at night time, for "connoisseurs". It is like admitting, in a certain manner, that whatever they show in day presentations is fiction for most of us, and that is why we never agree to dress like that. With Victoria's Secret and other presentations, we get back to normal – I'd say human - aspect.

I can understand now why older female fashion designers mostly produce weird clothing for the young boys they keep on a leash, and later on – what do you know ? –their apprentices become young gay designers.

Fact is they are successful and make a lot of money because we comply with this game: we have the fun, they get the money, everybody's happy! There is no one left to have the guts to say:

-     "Hey, look! The emperor is naked"!

WHAT IS THE CORRECT PERCEPTION OF MARRIAGE

The idea of bringing up this subject came to me after I listened more carefully to the Frank Sinatra's song "Love and marriage", used by the producer of the "Al Bundy" series – disturbingly realistic and full of hidden wisdom, beyond the laughs, if you ask me.

Of course, the idea also came to me after a remarkable experience in this …business, like 28 or is it 29 years? (WTF, I forgot "our' anniversary date again!). Hm, Hm – it is officially 29! I had a painful confirmation – do not ask!

Incidentally, did you notice the content of the next line – "like a horse and carriage" ? You did, right? Now I am going to ask a simple question: who is the horse and who is the carriage? I mean who is the one who works, sweats (even when making love, right?) and takes care for everything to go right? And who needs to be pulled, pushed, lured, and dragged, with some exceptions of course, when the charm of a golden credit card can change the life of a person ?

You can drop it – I don't need an honest answer; I don't want to shame all of you, brothers in suffering, but I want to clarify a few things, for my own peace of mind. And yours, maybe.

A friend of mine - who is a vet - told me something I found very disturbing.

We met late in the evening in a grocery supermarket; we were both tired after a day's work, all sweat and carrying huge bags. And he said:

- Hey. Look at us! We look like two paws of the same bear!

I was too tired to react and payed no attention to his philosophy; just smiled in an understanding way.

- Check this! He said:
- If you are diligent like an ant, work like a horse all day and finish by returning home tired like a beaten dog, then you should go see a vet, because you are stupid as an ox!

We start with the time when we were kids. We may have happened to see, at times, a very solemn Mum, speaking out loud and making noise in the kitchen, like trying to replace somewhere else all pots, pans and plates. Some of which may have broken in the process, meanwhile. During this time, Dad would be mumbling something, possibly stopping short of lighting a cigarette or opening another can of beer. He would be going in and out and around, like a frog stung into the ear, apparently without a practical purpose, then he would settle in the garage, where he would spend all his afternoon, sometimes even the night. Evening dish would be a little burned up, yet no one to complain. We would all eat in silence like at the church, and when finishing, Mum would fix us kids with the kind of "go to bed this instant" look. I don't understand how she has another look for Dad – or was it the same - who would sigh and bring his pillow and a blanket on the sitting-room coach. No TV that evening.

Apparently, there was a misunderstanding. Later on, I found out that Dad actually misunderstood the simple and natural fact that Mum was right. Like she's always right! Actually, years later in my life I understood that, when you are married, the wife is commonly, undeniably, naturally, rigorously and unavoidably right. And if by chance she is not right, she will keep talking and arguing until she is. And she will be!

The next day there would be a brief mentioning of this fact, lasting for no more than 3 hours or so, meant to fix it in the short memory of your tiny manly brain, and to convince you to use this thought whenever you feel like arguing again. Or – God All Mighty - nursing the crazy thought that maybe <u>You</u> could be right!

Tough when having kids though; it takes some effort to preserve your cheerful spirit. I took a coffee break with a friend one day. He looked very energetic and fresh, in spite of being just divorced.

- So how are you doing? I asked.
- Fine, dude! Real good! He answered, while looking deep under the skirt of our waiter. She had, indeed, a pair of fine long legs, grown "down from her tonsils".
- "How is your life?" he asks in turn, without even looking at me.

It was true we had spent some happy times together as students; all flavored with interesting girlfriend memories.

- Oh, you know, like everyday job, surgery, call duties, then home, the kids! Regular stuff. I like being with them a lot!

He seemed like being far away and not noticing what I was saying. Or that he couldn't care less!

- Aha! Yeah! Kids are…. a good thing! He lit a cigarette and puffed smoke away turning his head towards me. He was looking in my eyes when he said:
- You know, when she filed the divorce, we went to trial; judge called me to the bar and asked me: "Do you have any children resulting from this marriage?"

He took a sip of the coffee and puffed on his cigarette:

- I told him: "No Your Honor, sad to say, I have not! As a superior species, I cannot breed in captivity!"
- And?.......
- "Well, I got away with a 1000 bucks penalty for defying the Court. Haven't seen her ever since! But I miss my kids!"

However, marriage sounds romantic in the beginning. It is supposed to start by romance and the quest of finding the "love of your life". If you do happen to find her – like George, a friend of mine used to say - don't marry her! – you'll turn her into a freakin' monster – a wife!. Keep her for activities that do not risk to degenerate in household jobs that will scrub her hands and make her hair smell like a diner's table cloth.

Someone used to say that every man will - sometime in his life - find the love of his life. The most embarrassing part becomes hiding her away from the wife. Love is blind, deaf, dumb, and sometimes very weird. A gentleman comes to his gym instructor and asks, with a "secrecy" hint of tone in his voice:

- Listen pal, what type of device or workout can you recommend me for having more crush on chicks?

The trainer gets back a couple of feet, looks at him from top to bottom and then he says smiling:

- Try the ATM! At least twice a day – morning and evening! Especially on Saturdays and Sundays!

I once heard the story of some important professors we had at the university; he was the gentleman type, always elegant and per-fumed, close shave (old style), smart, working as a virus specialist in cooperation with WHO in spite of being resident of a communist country.

She worked in the same cathedra, as a successful and renowned bacteriologist and she was probably the best I'll ever know in this specialty. Unfortunately, she was ugly like the bad witch in kid's stories. Her coiffure was a bundle of slimy hairs stuck to her head, her possibly once interesting face was all wrinkled, she had nystagmus, so we, students, never knew where she actually looked and she had lost all teeth and carried total replacement dental prosthesis, both superior and inferior.

The bed-wetting part was those shark like dental prosthesis, which never agreed to stay together inside her mouth while she was speaking, during lectures, and made her yawn from time to time (it was no yawn, she was actually trying to catch back the loose one, using the counterpart) and unwillingly spit a little.

They say her rapid "growing old" was the price to pay for their "engineered" marriage and that she was much older than him, actually. He – on the other hand – seemed to have had an itch with younger dames. Rumor has it that once, when she was away at a convention, he invited a young lady, a student he was patronizing, at his home and they stayed together for a couple of days. The wife came unexpectedly, sooner than agreed, at a time when he was refreshing in the bathroom. His mistress was in their bed; the wife took her by the hand and threw her out silently.

Then, with all due discretion, she undressed and got in the bed, in the exact position where the girl was and put the blanket over her face. He went out of the bathroom, went to the kitchen and came back singing like to a kid: "Who's covered in silk, and wants a little milk?"

The effect was total: she unveiled from beneath the blanket and smiled with both false teeth prosthesis: "Me!". They say that was the time when he had his first heart attack! Or stroke! But maybe those were just rumors, as this could have been possible even if you didn't know her at all.

However, it would have been some explanation for the fact that she hated female students and they always had small grade in bacteriology, no matter how much they learned. Especially the good looking ones. Especially if they had a previous good grade in viruses.

Romance was the beginning of all!. I used to live – as a student – in an old people's house; they had an empty side of the house for rental. It was me in a room and another guy in the other. He married a girl who was our group leader in the university. They met at my birthday. As it was in November, we had some drinks. He went outside with a friend and they drank palinka – some sort of fruit brandy (commonly plum) very usual in Transilvania. But the stuff is so tough – over 50° anyway – that beats any traditional whiskey. I mean you can remember more or less adequately what happens until you drink – let's say – some 200 cc. On a full belly. On empty, 100 cc can knock you out. Beyond that, you fail to remember what you did or what happened. It is like a gap in your existence – total blackout. So Giovanni, my friend, after courting my colleague for a while, went outside to consume his manhood, by drinking the stuff with another friend in the bitter cold. By the time they came back – say half an hour – the fire of the stove inside had made the atmosphere very hot.

They took a minute to tell us, apparently normally, that they drank the whole half kilo bottle during this time. I told them to get out because the heat will torment them. They laughed at me and then Giovanni claimed Marianne is his wife and told us to stop starring at her tits, because this is his sovereign privilege. We realized he was almost done so we showed him out, where Marianne offered to see him to his room – where – knowing the effect of the stuff - I am convinced nothing happened. That's how they met and got married; twice. Meanwhile they divorced once and then decided to give it another try. I told Giovanni no more wedding – "I'm sure you kept the present I gave you first time – should be still working; the plug chord may need a change, but the rest is sturdy" I said. "These electrical devices have a 2 year warranty". Besides, a more cynical friend of mine used to say that bride dresses are white because that is the traditional color for any household device.

But we were romantic in those times. Not like now! My son is a medical student and when he comes from the University in weekends he sometimes shares with me some of his preoccupations.

He once told me he dated an older colleague, who is close to graduation. He invited her in a well - known and highly appreciated coffee bar, where they approached in their dialogue some life items while sipping on the good coffee. At a certain moment he asked her:

-       How do you like it?

She laid back in her seat, took some time to think, and said with unsure lower tone:

-       From the back, and with you pulling my hair gently! And she exposed a promising smile!

He then froze and said:

-       I mean the coffee! How do you like the coffee!

The thing is you need to carefully plan your step and avoid dating a girl that has been – the single cheerleader for a whole football team – to use a euphemism.

They say Dalai Lama was asked once a very trivial thing: "Why is it that a man that had many women is praised as a champion whereas a woman that made love to many men is still considered a whore?" The answer was really full of charm: "A key that opens many doors is priceless, but a room that opens with any key is worthless".

One other problem you have when thinking of getting married is: how will she look, say, after 25 years or so? You can easily answer to that question if you pay a visit home.

First – but you need to avoid any witness – you take a look under the rug. Just pretend you stumble or something. If there's some kicked away stuff under, you're in for trouble.

Then take a good look at the mother; without any subjectivity, ask yourself this: meeting this woman on the street, would I be interested to marry her daughter? Sometimes, mother is so hot, you may forget about the daughter – like in Maddonna's case, my preferred female artist!, but here we are in the situation you meet her first.

Naturally, if at her age (for sure if asked alone, she will be the thirties) she looks like preserving normal human proportions, then you have a go.

If she is easier to jump than circle around, than it is time to move on to another flower.

Too much of a good things can produce damage, as some people would say.

A guy decides to attack the local bank. He takes a mask and a gun and steps in: everybody is terrified and leans on the ground. He takes the money and before running away decides to give an example for the audience. He grabs a guy from the lot and asks him:

- Hey, did you see me?
- The terrified guy nods unwillingly and admits: Yes I saw you!
- Well, let that be a lesson to you and the others – says the burglar and shoots him in the head!

He then grabs the second guy and asks the same question:

- How about you? Did you see me?

The guy is yellow pale and he talks between clinched teeth:

- No, I am sure I haven't seen you, and that is nowhere near as to be able to do a description!

The perpetrator relaxes and starts heading towards the door, as police sirens approach howling, when the second guy raises his voice:

- But my wife did!

I've been with my wife 29 years now and I can't say I am bored. Boredom has nothing to do with it. She would find every day a new idea or a new objective that you have to run for. Sometimes, this is how guys got into presidency. Other times, this was the way they gotten into deep shit or the can.

My mother in law is a dear, even if not a stupendous beauty and with some health issues, she is a distinguished woman for her age – she would be 85 soon, I guess tomorrow. I meet all my wife's folks, some of them would come to my office and say: Hi cousin! Remember me, I was at your wedding? OMG – I answer, is it really You? Obviously, I didn't notice him even at the wedding, so it would have been highly unlikely for me to remember him after 28 years or more. "You changed!" – THAT never misses after all this time! "How's your wife? And the kids?" – I score again with things that cannot miss. Be careful not to mention kid's gender, as you may fail to remember if the person has a boy or a girl; you must be more elusive, like "kids, younger generation, hears, junior(s), future generation, etc.

"Wife divorced me, don't you remember?" Of course I didn't, I didn't even notice when he got married, nobody informed me about his love life. Besides he was so boring I wouldn't understand why a decent women would pick him at all - of all the men available on Earth! "And I don't have kids!" "And I have this cirrhosis and a fractured elbow, which brings me to you as a doctor – I have this plaster cast problem!"

Ahaaa! ….F-ck!

Speaking about mother in law, a friend of mine told me an old story over a cup of wine.

- I was once present at a trial; you know Billy, our college friend, staying in the next room.
- Yeah, I remember him!
- Well, he was booked for family violence – he'd been beating the crap out of his mother in law! ….. Yeah! But he made bail, finally!
- OMG! Why would he do such a thing?

He gave me a bored look:

- Probably character mismatch! – WTF? Does it matter? He mumbled. A neighbor was called in as witness for the victim. Check this out! So this neighbor walks in, smiling, swears on the Bible and sits down. Still smiling.
- Well Sir – asks the Judge – did you see what happened?
- Yes, Your Honor, I really did, says the guy in a hasty voice! I saw it all, from the beginning to the end; I haven't missed a move!- It was a big time show! Never saw something like this on our street! I mean never since I moved in! And I moved in quite for sometime!
- Then why did you stay there, without interfering? Judge asked.
- You see, Your Honor, at first my spirit of justice and human respect pushed me to react and I felt inclined to interfere, but when I saw that he can easily handle the situation by himself, I relaxed and stayed around, to help him just in case.

Which reminds me of "mother in law" story I was told by a guy who was a member of the NRA.

Johnny comes home on Mother's Day, and, unlike other years, he goes straight to his mother in law and hands her a present, a little parcel.

She looks at him in disbelief, then takes the parcel and slowly opens it, as if trying to prevent an explosion. But whatever she sees inside makes her smile:

- Oh Johnny! A pair of ear rings for me! How sweet of you! After all these years you started to care! Come on, let me give you a hug!... Errr, but Johnny, what are you doing with the shotgun?
- Thought'ya may need'em ear-ring holes, Ma', don't ya'?

Things are not so simple. Having kids can be dangerous, like my friend Tom can state. He once had a hard time in his marriage because of the "holly search for truth".

A good old saying goes like this: "What you don't know, won't hurt you!".

One day, Timmy, his little boy, comes from school. He noticed that his wife was a little nervous, but would keep this state of mind for herself. She was doing a lot of noise in the kitchen, looking busy. He was wondering what would follow. As soon as Timmy sits at the table, his mother starts questioning him:

- Ok, Tim, now I want you to tell me again what you saw yesterday!

Mouthful Timmy complies, chewing food undisturbed:

- I saw Dad and our neighbor Sandra in Sandra's house. I was in the garden and I climbed the apple tree, so I could see the bedroom….Ooppss! He then looks carefully around – Like it happens sometimes….when I climb for an apple!

And Timmy bashfully chews on his steak as if trying to bring it to amino acid state..

- Never mind that! Mother decides the important tip is somewhere else. And what did you see they were doing?

Timmy, a little more cautious and looking at his Dad, who fixed him with his eyes over the opened newspaper, in the next room:

- Like I saw what they were doing! They were doing exactly the same thing you and Uncle John did in our upstairs bedroom, while Dad was away for the army training week last year!

I once sat at a cup of coffee and a glass of wine with an old sailor, a guy who used to know my Dad – Lord have Mercy on his soul!

This guy had been a ship Captain, not an engineer. Ghiorghieff by name, he used to say he had Russian origin, but I suspected he was in fact Bulgarian, which didn't really matter. He had a couple of white hairs on his skull, never mingled in a decent haircut and quite slimy in the summer breeze.

He must have had a whole barrel of wine that night, not to mention what he'd been drinking over the day, enough to power a tug boat for 2 hours.

He was retired and ended up manning an old bucket – a small tourist boat on the city lake. However, he was preparing for every trip to the island in the middle of the lake like it were a trans-Atlantic trip. The island was tiny, a few acres, jammed with gardens and an open air restaurant. Plenty of rats last time I checked. It has been historically established that the ancient Roman poet and philosopher Publius Ovidius Naso had been exiled and actually lived his last years on that island, while Dacia – the former name of my country – was finally being conquered by the Romans led by emperor Trajanus – the Spaniard – following the war in 105-106 A.C.. You can visit a monument – a huge column - dedicated to this victory, in downtown Rome, not far from the Colosseum, and close to the Emmanuelle the Second Palace.

So Gheorghieff was telling me about how marriage goes. He started by describing women as animal lovers:

> - Mario, my friend, they are very fond of nature and animals. Their soul is like a Public Zoo: they would like a fox around their neck, a tiger in their bed, a Jaguar in their garage and an ox, around the house, to work and pay for everything.

Ghiroghi Ghiorghieff was speaking his soul out, after having been married five times. Or maybe six.

- But Ghiorghi, I understand what you mean. I once met a guy who said: "Any grown up man who is passed 30 and is endowed with some wit, will manifest - whenever a beautiful woman is around - the same sense of danger that only a previously beaten dog experiences! How do you explain that – I mean you were married 5 times already?
- Nonsense my friend! And – by the way - it was six, not five! When you see the chosen one, your dick is helplessly dragging you on the trail of lust like a Big-Boy-Challenger locomotive uphill. If you ask me, I get carried away too quick and my strategy does not visualize farther than the first, maybe the second fuck! Definitely the second, too! That's the best! After that, it goes downhill! But I honestly loved all of them – says he smiling like the Equator line and displaying some solitary old teeth like mumbles for ship mooring, while exhaling the darkest cloud possible out of his clay pipe. Its smell resembled wet oak leafs, a household burned broom, possibly some freshly cut finger nails, a vacuum cleaner burned bag, some dry old carrots and potatoes, a bundle of wet hairs from a stray dog and a vague hint of garlic, mint and some chicken shit. Possibly some ginger and horse radish essence, but I wouldn't know where to locate them.
- What's that stuff, Ghiorghi, kinnikinnick? – I asked, tears rolling down my cheeks while sneezing like a cat locked for 2 days in a garbage collector.
- Nope! - he said, in a dreamful attitude - it is my favorite mixture; I do it myself! I like the way it goes smooth on my throat! Not like the shit they sell at the shop these days! Makes you bark!
- Did you try to settle and flavor the mixture down in something, I don't know, like an acid bath? Jet fuel,

peroxide, maybe liquid Nitrogen? He looked at me in disbelief. Which made me insist:

- It might take away the sting and smoothen it even more! – That's all I could say, trying to encourage him, before another coughing round. But his mind was already miles away.
- Listen greenhorn! All they do – them ladies – is fake! They lie and cheat like they breathe! Check this out: fake tits, fake ass, fake lips, fake hair on the head, fake color of hair and skin, fake fingernails, fake eye color and fake noses by surgery, everything's fake, but when it comes to men, they want a genuine, REAL man! Ha! And he ended the phrase with a typical sailor spit in the harbor water, next to the pub. Possibly aimed at a fish.

He recovered his breath, puffed vigorously from his short pipe and we were both lucky the wind blew the toxic cloud across the water, so we could not see the dead birds fall and the poisoned fish raise to surface.. He took a gigantic sip from the wine jar in front of him and carried on:

- You know I got me a daughter! Told her once and again to be smart and not to believe us men. I said: when he says you're good, he thinks of your ass, when another one says you're nice, he thinks about your spread feet, not your nose, and when another one yet says you're pretty – that means you have a good soul and let him in. Now listen to me – I told her – no matter what everyone says – all they want to – all the three of them want to – is to screw you, nothing else. So don't fu__ing get married ride away! 'Cause they'll do to you what I did to my wives – I forgot about them when I met the next one!
- But Ghiorghi, tell me, did you ever feel sorry for this?
- Har, har, har! He laughed like a pirate. I do not think so. See, they all said they loved me just for the way I was – and you know I was no Prince Charming and definitely

no Einstein even in my earlier times, but as soon as they had the darn golden ring on the finger, all they wanted to do was to change my way – the exact way they initially loved, and kept on doing so until they started tormenting me. Retribution came, har, har, har! Say, remember the story with the guy who got his wife caught stealing at the grocery? She stole a jar with pickled peaches or compote something. When she got in front of the judge, he said:

- "Madam, you should behave like an honorable house wife! Let this be a lesson to you! I will sentence you to serve one month of jail for every peach in that jar!"

The husband, sort of passive meanwhile, suddenly woke up and said: "Your Honor, excuse me, but nobody observed she also stole a jar full of green peas…!" Get it? There comes a time when they no longer let you be! That's the time to go – and never look back!

- You're a funny guy Ghiorghi! Should I order another wine?
- Nope – he swung in an approximate standing position. The youngest Madam Ghiorghieff awaits for me at home!
- So you got a fixed hour, like college girls?
- Bullshit, man! That's no way to speak to an old sea wolf like me! I could be your father – or an uncle, something! But you know how sensitive I am to love gestures: she said something that bothered me. She said "Mr G" – that's how she nicknamed me – Mr. G! Like the G spot! Har! Har! Ain't she funny? Mr. G – she said – you have your ship rules, I have mine! My rule is at 10 o'clock at night it is sex time! So make sure you get back before that, or else…So you don't want me to be late, don't you?
- Why Mr. G? I entered his game. What "else" is gonna happen? She might start without you, which should be a sight to see – sorry pal! Or she might start with somebody else, someone who manages to be available… By the way, Mr. G, how old is she?

\-   Oh, she's much younger than me. I'd be 75 in March and she's 25!

I was wondering for a moment what did she see in him, besides blindfolded love and 20 second intercourse, if any. The lone sea wolf might have stashed aside 1-2 hundred K while sailing the seas. I was fond of the old buccaneer and I hoped he did not really believe in her loving him dearly and sincerely. But after 5 – sorry, 6 marriages- he might have figured out the right answer. While he put on his coat and hat and was about to leave I asked:

\-   Hey Ghiorghi! If your wife is 25 now, how old should be mine?
\-   Har, har, har! Relax boy, your true love isn't born yet!

He took some steps into the dark, then turned around and shouted:

\-   And your wife to be, either! Har, Har, Har-Har-Har.. – he laughed departing in a cloud of stinking smoke, like an old steam tug into the evening mist.

A friend of mine used to say "marriage is a workshop where the husband works and the wife shops". He also told me once he asked his wife what is her favorite position in bed. She answered - next to the plug-in so I can charge my phone.

A guy I know went to the can. Some financial mumbo-jumbo, as far as I remember, and the IRS picked on him. He was sentenced to do one year – "the longest year of my life" he used to say afterwards, "but I felt somehow free!". We met over a cup of coffee once and he would tell me some of his prison impressions. One of those days he would think and stare at the white wall in front of him. Without intention, he had gotten the habit of picking his nose. So that day he would pick his nose again.

His room-mate said:

- Stop doing that!
- K!

After a few minutes:

- Stop doing that already!
- So what's the big deal? If it bothers you, turn around and pretend you don't see me!
- No moron! Stop doing it because we have a saying inside – whenever you pick your nose that means someone else in banging your wife!
- Really? Do you believe it?
- Sure I do!
- Then I sure hope my wife never gets to pick her nose!

Les is my friend in Pittsburgh, and he tells me all sort of funny stories. He once told me about a scary night he had with his wife, years before.

They had dinner and watched some TV, a football game as usual (he was totally addicted to it) then went to bed as they did every day.

After a few hours – like it was maybe 3-4 a.m. – his wife suddenly sits up in bed and stares at him. After a few minutes she turns on her head light. He turned to the other side to avoid light.

- Leslie! She says gently. Leslie, are you asleep?
- Mhmmm! Yeaaaah!
- Leslie, when was NFL founded?
- Zzzzzz! Like in the 20s as a football league, but the NFL as it is in 1922…zzz,zzz!
- Leslie! What was the longest run in the history of NFL?
- Hmm! Zzzzzz! Tony Dorsett, Dallas Cowboys, 99 yards, 1983….zzz, zzzz,
- Leslie! Which teams of the NFL do not use cheerleaders?
- Hmmm! Bears, Browns,…hmmm, Lions, Giants, Steelers and….hmmm! Packers!,,,,zzzzz, zzzz
- Leslie? Can you hear me?

- Zzzzzz, zzzzzz….what? Ok! Yeah!
- Leslie! What was the last scoreless game in NFL?
- Zzz, zzzz Detroit Lions versus New York Giants errr… 1943 zzz,zzzz…
- Leslie, was there any team that finished a whole season undefeated?
- Hmmm, Miami Dolphins in..zzzz…..in 1972!

At this moment, his wife took the pillow and smashed it to his head!

- Hey, he woke up all boiling, what's that supposed to mean?
- You cheap lying no good feeling bastard! Despicable moron, you!
- What? What do you want?
- Yesterday it was my birthday!

One day, while waiting for my young daughter, I witnessed an interesting dialogue between two kids at the kindergarten door:

- My father is better than yours!
- Not true!
- My dog is better than yours!
- Not true!
- My Mum looks better than yours!
- That's true! My dad says it all the time!

I once had a conversation about marriage with a Muslim friend; he actually was my group colleague in Medical School and we knew each other for a long time (like 34 years I think). He is a resident of Iraq, but lives in the Turkman community in Northern Kurdistan.
He said :

- Do you think it is easy for us Muslims to have the adequate number of wives? (Which is 4!). Very few people dare to do it, and it is not because of social pressure. The Islam law says you have to treat them equally! Now imagine I buy a Swiss watch to one of them – maybe the one I like most! It makes no difference – I have to buy another one - the very same type – for each of them! So I have to spend 3 times more money!

- That must be less of a problem for a rich Saudi, I said! Because, a rich guy – Allah Y'yn! – can afford to pay 4 times a gift!

- You are a definite square-head like all western people, like the Americans. You think everybody is compelled to think your way. Look what the Americans did with the Arab Spring! Their obvious intention was to mow down all Arab leaders and dictators acting under Russian influence! Who were those? Prominent leaders of the Baas Arab Socialist Party, sustained by Moscow. Starting with our Saddam Hussain, then Gaddafi of Libya, Algeria, Tunisia and Egypt and there's only Bashar al Assad of Syria who still kicks, openly helped by the Russians. It is and it was all about oil and only oil! Money!

- Yeah, but the leadership was changed for the benefit of people and democracy!

- Democracy! Shnemocracy! He asked, laughing hysterically. Arabs were tribal peoples, living on animal farming, war and hunting until one or two decades ago. For them democracy is weakness and Parliament is a gathering of whining morons (I think we could have agreed on this one!). Arab people do not understand voting, democracy, elections or women who drive cars and wear jeans. They will respect the man with the sharper sword and better gun, the one who is powerful enough to subdue all tribes. That man- and only him - will be President and maybe even dictator, they do not care how you call him. They will respect only power and fear, and they are used to the power that comes together with abuse, disrespect for human rights or life! And money, of course! They will not respect a senator or a congressman in a million years the same way they respect a dreaded leader. You do not understand that your system is not working here! What was the result? Opposed leaders took over and now Americans had the ISIS / DAESH or Al Qaida leaders who became prominent and efficient political leaders. The lack of effective power was promptly taken advantage of by extremist and fundamentalist Islamic organizations and entities, none of which committed to democracy and public welfare.

- Ok, I get your point! Now which is the tip with the wives?
- Well, imagine you feel like screwing one of the wives on Thursday! The next three days- or should I say nights - will be assigned, too. Not to mention that the order you establish can lead to interpretation. Can you handle this?
- I feel inclined to say yes! I think I can handle 4 nights with different women!
- You are truly stupid! They have a different temper, different style and different needs! There are some that can squish you dry after one night. They are like Dutch cigars – if you remember what Jerome K. Jerome said in "3 on 2 bicycles" - after you smoke a Dutch cigar, you are fed up with smoking and won't feel the need to smoke anything within the next week or so. What do you know about our women? You see them covered in black but you cannot guess their soul!
- That's true! I don't even try to look at them; they might feel offended!
- That is nothing! You are superficial enough to overlook the most important angle of this complicated problem!
- Which is?...
- Having 4 wives may look fun, but there are 4 mothers in law that come in the same package! It's all included in the same package, mister! Now I'd like to see how you handle those! No Sir, one is more than enough! Take me, for a fact, I couldn't do it and I confess that publicly! By the way, can we go outside to smoke a cigarette? I don't want my wife to see me! She says that whenever I smoke I am

probably thinking of another woman! Give me the lighter, man! Don't tease me!

Zsa Zsa Gabor used to say: "Personally I wouldn't know anything about sex; I've been married all the time!". Sharon Stone, on the other hand, admitted: "Women can mimic orgasm, while men can mimic a whole relationship!".

I have seen the delicate balance of power in a family! Like a friend of mine used to say: "If the man in the house is silent, that means he is thinking! If the woman gets silent, on the other hand, the thinker…. is so fucked!"

It is very easy to start a fight in a couple – so easy that we can give a thousand examples, but so hard to end it! For instance, I was in a philosophical debate with a friend of mine; he was convinced he has all the answers. He said:

- I can give you at least a dozen motives for a serious fight with your woman, and you ain't gonna have answer to them!

I thought he is being presumptuous and laughed; "Well buster, try me!"

"OK" he said. Check this out:

"I'm staying in bed near my wife and watch – with less than full interest, I guess – the "Want to be a billionaire?" game. Being kind'a bored, I asked her: Hey! How about a quickie? She was watching the show attentively and answered almost mechanically – Nope! I insisted: Is that your final answer? She says: Yes! Eyes on the TV! Then I say: Then I would like to call a friend! And the fight starts….!

- Yeah - I said – but you twisted the meaning…..
- I twisted nothing! He says without blinking. Here's another test"

"I am next to my wife in bed and do some channel drifting!.
At a certain moment, she seems to realize there's no sound and asks ;
Honey, what's on the TV?

Half asleep and careless, I answer: Dirt stuff on top! So the fight
begins...."

- This is silly I say – it is merely a word problem.
- False! Just listen!....

"My wife was desperately trying to suggest what she would like
to receive for her next birthday: I'd like something shinny that goes
from 0 to 100 in 3 seconds!

So I bought her a battery scale - in Kilograms - ..... and the
fight begun!"

Had no answer to that, so I dared him to continue.

"Last night when I got home, my wife told me she wanted to
go in an expensive place! So I took her to the gas station – and the
fight begun!"

- Have you got more? Can't be that bad! I said.
- Oh, you've seen nothing yet, my poor lad! He says.

"When I retired, I went to the social security office to register!
The lady at the office asked for my ID, which I had been leaving at
my home. I told her I really am that age and she said: ok! Unbutton
your shirt!. Upon seeing my grey chest hairs she admitted I was old
enough to fit in the law. I told my wife how nice the lady was to spare
me the trip home and she said: Why didn' t you drop your pants off!
She might have registered you for severe handicap! – and the fight
started...."

"I was seated next to my wife at the 20th celebration of their
class prom, when I noticed this guy, sharp dressed and apparently
drunk, gently spinning his Champagne glass between his fingers and

looking towards us from time to time. I said: hey! Who is this guy staring at us Do you know him? She smiles gently and whispers: this one was my first true love in college! He loved me very much, that when I left him and married you he started drinking, and they say he is still drinking because of that until now! God forbid, I said! I never saw someone cheerfully celebrate for so may years!... and the fight started!"

-    Did you have enough?
-    No way! I said! They all were misunderstandings!
-    Ok! Here's one more!

"Saturday morning I gotten out of bed gently, went down to take my parcel, dressed up and entered the garage to put my fishing gear in the car. The weather outside was agonizing! Rainy and windy like in a bad dream. I made up my mind and decided it is not a good day for fishing! I left gear in the garage, went upstairs, took of my clothes and got into the bed as gently as I could, but she felt me. I whispered: the weather outside is so bad – wind and rain! Half asleep she replies: Can you believe that my moron of a husband went fishing on this weather? – and the fight started."

"It was our anniversary and I asked my wife: Hey Honey! How about going this year some place we have never been before? She smiled and accepted immediately, so I took her to the kitchen – and we started a fight!"

-    I say, you have to finish sometime!
-    Wait I have a good one for you!

"Two years ago I went to my parents in law to pay a Christmas visit; I didn't know what to buy to my mother in law so I bought her a place in the local cemetery and handed her the papers. She acted very civilized about it, possibly because she was a practical person. This year we went again to them and had a good time. At a certain moment, my mother in law asked me: How come this year you didn't bring me a present?

I smiled and said: well, considering the fact that you never used the gift I gave you last year, I thought you don't need one..........and the fight begun.

The funniest conclusion of these stories was given by another friend of mine, who used to say: "some marriages have a happy ending by divorce, but not all of them".

What can I say? I've been a happily married man for 29 years – half life – but one thing I know for sure – I could never leave my kids.

THE UNIVERSAL PANACEA

"Terribly exhausted, all sweat and with his beard and hairs mingled with the local thistle, but with his hand firmly grasping the bleeding stone axe, the primitive man was watching the hunted animal at his feet, dead game looking and smelling as bad as he did.

He was already salivating – as we'd probably do, under the same kind of circumstances – thinking of the chunk of meat roasting and sizzling in the cave fire, surrounded by the admiring but also coveting tribe member's looks.

There had been a fierce battle, that needed to be traditionally told to the whole tribe before eating, and his arm, lacerated in three places, stood proof for the narrow escape; that critical moment when they have finally decided – face to face - who's gonna' eat who! After he made sure the creature is dead, by pushing it with a stick in some very sensitive places (you were never too careful in those times!), he slowly walked to the bur and plantain bushes around and collected a fistful of leafs, which he stuffed into his mouth and started chewing on them. A vegan? You will hastily say; why did he kill the poor animal for, then? Animal cruelty came with human society, n'est ce pas? After a time, he extracted the green mixture from his mouth and gently spread it on his wounds.

No ER, no GP, no county hospitals! Within a few days he is sure he would be able to hunt again. We are not lucky to get such hasty treatment these days anymore, do we?"

This is the way it must have happened about 200 000 years ago. Now you just go to Walmart or Costco and buy a wound dressing patch; such activity should be less dangerous, in theory. Lucky guy had the means to treat himself back, sound and safe, without waiting for hours at some ER of a county hospital or a few weeks, till he got an appointment with his neighborhood shaman (that would be the GP).

The influence of the tribe's shaman or witch, and his qualities and demands as a family / tribe physician penetrated the Neolithic culture only later, and generated the implementation of the first rudiments of the Obamacare health system.

How else can we consider reciprocal grooming in primates - when we clearly see it is not a random gesture or the trivial "you scratch my back, I'll scratch yours! Capisci?" - but tributary to a social behavior that respects a certain hierarchy?

The essential thing is that it kick-started; the cause-effect relationship was eventually observed – not necessarily understood – even by the inferior species, so it was to be expected that our ancestors realized that some events in their archaic quotidian had the power to damage their biological status or even kill them in the process. Such life events could have the power to make them look like their game before being eaten, at the best, and all biologists agree after that, after all, death is a fact of life.

How many primitive lives have been wasted in the past 5 million years to infected wounds, while at present day we have such simple cure like antibiotic pills?

Is it possible that Lucy – now, questionably being the first humanoid – died because of a neglected whitlow – inflicted by the leopard trying to fix her pedicure?

How much sacrifice was it necessary until they finally understood that bur and plantain are good for inflammation and healing, and decided to pass on this knowledge from generation to generation?

How many of the Sapiens species must have died before we understood that chamomile disinfects, digitalis strengthens the heart, hyosciamus calms down spasticity and vomit, and wait to see what happened when we discovered that poppy can put you to sleep or Mary Jane can be found at the corner shop for two bucks a joint!

When did you first find out that basil and lavender are able to kill the tuberculosis bug? You just did, right? Oh, all of you, drinking lime tea with honey when you catch a cold, take a bow and thank the unknown ancestor who used them for the first time. Oh, and all of you suffering intensely, shivering and farting on your toilet seats, because of a fermented Coke or a spoiled ice-cream, or a slimy hamburger during summer, please send a respectful thought to the Neanderthal who was first to use mint tea (toilet paper relief supposedly came later and did not meet universal acceptance!).

The human yearn for finding one answer to all questions or one medicine for all illness, did not stop here. Any small derangement ended up being treated with a specific cure. The prescription was commonly so complex in ingredients, that you could end up healing spontaneously or not remembering any more why you were searching for them in the first place, before completing it!

One by one, for severe diseases like plague, leper, black pox or other conditions like baldness, love, stupidity and impotence, various mixtures were tested. They ranged from vegetables that needed to be harvested on full moon by naked maidens (that would have been a sight to see, if you happened to be a leprechaun!), to the more common lizard eyes, bear teeth, rooster blood, rhino horn powder, tiger's penis, sea-goal tongue or chest hairs from Dwayne "the Rock" Johnson.

Perhaps we can ultimately blame the alchemists – eternally optimistic when trying hard to turn almost everything into gold - for this converging Middle Age tendency of finding a cure that can heal any disease, and all of them in the same time.

This tendency has even taken a leap towards other corners of our economic life, as we can see the great commercial brands trying to sell us their junk as novelty or quality merchandise.

With this goal in their minds, their specialists spend vast amounts of money on promoting their stuff and when we do not seem convinced enough, they find multinationals to swear that product a or b is good for our health.

When that doesn't work, they get simply sordid: "You are beautiful!" they whisper to any ugly spinster watching TV, and if you want to stay that way, you'd better buy our stuff and swallow it or you'll end up in a Trump-care hospital (whatever that may stand for!). I take the liberty of discussing this promotion / commercial subject on another occasion.

Our Government is sometimes acting like alchemists; the finance specialists keep on trying to demonstrate that budget loss is in fact beneficial for the citizens, as it prepares our economy for the next re-launching of a stronger and more efficient financial effort. It is like the Nazi radicals "explained" German withdrawal towards the final months of the WW II – "Our Wehrmacht is redeploying troops and war machinery on previously established retreated positions and concentrating in view of the decisive attack that would bring us Final Victory!"

The regular slow- grazing, horned & hooved buffalo foreheaded - citizen understands nothing and gets publicly invited to share the abundance of the next salary raise, like the stork was invited by the fox to eat from a plate.

Take the regular financial advisor from the IRS; news of tax increase can make him smile, retro-active application of a tax makes him laugh, a new tax gives him a boner!

With the next semester, the regular grazing citizen finally understands who's gonna' get it! Our citizens were passively waiting to join the EU, while smoking plain or smuggled cigarettes, or for the Americans to somehow come to Europe.

They'll have to wait some more, as the Americans are quite busy right now! First, Bin Laden got "nominated city-architect" for New York, and this led to war with Afghanistan and then Iraq. Plenty of new warfare was invented and sold to third parties, after being on "display", and in the same time, the number of national heroes awaiting for family visits in Arlington painfully increased. Fighting terrorism far away from our borders was a successful strategy in the past, now we have to brace for closer and more unexpected encounters.

Americans were so busy that they did not react when Putin was "nominated" for counting the votes for the last presidential elections. Now the Americans have another problem – the Chinese have been able to annihilate Trump's bold power rhetoric over the North Korean nuclear danger, by encouraging the two Koreas to join hands and make peace.

Obviously, the only one able to profit from local peace there is China, who will do it economically, and the Americans will be free to watch the show. The subtle Chinese game bewildered both American and South Korean diplomacies, as they understood only after the meaning of the circus put up by comrade Kim-Jong –Un.

And he didn't have to use any of his fireworks; I can still see the American generals seriously re-assuring citizens that American counter measures are perfectly able to take down any ICBM from North-Korea, while they had trouble even to make them take off. The cure to war and poverty is not medical, and we have a hard time defining it.

In our country there will come a time, when we will find the saving solution, which will be administrated orally, injected or somehow inserted through the "back door", like a generous laundry soap enema (by the way, it works wonders when nothing else is available, trust me!), and justice, welfare and satisfaction will once again be restored, as it had been a thousand times before.

The retired old people will smile with happy and fat faces and so will do orphanage kids, finally cured from dystrophy.

A miracle cure will be available for the jobless and the eternally assisted. It is true that in a normal situation, they should have perished long ago or rallied in front of the rich palaces built overnight, like they did under the communists, when shouting for chicken claws at 4 am in front of the supermarkets.

Apparently paradoxically, many of them behave like patients in state hospitals, who are healing in spite of any treatment they might receive. They obviously find something else to do under the counter and survive. I always said our jobless are, by far, better oriented than their capitalist.

The miracle all-cure medicine was re-invented during the communism, when the Dictator's fixed ideas about over-working the population met his wife's fixed ideas about starving the population.

It is a pity they did not survive to see both ideas worked beyond reproach. Meanwhile, we kinda' dumped working habits, but eating has proven to be a depraved habit impossible to eradicate, no matter how hard you try.

After our revolution, we received various medicine: terrorist droplets with lead (remember the story about little Mike who was asked by the secret police how did his father die: "He got 'neumonia!" little Mike said. "How is that"? "He got shot in the chest and the bullets were hot, but the air coming in through the holes was so cold in winter!").

We also received base-ball bat- syrup from the miners, who were called in by our next pro-Russian president. The intellectuals were especially targeted, because they complained of rebel migraines and they further underwent more exquisite treatments like the massage "a-la-gendarme", surprisingly still working in 2018 – and tested in the 10th of August diaspora rally.

There was a new infusion of modern cure for boredom and poverty: the pyramid games and the eternal Bingo, but with the local touch of a national lottery. All those chimeras were enveloped in the wrapping of "safe –solutions-to-make-big-money-spending-almost-nothing" because you were the "fortunate-dude-who-found-out-first-and-is-bound-to-succeed, in spite of others".

There were people who invested all their savings and even social security funds in those scams and in the end, the only effect they ever noticed while shaving in the morning was they grew horns and big ears and started to baa! Or hanged themselves.

The economical Romanian panacea has a deep Balkan spice secret: it needs to be taken frequently, to fill your belly and your pockets and to never require work.

Boy, if we ever get to catch the little ol' gold fish (you know, the one that grunts you three wishes). He's going to grunt us thirty or perish in a lousy soup! Speaking of which, many of the most preferred drugs contain subtle quantities of alcohol, which makes some prefer the diluting agent to the active substance itself.

Our wishful thinking can "build" jaw-dropping qualities to medication and other items. I remember the story of this old lady, living in a small poor cottage near the river. One fine day she was fishing for her lunch and she catches the golden fish. As usual, the fish starts screaming and crying asking her to throw him back into the water, for which he will gladly grunt her three wishes. She became interested and asked: "Hey buster, how is it gonna be? Do I throw you first and then get the wishes or should I keep you here meanwhile?" The fish looked terrified and politely answered that, considering her background and life experience and accomplishments, a substantial amount of indecision and uncertainty is bound to characterize her deeds333, and by his calculation, he will consequently be suffocating in free air long before grunting her second wish.

And he is bound to do so, if she decides to keep him like this any longer, chatting about sterile stuff. The two agreed on immediate re-immersion of the fish. After gulping fresh water through his gills, the fish came back and said:

- See, I'm a fish of my word! Tell me your first wish!
- Well, fishy, I think I was poor long enough! So why don't you make me filthy rich?

The fish flipped tail twice and a giant and rich palace rose instead of her tiny cottage. Dozens of servants swarmed cleaning, carrying stuff and doing all sort of things and an elegant coach with 6 black horses came near her, driver inviting her in!

- What's your second wish, my good woman? Said the fish, smiling at her stunned face.
- My … second … wish? She seemed like waking up. She instantly produced a mirror from her pocket and said:
- Look at me! I'm a ruin! I could scare crows myself! What is the meaning of my fortune if I die before enjoying it? I want you to make me young and beautiful again!

- You've said it! The fish flipped tail twice again and a silver cloud engulfed the old lady. When the steam and smoke scattered, there she was in her sweet six... er, let us say twenties. Black hair, blue eyes, big boobs, rosy lips and curvy hips, all dressed in style and rattling with gold jewelry.
- Ohhhhh! She said! Looking in the mirror. I am so nice! You're good, you know! You should come more often these parts!
- That, my dear madam, makes me very proud! Your appreciation is most welcome, but you still have one wish left. Think well, as this is your last one!
- Hey, don't be rude to me! Don't push it! I'm still older than you, no matter how I look now! Let me think! ... Oh yes! What's the joy in being rich and young and beautiful, when you're alone? I want you to turn my Tom cat over there into a young man for me!
- Ok! The fish flipped tail twice and the Tom cat disappears. Out of the silver cloud he comes as a young man: tall and athletic like Tarzan, with the intelligent eyes of Dwayne –the –Rock Johnson, non-smoker, working out every day, with a new CEO Job proposition in his pocket, dressed like a prince and obviously looking like being in love with her.
- Oh darling, she says, I've been waiting for you all my life! Take me and love me eternally!
- Oh my beloved one! He walks to her and embraces her gently, kissing her neck and face languorously, then whispers to her ear:
- Ain't it a pity you had me castrated last week?

When it comes to medication, we have the same great expectations like from a wizard's witchcraft. You fill bloated? Take this pill and within 3 days you'll get slim like Christina El Moussa! You need strength? Take these injections and you'll coil Schwartenegger on your wrist like he were your garden hose (after he "will be back", of course!). You need courage? Take this pills and you'll take the first plane to Pyongyang and slap Kim Jong Un on his rosy cheeks (I meant the face!). You feel sick about politics? You take this injection that will make you look like Hillary and sing like Frank Sinatra while doing a lap dance for Trump! And I said lap dance not pole dance! We have everything! Remember the times when they would sell tablets that you put inside a can of water and turn it into gasoline?

The diseases may have weird ways of action. I remember a question after the Chernobyl radioactive accident: "Is it true that the people in the area of the accident lost their teeth?" KGB answered – "Ofcourse, it is not true. Only those that didn't keep their mouth shut!".

Sometimes we may think we found a cure for everything right in our closet! Check out alcohol! You can of course drink it and you will get happy! Well, alcohol can have this sort of action upon you! One man from South parts once said to his friend:

- You know what? When I drink something, I get very brave! You know, like very, very brave! I feel like I ain't afraid of no one!
- Crap! You ain't afraid of your wife?
- Ickes! If I come to think of it, I never got that drunk!

Alcohol can be used to rub your back when you have chills, or heat it on the stove and serve it as grog! Japanese men walk all day in a pair of socks they call "tabi" sleep on the floor on a straw mat they call "tatami", with a wooden pillow, in a house with painted paper walls they call "shoji", and the next day they wake up good and ready and that's because they drink that hot rice booze they call "sake".

I once went to a wedding; one of my younger colleagues was getting married, so he invited us to "mourn" him! Like usual, we were going to start with a serious dose of whiskey. An older lady with a bored nun face comes inside the room like a ghost, shaking a bottle of whiskey in her extended hand, like Lorraine Bobbit the trophy of her household war:

- Anyone else want more alcohol? - She says with a grin and a harsh voice that displayed all her despise towards alcohol, alcohol products and derivatives, the producing factories and distilleries, the grapes, fruits and cereals liable to be transformed in alcoholic drinks, the distributors who make a living on it and even the customs agents that grunted import, along with the IRS agents that tax it.

We starred at each other like an A.A. group on the first meeting and shook our heads like the Indians say "yes".

- Goooood! She says – with a satisfaction grin on her face, and leaves the room like she was rolling on ghostly vapors.

Later on, I understood the weird old lady was his mother (and she was sick), and he brought two more bottles of whiskey when we moved to another place to keep the party going.

The French never made a secret of the fact they enjoy wine. A lot! From morning till dusk! From primary school to retirement and after! Anywhere, anytime! They go as far as having a certain type of wine for a certain type of dish! I saw pictures of a French restaurant where a "grand chef" – great cook, that is, placed a dead duck in a horrible pressing machine and squeezed until all fluids went out of it. He used the disgusting dead bird fluids to cook an exquisite sauce for the duck breast that he called "canetton" and informed us that eating that would cost us 200 Euro per person. More than that, this did not include the specially selected wine, a bottle of rozé "Chatteau Noeuf du Pape" that would make another 100 Euros. I can starve on those 400 bucks, as I do not eat duck! Not butchered like that or killed any other way. Me and ducks would live together forever on a deserted island! I can imagine the news afterwards: "a dangerous species of carnivorous ducks evolved on a deserted island in the South Pacific. Unfortunately, there was no human left on the uninhabited island to tell us how that happened!"

In the early history of the US, there was a great efficiency of the local shamans: no matter what disease you had, they would recommend scalp treatment! This made the early English colonists to bring with them their big white "Whigs".

I suppose we shall never get tired of hoping to solve all problems in a single way, and that is because of our laziness. We'll soon find the miracle formula of the perfect medicine, which, paraphrasing Jerome K. Jerome, will cure our stomach ache, dandruff, fungus, myopia, will help us spice the steak, clean the TV set screen and the computer keyboard and we can use what's left to clean the cooking stove shining!